PHANTOM WARRIORS
THE DARK KING

JORDAN SUMMERS

Phantom Warriors: The Dark King

Copyright © 2012 Jordan Summers

Formatted by IRONHORSE Formatting

ISBN-13: 978-1-942237-00-6

Taylor Shelley has always had the worst taste in men. When her latest ex turns out to be part of the Russian mob, she's offered the chance to start a new life…on another planet. No more bad boys for her.

Hades, The Dark King is both feared and rejected due to his mixed Atlantean/Phantom heritage. As King of the Phantoms, he rules his land via blood and claw. Hades doesn't have time to watch over a human female, even one as enticing as Taylor, but a debt is a debt. If keeping an eye on the woman for a week will clear the slates, then he'll do it.

Taylor isn't sure how a cage-fighter ended up on the throne, but she wants nothing to do with this royal bad boy.

What starts as an obligation, ends in a game of seduction where the players are evenly matched. There's only one rule to remember when playing with the Dark King—the house ALWAYS wins.

The warrior slipped into the communications room during the shift change and shut the door behind him. Not that his presence would be questioned if he were found. No, the guards wouldn't give him a second thought. But treason was best performed without an audience. He had minutes before the new guards arrived.

The red and white communication's crystals sat upon a metal table in the center of the room. They glowed and pulsed, indicating that they were ready to use. In the corner, a green crystal coruscated, verifying that the energy field around the Walled City was active. Had the energy field been expanded to cover the surrounding areas, the crystal's green color would've morphed to gold, signifying that they were under attack.

The warrior ignored the crystal in the corner and picked up the red one nearest to him. He moved the crystal to the right of the white ones. The change in position caused the red crystal to vibrate and give out a high-pitched tone. He quickly moved another red crystal to the side. The tone changed and became a steady beep.

With a careful twist of his wrist, the beep turned into a signal, a beacon projected into space. The type of distress beacon a Slaver ship would be unable to resist. The warrior waited as long as he dared to ensure the message had gone out, then returned the crystals to their original positions.

It was done.

Time to see how the Dark King handled unwanted company.

Once the Phantom people saw how unsafe their city was, Hades would have to accept his challenge for the throne.

*****

Chapter One

Linx strode into the dank cavern. Flames lit the walls, casting long shadows over the wet rock. The musty air tickled his nostrils, making him want to sneeze. The ground crunched as the rock beneath his boots crumbled under his weight. Behind him, his mate's sister, Taylor stared wide-eyed into the darkness. She hesitated at the entrance for a moment, then followed him inside. Her kitten heels tip-tapped on the stone as she rushed to catch up.

"Remember what I told you about the Dark King," Linx said.

Taylor glanced at him. "I will, stop worrying." She rubbed her hands over her arms to ward off a chill.

"I know it looks bad, but it's not as bad as it appears," he said.

No, it was worse.

These days Hades loved to rule his Kingdom like some dark lord from the underworld, but that hadn't always been the case. When he'd first risen to the throne, he'd railed against the voices of dissension. Strove to bring his people together. But eventually he became disillusioned by what the Phantom people were saying and decided to become the abomination they accused him of being. Neither the Phantom world nor the Atlantean one fully accepted him, but very few were stupid enough to challenge him.

Linx looked at the woman beside him. Perhaps her being here would create change. "I'll bring Tabby as soon as I'm able to petition the Atlanteans for your status upgrade. I have no doubt that once they hear the circumstances under which you came here, they will accept you as a citizen of New Atlantis," Linx said. "But it will take time."

Taylor snorted. "Nice to know that bureaucracy exists everywhere in the universe."

Linx smiled, but his grin faded as a regiment of towering guards came into view. The men were all Phantom Warriors. A bit of a surprise given the King's mixed heritage. The guards stood in front of a massive metal door that looked like something from medieval earth. Linx stepped forward. "Phantom Warrior Linx. I'm here to see the Dark King," he said in a loud voice, officially announcing his arrival.

"State your business, Phantom," the nearest guard ordered. His red eyes glowed in the darkness, but held all the warmth of a glacier.

Linx felt a clumsy touch in his mind as the Phantom tried to read his thoughts. He fought back a smile, then pictured himself in a state of undress.

The guard's face flushed and his gaze narrowed accusingly, then he straightened to attention.

Linx kept his expression innocent. "I have an appointment with the King. As for what it's about, that is none of your business. Just tell him that I'm here," he said. If things went well, he'd leave his Royal Crankiness with more than a new charge to care for. It was time the Dark King joined the land of the living again.

The guard's jaw clenched and unclenched as an internal struggle took place. Eventually reason won out and he said, "One moment." The other Phantoms continued to block the entrance as the lead guard stepped away.

It took fifteen minutes for the guard to return. Linx was sure that he'd kept them waiting on purpose. The Phantom barked an order and the guards slowly parted to reveal another door, this one made of thick stone, beyond the metal one they were blocking.

*****

Taylor had never been more terrified in her life. Not even when the Russians were torturing her sister, Tabby, which was saying something. She had no idea what was on the other side of that great stone door, but if it was anything like the entrance to the cavern, then it wasn't going to be good. Whose idea was it to build a palace—scratch that—fortress inside a mountain? She didn't think things like this existed outside of the movies.

She'd been moved from what amounted to a windowless shipping container straight to Linx's transport. He had made her duck down to avoid detection, so she hadn't seen much of New Atlantis or the Walled City. Heck, she'd barely gotten a glimpse of the light green sky. What she wouldn't give for a little sunshine. If it weren't for the tanned skin on the warriors they'd passed, Taylor would've thought she was being dropped off in the land of the mole people.

Linx looked back at her. "Ready?"

"As I'll ever be." She took a steadying breath.

"Before we go in, take this. You'll need it if there's any trouble." He handed her a small round disc that looked like a black pebble.

"What am I supposed to do with a rock? Throw it at him?" From what she'd seen of the Phantom Warriors, she'd need something a lot bigger than a pebble to stop one.

Linx didn't bother to hide his impatience. "It's a communication device. You can reach me any time by touching the top. Your sister made me promise to give you one. I'm pretty sure that Hades won't hurt you, so hopefully you won't have to use the device."

The mention of her sister, Tabby, made Taylor's heart clench, which was why it took her a moment to register what else Linx had said. "Pretty sure?" As in he had some doubts about her safety. "Your lack of confidence in the Dark King is not reassuring," she said.

Linx sighed. "I'm positive he won't. No Phantom Warrior would ever raise his hand to a woman. The punishment for such things is...*severe*." He eyed her critically. "Besides, you're kind of his 'type'. He has a thing for long hair and full breasts."

Taylor arched a brow. "Don't most men?"

Linx grinned. "Good point. Ultimately his taste in women matters not, since you'll be under his protection and you'll only be here a week tops."

How reassuring, Taylor thought.

"I think the King and I will be able to resist temptation for a week," she said dryly.

Linx's expression turned calculating. "Your sister didn't last that long."

She pulled a face. "Ew, too much information."

Linx grinned.

The hair on Taylor's arms rose. *What was that cat up to? And why didn't she think she was going to like it.* "Thanks for the device." She tossed the communicator into the air and caught it, then shoved it into her pocket.

He stepped forward. She followed close behind. More guards poured out of the shadows, blocking their entrance. Their fierce expressions never wavered as they frisked them, before they were allowed through the stone door.

Linx glared at the guard, who was a little too thorough in frisking Taylor, but he didn't say a word. She gave him a small reassuring smile, but she was trembling by the time the Phantom finished. Taylor was used to men trying to cop a feel, used to them ogling her. When you take your clothes off for a living, you get used to a lot of things. But dealing with men and dealing with shape-shifting aliens were two very different things.

She thought about the pain and horror Tabby had gone through because of her poor judgment in men. If her twin could live through torture, then Taylor could survive the next week. Tabby may not think she was strong, but she was wrong. Taylor had learned to be strong, learned how to survive. She'd had to when she had gone into exotic dancing, since it wasn't exactly an accepted profession.

People looked down on her, but Taylor refused to look down upon herself. In her mind, she had nothing to be ashamed of...at least not until she hooked up with Sergei. Her mistakes from that day forth had piled up until Taylor was convinced she'd never see daylight again. Fortunately, her sister and the man—make that alien—standing beside her had saved her life, given her a second chance, and she was determined to make the best of it.

No more mistakes. No more screwed up relationships. A proper 'do-over'.

Linx stepped through the door. When she reached his side, he took her hand and placed her palm upon his arm before escorting her deeper inside the room. The move was oddly formal and caused butterflies to attack her stomach.

Taylor frowned, but didn't say anything. They walked side by side into the Great Hall. Had he not been holding her, Taylor would've stopped, shocked by what lay beyond the cavern door.

The journey in had been all craggy cave, wet walls, and musty minerals, but somehow the stone door had transformed the cave from something out of Middle Earth into a sultan's palace. Plump red pillows lined the benches that cuddled against row after row of long tables. Rich tapestries clung to the walls adding vibrant color to an otherwise slate room. Thick black rugs brushed the cobbled aisle, giving it a polished look. Taylor visually followed the stone pathway to...she squinted. Was that a throne?

Of course it's a throne. You're about to meet a King.

She'd never met a King before. Oh sure, she'd entertained a few Saudi royals at Sergei's club, but she doubted that a King would be expecting a lap dance. Such things were beneath them. Weren't they?

How did one behave in front of royalty?

Every culture had its own version of royalty. Each with its own set of rules when it came to dealing with them. Taylor had seen Kings and Queens on the television, but were they the same here? Did they even have Queens? She had her doubts. The cultural differences she'd witnessed thus far on Zaron were in stark contrast to the ones she'd left only a few days ago.

Had it only been a few days? It seemed like a lifetime.

Taylor cut that line of thinking off at the knees and dumped it in a shallow grave. She was done feeling sorry for herself.

The door shut behind them with a thunderous boom. Her palms began to sweat as Linx led her forward. She rubbed them over her jeans just in case she had to shake the King's royal hand.

Blood roared in her ears as her heart tried to pound its way out of her chest. This was a mistake. She shouldn't be here. She was a stripper for goodness sake! Wasn't there a hotel or motel she could crash at until Linx cleared up her 'visa' issue?

The empty throne came into sharper relief. Fear and trepidation slowed her steps. The royal seat was neither gold nor silver. Taylor expected to see jewels at least, but there were none. The seat was a spider web of steel with spindly legs and humanoid skulls for feet. If she hadn't been told it was a throne, Taylor would've thought she was viewing a torture device.

Was this some kind of joke? She looked at Linx, but he wasn't laughing. Her gaze slid back to the empty-eyed skulls. Their grotesquely pointed teeth seemed to grin mockingly at her.

This wasn't the throne of a King. This was the throne of a barbarian. What had she gotten herself into? The urge to turn and run away nearly overwhelmed her.

Linx must've sensed her unease for his grip tightened and he kept her moving.

A tawny-haired man with a fight-carved face lounged insolently against the base of the throne in the shadows. He was a study in muscle, though Taylor doubted that he'd ever stepped foot inside a gym.

Was this one of the King's private guards? His bodyguard perhaps? He looked the part. Built for sheer brute force without all the frivolousness of subtly. One glance told her that the man could crush skulls with his bare hands until all that remained was bone dust.

His lazy gaze started at the top of her head, resting momentarily on her full breasts until her traitorous nipples hardened in awareness, before proceeding to her toes. He reversed direction without saying a word and stopped when he returned to her face. Taylor shivered under his uncompromising regard and hated that her reaction wasn't all because of the cool, damp air and fear.

In her old life, he was the type of man that she would've been attracted to. His rock hard body and edgy vibe would've turned her on. The old Taylor would have wanted to lick and touch every one of his bulging muscles. And even if she didn't surrender right away, the promise of mind-blowing sex would have been too tempting to resist for long.

Taylor would've gone out of her way to catch his attention, lure him with her body, and seduce him into her bed…but not anymore. She'd learned her lesson and it had very nearly cost her everything she held dear. Taylor forced herself to meet his eyes. Something odd flared in the icy blue depths before being carefully banked. The man's unflinching gaze slowly moved from her to Linx.

"What do you want?" His clipped words made the

temperature in the room drop.

Linx arched a brow and looked at the *guard*.

"I thought you said the King was expecting us," Taylor said in a hushed breath, hoping that only Linx could hear her. Had they come on the wrong day? Had the King changed his mind about seeing them? What if he did? What would she do then? There were only so many places she could hide on Zaron without risking discovery and deportation.

"He is," the guard said. He rose slowly and walked to the front of the throne, then sat, resting his meaty hands on the thick metal webs.

"Your Highness." Linx's lips kicked up at the corners in amusement. He gave the man a short bow.

Taylor gaped. This was the King. It couldn't be. Kings didn't look like cage fighters. Kings were soft, well-spoken, pampered. She glanced around the room at the lush red pillows. Okay, so maybe he did pamper himself a little, but that was as far as the stereotype went. Her gaze returned to the fierce looking throne and the even fiercer looking man seated upon it.

"If I grant you this favor, then we are even," the Dark King said.

"I wouldn't exactly call it a favor, Your Highness. Perhaps a gift."

Gift? What did Linx mean by that?

The King's eyes narrowed dangerously.

"But you're absolutely right, we're even now," Linx said hurriedly before the King could speak. "I will be back to retrieve her within seven days." He gave Taylor a warning glare and indicated to the King with a jerk of his chin.

Nothing like being forced on someone, she thought wryly.

Taylor dropped down onto one knee. "Thank you for allowing me to stay, Your Highness, and for putting me under your protection." She recited the words Linx had made her memorize. Taylor must've done it right because Linx smiled at her when she finished.

"What are you called, Earthling?" the King asked, drawing her attention away from her sister's mate.

"Taylor Shelley, but Taylor is fine." She tittered nervously, then clamped her mouth shut.

"You may call me Hades."

Taylor stared at him for a few seconds. She couldn't have heard him correctly. "I'm sorry, did you say Hades?" She frowned. "Like the god of the underworld? Is it because you live inside a mountain?" She indicated to their surroundings.

"No." He shot a pointed look at Linx. "It's because it is my name."

"Oh, that's a good reason, too," she said.

Linx sighed. "Forgive her impertinence, Sire. She's never been presented to royalty before and doesn't understand our culture. She meant no offense."

"Fascinating." The King looked at her again like she'd just sprouted ram horns out her ears. It was obvious he wasn't used to receiving 'common' people. He continued to stare, his aqua blue eyes boring into her until Taylor felt naked. Finally, he deigned to speak. "The Phantom Warrior tells me that you have given up your wild Earth ways and plan to start a new life here on Zaron, if King Eros grants his permission."

Wild ways? Taylor glared at Linx. What in the world had he told Hades? She wasn't wild. Just because she'd chosen an unusual profession didn't make her a slut. She resisted the urge to hit him, then turned back to address the King. "That is correct, Your Highness," she said through gritted teeth. Why was it when men were 'wild' they were considered studs and when women were proud of their sexuality they were called much, much worse?

The King stared at her, no doubt judging her like so many of the men that she'd met in her lifetime. Would he consider her unworthy to stay in his kingdom? If he did, what would that mean in terms of her fate? She lifted her chin and stared right back at him. Taylor wouldn't let a King or any other man make her feel inferior.

The silence became painfully uncomfortable. Sweat broke out on her forehead as they continued their staring contest. Taylor was about ready to repeat her answer, when he spoke.

"Pity, that you decided to make such a change now," the King said, clearly bored with the whole conversation. "I had hoped for a *distraction.*"

Hoped for…what the hell?

Taylor's temper flared before she could rein it in. She shot to her feet. "Well you won't find one here," she spat.

The arrogant jerk!

She should've known by looking at him that he'd be an ass. Taylor had thought that traveling a hundred light years would make a difference. When would she learn to ignore her hormones and see people for what they truly were? Men were the same no matter what solar system they lived in.

Linx's eyes widened and he glowered at her. "You are speaking to a King," he hissed. "We talked about this. You forget your place."

"My place? My place is a hundred light years from here." But he was right. Hades was doing them a favor by letting her stay here. The least she could do was be gracious. Taylor opened her mouth to apologize, but one look at the King's arrogant expression changed her mind. She crossed her arms over her chest and glared right back at him. He could take her apology and stuff it up his tight butt.

Yes, she'd noticed that he had a great butt. She might be 'reformed', but she wasn't blind.

Hades laughed. "Don't underestimate yourself. I have a feeling you could be quite distracting, if you put your mind to it," he said to Taylor, then glanced at Linx. "You are dismissed."

"I thought perhaps—" His words died mid-sentence at the look upon Hades' face. Linx hesitated, clearly torn about whether he should stick around. He shook his head, then gave the King another short bow. "As you wish." Linx took a step back. "Behave," he grumbled under his breath to Taylor.

She fumed silently. *He had started it.*

Linx waited for her to respond.

Taylor sighed. "I will," she said reluctantly. "Maybe you should give his 'Royal Badass' the same advice. I think he could use it."

"Nice to see you two hitting it off. I'll give Tabby your best," Linx said, then hightailed it out of the cave like a scaredy cat.

*****

Hades wasn't sure what the cat was up to, but he was grateful to have his debt satisfied. He sometimes wished that he had taken the knife to the chest. It would have been far less painful in the long run. He didn't like owing Linx or anyone else.

He stared at the Earth woman that he'd promised to keep safe. She was full of fire like the long, flowing dark red hair that framed her pale face. Odd colored eyes, neither brown nor green but somewhere floating in the middle, stared back at him in observation...and defiance. Her looks bore no resemblance to the Atlantean women or the Phantoms, but they were striking in their own way. He felt himself drawn to her, despite her anger and her obvious human shortcomings.

He'd read Taylor's thoughts easily, when she stepped forward into the chamber. She hadn't believed him to be a King, but that was nothing new, since half the Atlanteans and Phantoms agreed and chose to follow King Eros instead.

In their eyes, Hades would always be a Half-being, neither Phantom nor Atlantean. A mistake. A 'Royal Badass' according to Taylor, though he kind of liked that term. Feared, but not necessarily respected. Their opinions would change quickly, if Zaron were ever under attack. For Hades was good at one thing, better than anyone else on the planet.

War.

He knew how to fight, how to use every weapon. His strategies were beyond compare. He'd been raised as a warrior from the start and did not fear death. Nor did he court his demise. Hades would do whatever he must in order to win, to keep his people safe.

Eros would never be able to say the same. His family made him soft. Weak. Made him forget that he was a warrior first and foremost. That particular failure would never happen to Hades.

He ensured it by keeping his distance from female entanglements. Oh, he enjoyed a good fuck as much as the next man, maybe more so since his dual bloodline gave him an insatiable appetite, but he never let sexual gratification lead to bonding. Hades didn't think with his dick. Never had, never would.

The Phantom people regularly pushed for him to take a mate, but Hades vowed never to do so. His refusal caused strife, but it was a strife that he could live with. He was satisfied with his life. Happy even.

So maybe he got bored on occasion. As King, it was his right. And maybe the women he bedded were becoming interchangeable in his mind. That didn't stop him from enjoying their company. And it certainly didn't mean that things needed to change.

His mood soured as his thoughts switched course. He glared at the human. It was her fault. He wasn't a damn nursemaid. He was King. Kings didn't babysit wayward females. He should call Linx back this instant and demand he come to retrieve her. Debt be damned! Hades noted the rebelliousness in Taylor's eyes. It sparked something primal inside of him.

Perhaps she was an exception...

She finds you arrogant and thinks you're an ass.

Hades snorted. Her words were strange, but their meaning was clear. She was right. He was an arrogant ass. Those were two of his *good* qualities.

Why wasn't she lowering her gaze?

Didn't she know about the beast lurking beneath the calm facade of every Phantom Warrior? He may only be half Phantom, but his beast was strong—and dominant. It didn't like to be directly challenged. Yet, Taylor wasn't backing down or looking away.

Hades continued to stare, shocked and oddly *impressed* by her brazen display. Something inside of him rose to accept the challenge she unwittingly tossed out.

Taylor Shelley was different. She'd made that abundantly clear with her barely veiled disdain. If he hadn't sensed her fleeting attraction before she'd realized who he was, Hades might've been able to leave her alone for the week.

But he *had* sensed it. For a moment, she had wanted him. She had fantasized about stripping him bare. Now he could think of nothing but doing the same to her.

The flash of awareness coupled with her flare of temper intrigued him. Most women fell over themselves to please him in the hopes that he'd make them his Queen or at least bed them, but not Taylor. She wanted nothing to do with him. The question was why?

He knew it wasn't because she'd been forced upon him. He'd read that much from her thoughts. No, something else held her back. Hades immediately strategized, running all the options, evaluating the various outcomes. In the end, the answer was always the same.

He would protect her like he vowed, but Taylor would learn to bow before the Dark King…like all the others who'd come before her. Hades knew his way around a woman's body and took great satisfaction in bringing them pleasure. Taylor would be no different, even if he had to wait for Linx's return to take her.

Who knows, he thought. *She might even learn to like his*

touch.

Hades gave her an evil grin infused with sheer determination. Taylor's full breasts quivered delectably beneath her shirt. She shifted her long, sensuous legs, which appeared to be poured into the thick blue material she wore, and glanced around as if she'd flee given half the chance.

Perhaps she was smart after all.

He inhaled through his nose and mouth. A rich, spicy scent tickled his sensitive nostrils. Hades' eyes fluttered closed and his head spun as he drank her in. If Taylor tasted half as good as she smelled, she'd be delicious. His tongue darted out over his lips. He could almost taste her. He breathed in again, this time deeper. Now there was nowhere that she could hide that he wouldn't find her, but it was going to be fun to try.

"Run!" he ordered.

Taylor squeaked and took off in the direction from which she'd come.

Hades watched her go, her full bottom twitching from side to side as she ran. Anticipation rose as he prepared to give chase. His beast prickled beneath his skin, scraping its claws down his spine. He looked forward to giving Taylor her first lesson in obedience. He had no doubt that when he caught her there would be a battle of wills. Hers cast from Earth's soft soil and his cast from iron.

He might bend to get his way, but the Dark King would never break.

Hades wondered if the same could be said for Taylor Shelley. There was only one way to find out. He surged up from the throne and roared.

*****

CHAPTER TWO

The ear-shattering roar echoed through the Great Hall. Taylor screamed and ran faster. She should've apologized for insulting the King when she had the chance. She was afraid to look back. Afraid of what she might see.

She'd witnessed Linx and Riot in their Other form. Seen them in action, while they fought the Russian mob. Their physical change had scared her silly, but from the sounds of it, Hades was something *far* worse.

Taylor reached the heavy stone doors and grabbed the carved out handles. Her muscles strained as she pulled on the massive slabs. Linx had made opening the doors look easy. She should've known.

She could feel Hades' heated glare burning through her shirt, searing her back. It scrolled down her body, resting on her ass. The sensation only made her pull harder. The door inched open. She glanced over her shoulder and saw what could only be described as a giant *liger* coming toward her.

Taylor screamed.

She put her hands in the door crack and pried it apart, until she could squeeze her body through. She'd barely made it into the hall and shut the door behind her, when something large hit the stone on the other side and made the rock tremble.

Oh God, she had to hide. But where could she go that he wouldn't find her?

*****

"Your Majesty," Opal called out, so she could be heard over the massive claws scratching the Great Hall doors.

She'd watched the flame-haired woman escape the King's grasp and hadn't thought much of it, since Hades was known for having a rather *large* sexual appetite. He'd be bored with her soon enough. She wasn't the type of woman that held the King's attention for long. It was a pattern Opal had seen repeated multiple times over the years.

Hades continued to claw at the doors, his big paws unable to slip into the carved out handles.

The woman must've really gotten under his skin. He rarely put any effort toward pursuit. Hades preferred that women chase him, since it kept misunderstandings from occurring. Opal cleared her throat and raised her voice. "Your Majesty!"

As the King's Righthand, a position she fought tooth and claw to reach, it was her duty to give him a daily report on happenings within the Walled City. It also gave her a chance to be alone with Hades. Opal cherished those moments, even though they passed quickly.

Normally, other than minor disputes, there wasn't much to report. Hades didn't tolerate rebellion and most warriors were smart enough not to challenge him in the Pit for the throne. Today was different. A slaver ship had been spotted doing a reconnaissance flight over the area.

Neither the Atlanteans nor the Phantoms could afford to lose any of their women to the Slavers. The fact that the Slavers sometimes sold the women for their 'body parts' only made the situation graver. And if that weren't bad enough,

Perseus was up to his old tricks. He'd always been a discontent, but now he was rallying men to stand with him. It wouldn't be long before he presented Hades with a formal challenge.

Opal shook her head. Perseus was a fool. A fool that would get himself killed if he kept up his machinations. He misjudged Hades' tolerance for weakness. Nothing could be further from the truth.

Her gaze narrowed as she focused on the closed door. Was there a connection between the mysterious woman, Perseus' sudden move to take the throne, and the appearance of the Slavers?

For the woman's sake, there better not be. Opal didn't tolerate disloyalty any more than Hades did. And since she intended to be Queen one day, she took all threats to the kingdom personally.

A large paw hit the stone door, sending shards of rock crumbling onto the floor. Even in his half-shifted form, Hades was magnificent. Opal had thought so the moment she had laid eyes on him. Five years later, her feelings hadn't changed. If anything, they'd intensified.

Opal loved Hades. She loved him with both her hearts and knew eventually, if she waited long enough that he would discover that he loved her, too. Or at least respected her enough to make her his Queen. Either way worked for Opal, as long as it ended with her on the throne beside him.

Like all men, Hades was stubborn and blind to what was right in front of him. Opal however was not. She'd worked hard to put herself in her current position. And she'd work even harder to land on the throne. Failure wasn't an option. It's why she let Hades take her body whenever he wanted and why she looked the other way when he bedded other women. A good Queen knew when to overlook a King's indiscretions.

She watched the muscles in Hades' back bunch, rippling the pale yellow fur with light black stripes. Opal had felt that fur beneath her fingertips and beneath her claws. It was deceptively soft, not at all like the power lurking behind it. Her gaze dropped to his lower half, which remained humanoid. Leather pants lovingly cupped his firm ass, leaving little to the imagination.

Hades was a ferocious lover, passionate, talented, and giving, but he also demanded the same back from his partners. It had been no hardship to spread her thighs for the King. She'd spread her legs for his entire army if it guaranteed her a position at his side.

What was it going to take to get him to mark her? She'd done everything she could think of short of stripping naked in the Pit and challenging him. If Opal knew for certain that he wouldn't kill her, then she'd have done it already. But, the King was unpredictable. Like other Phantoms, she blamed his mixed bloodline, his *handicap*.

The giant cat let out a loud yowl and tried a final time to open the door. If the King shifted back to his human form, it would be no problem to open, but that would be too easy. Hades was a big cat through and through. Opal waited patiently for him to give up.

When he didn't succeed on his final try, Hades slowly turned to face her. His massive erection filled the front of his leather pants, threatening to burst the seams. Her mouth watered as she recalled the feel of that rigid shaft filling her, stretching her to the point of breaking.

Hades' chest heaved with exertion as he fought his beast for control. He rumbled deep in his throat and his odd blue eyes flashed in frustration as he glanced at the door one last time. The change in color was a quick, but efficient reminder that he was half Atlantean. Not that his thought-reading abilities mattered to Opal. She'd learned to shield herself as a child from all Atlanteans, the King included.

"What is it? Can't you see that I'm busy?" The questions came out garbled as his beast struggled to form words.

"Do you want me to go after her? I could bring her back

so that you could fuck her on the throne," Opal said dryly.

Since when was chasing new *tail* so important that he'd willingly set aside duty to do so? She frowned. The woman's quim must be lined with space blossoms to drive the feline King so crazy. Opal almost laughed aloud, but she didn't think that Hades would appreciate the humor.

His shocked expression was almost comical as he glared at her, then his face closed down. "That won't be necessary."

Hades shifted back to his human form. Muscles in his upper body appeared to fold and shrink before her eyes. It took but a second or two for his fur to fade. When the shift to his humanoid six foot four frame was complete, he stalked toward her. "What do you need?"

He made no apologies for his behavior and Opal hadn't expected any. It would have been more of a shock if he had. "I have the daily report ready for you to go over." She didn't wait for him to respond. She pressed a button on her wristband and a holographic screen appeared in front of her, displaying Hades' kingdom.

"Can't it wait?" He glanced back at the door and rubbed his clawless hand over the furrows he'd carved into the rock. When he turned back toward her, there was a frown on his face.

Opal shook her head. "Not today. One of the guards spotted a Slaver ship in the area and Perseus has started to rumble again. I believe this time his vocal disgruntlement will end with a bid for your throne."

Hades' body stiffened and all sense of playfulness disappeared. "Where? Why wasn't I informed about the ship immediately?" He pushed away from the door and strode down the aisle toward her.

"I came to you the second I received the report," she said. He'd ignored the news about Perseus like she'd expected.

Hades reached her side and dropped onto the throne. "Show me where the ship was spotted."

Opal put her finger on the hologram and the view

changed, zooming into a remote mountainous location. She knew the area well, since it was where she'd been born. She pointed to the ship's last known position. "The scout who spotted the Slavers said that the ship was flying low over the trees, keeping to the valleys between the mountains. It was as if they were searching for something."

"Are we missing any craft?" he asked.

"I thought of that, so I checked," she said. "All ships have been accounted for."

"Did he notice any other Slavers on the ground?" he asked.

Opal shook her head. "No, only the one. But there could be more. Slavers are like Zaronian spores. You spot one, the next thing you know you have an infestation. Thanks to their advanced shielding tech, they slipped into the atmosphere without detection. Do you want me to alert New Atlantis and King Eros?"

"I can take care of any threats to *my* Kingdom," Hades said. "Or do you suddenly doubt my abilities?"

"No, Sire. Never." She dropped her gaze momentarily. "I was simply concerned that the Slavers might enter Atlantean airspace."

His lips thinned. "We'll notify Eros if, and only if, it becomes necessary. I want to know what we're dealing with first."

"What about Perseus?" she asked.

Hades appeared confused. "What about him?"

"I believe he's going to send forth another formal challenge for your throne."

Hades scowled.

"This one you cannot ignore, Sire. You've already passed on his first two challenges. There is talk—I'm sure instigated by Perseus himself—that insinuates that the reason you have declined up to this point is because you believe that you will lose."

Another rumble came from his chest. "This wouldn't be

happening if I were a pure-blood," he said in disgust. "It's only because I'm a Half-being."

She stared at him. It was the truth, but there was no sense in confirming the obvious. So instead Opal said, "What would you like me to do about him?"

Hades glowered. "Nothing. We must await his challenge, and then I will decide what to do. You and I both know this won't end until one of us leaves our blood in the Pit."

Opal reached out and gently touched his arm. "Do not fear, Sire. Perseus is a fool. He cannot defeat you."

Hades bristled beneath her hand and pulled his arm away. "I do not *fear* Perseus. I am the Dark King." He slammed his fist onto his wide chest. There was a thick thud as bone met slabs of muscle. "It is my birthright to sit on this throne. Half-being or not, I will hold what is mine."

"I never doubted you, Sire. You just need to know that there are those who do." Opal glanced at the door, staring at the claw marks, her earlier concerns rushing back. Was it a coincidence that the Slavers appeared at the same time as the unknown female? She didn't believe in coincidences. The King couldn't afford any distractions, not when his throne was being threatened. "Who was that woman? I didn't recognize her."

Hades stared at the map, studying the terrain. "Have the scouts check out these two areas." He pointed to a couple of ravines. "Those locations would be easy spots to hide a ship the size of the Slavers' craft. Make sure at least one of the scouts is from the Tooth Clan. Use a member of the Claw Clan as backup."

Opal hid her shock well. He hadn't answered her. In fact, if she didn't know better—and she most certainly did—she could've sworn that the King had purposely ignored her. The question was why?

Normally Hades was quick to name his bed partners, even the future ones he had his eye on, since momentary pleasure was all that mattered to him. He'd spoken with Opal often about how skilled various women were when it came to bed-sport. It was as if on occasion, he forgot that she was a woman, too. His oblivious nature had only made Opal more determined to please him and win his hearts. She was convinced that the way to the throne was through his hearts, but Hades kept them as guarded as he did his prized weapons.

She glanced at him, his face a picture of concentration. What was he trying to hide? This wasn't the first time they'd had Slavers sneaking into the kingdom or someone had wanted to challenge him and it wouldn't be the last. As news went, it was serious, but thus far not a direct threat.

"Sire, the woman?" Opal persisted, her curiosity getting the better of her. Before she'd been mildly interested, but thanks to the King's evasion she felt like she needed to meet this mysterious stranger to find out exactly what her intentions were. Opal would set her straight quickly, if she had her eye on the King and his throne. She'd run off several of Hades' playthings over the years. All for his own good, of course.

But none of them had made Hades want to claw through a door.

The King's jaw clenched and his muscles corded. "I do not appreciate being questioned." His blue eyes flashed ice, when he looked at her. "Not even by my Righthand. Have I not made my orders clear?"

"They're clear, Sire." Opal swallowed hard, but held her ground.

"Good!" Hades said. "Now finish your report, so that we can send the scouts out right away."

"I could go myself. No one knows that area better than I do. I grew up playing in those ravines," she said.

"No! You're needed here," he said.

Happiness swelled within her. He did care. This proved it. Opal didn't bother to hide her changing scent. Hades' pupils contracted as he inhaled and she saw his cock swell once more.

Opal moistened her lips. "I could remedy your condition before I go." She allowed her gaze to linger on the impressive bulge straining his pants.

Hades shook his head. "There's no time. I don't want Slavers believing that they can enter my realm whenever they feel like it with impunity. No one comes into my kingdom without my permission. Now go!"

Stunned once more by his refusal, Opal bowed. "As you wish."

*****

CHAPTER THREE

Meanwhile in the city of New Atlantis...

Dr. Rachel Evans, Jaclyn Ward, and Brigit Taylor sat around the communal table, picking at the Zaronian fruit in front of them. Rachel's two children, Loki, a boy who looked just like his father, King Eros and a dark-haired girl, Persephone, who was the spitting image of her mother, played rambunctiously with Jac's son, Titus.

"Not much has changed," Rachel said, glancing at her friends around the table. It was of course an understatement. Their lives had been turned upside down and blended for good measure, before being tossed to the other side of the galaxy.

Brigit looked down at her expanding belly. "Are you blind?" She pointed to her obvious pregnancy for emphasis.

Rachel giggled. "Relax, I was kidding. Maybe a few things have changed."

Brigit snorted, then touched her nose to muffle the sound. She picked up a spear of fruit and nibbled on the end.

"Titus, what did I tell you about hitting Loki?" Jac shouted. "Don't make me come over there."

The dark-haired boy stopped and looked at his mother. His green eyes sparkled mischievously before he replied. "You said, don't hit anyone unless they hit you first."

Jac rolled her eyes and looked at Rachel and Brigit. "I didn't say that."

"Sure you didn't," Rachel and Brigit said in unison.

Jac grinned. "I swear that boy is his father's son. If I didn't love him so much, I'd throttle his father for getting me into this mess."

Brigit and Rachel laughed. Both of them knew that Titus might 'look' like his father, but his personality was out and out Jac.

"Doesn't it seem like we've done this before?" she asked, indicating to the lunch on the table in front of them.

Jac snorted. "Yeah, but the last time we were sitting in the Met Museum in New York, bitching about your latest boyfriend. What was that loser's name again?" she asked without waiting for an answer. "I still can't believe you *fucking* talked me into leaving Earth." Her voice dropped to a whisper, when the curse slipped from her lips. She glanced over to make sure the children hadn't heard her.

Rachel arched a brow. "I didn't talk you into anything. I *asked* if you'd come. Besides, you looked pretty willing to me, especially after Ares got you naked. We heard you screaming out your orgasms halfway across the jungle."

"Yeah, well, by the time I found you in that craptastic jungle, Eros had already knocked you up. So you're one to talk, *slut*!" Jac said, whispering once more.

"You're such a bitch!" Rachel countered, not bothering to be quiet.

"Mommy said a bad word," Persephone said.

"Bad mommy." Brigit burst into giggles. Her laughter was followed by a wave of tears. "Ignore me. I can't seem to control the water works."

"It's okay, Brig. We understand." Jac shrugged off the insult and smiled. "At least I had a good time, before my man came in and swept me off my feet. God, I can't believe I just said that out loud. I'm pretty sure that confession made me vomit a little in my mouth."

Brigit's tears dried instantly and she cracked up again. "You're so gross."

"Hey!" Rachel's brow furrowed. "I had fun."

Brigit rubbed her belly and chortled. "With all the losers you used to date? Doubtful. I remember her mentioning something about small dicks or needing a dick. Don't you, Jac?"

"Yes!" Jac's blue eyes widened dramatically. "Vividly."

Rachel chucked a piece of fruit at Jac's head. Her friend ducked easily. "Okay, fine. Go ahead and gang up on me, but it's not going to get you out of helping me host this Christmas party," she said. "I'm tired of just celebrating Atlantean holidays. I want some of our own."

"God, I was hoping that you'd forgotten all about that idea." Jac slumped in her chair.

Brigit pulled a face. "It's not Christmas yet. Not sure you noticed, but the Atlanteans don't even celebrate Christmas. If it weren't for all their surveillance recordings, I wouldn't even be able to get my horoscope."

"Oh the horror," Jac said.

Rachel sighed. "I'm not talking about horoscopes. Christmas is a major holiday. If more and more human women are going to be living on Zaron, then the Atlanteans and the Phantom Warriors are going to have to do more than *learn* about some of our customs. They are going to have to accept them and participate."

"Where are we supposed to find a Christmas tree?" Jac picked up a piece of fruit and popped it into her mouth. "This stuff tastes like crap. What I wouldn't give for a good espresso right now."

Rachel gave Jac the stink eye. "You can't have caffeine in your condition and you know it."

Brigit sat up abruptly. "What? Are you saying... Are

you?"

Jac's pale face turned bright pink.

Brigit crossed her arms over her growing chest in mock disgust. "Why am I *always* the last one to know? So not fair." She rolled her eyes. "Your horoscope didn't mention anything about an impending arrival."

"I don't want to talk about it," Jac growled.

"You don't have to, but eventually you're going to show," Rachel said. "Then everybody will know that you let Ares 'sex you up' again."

"Still not talking about it," she said. "I thought you wanted to plan a party."

Rachel let her friend off easy. The pregnancy had been a shock to Jac, since they hadn't been *trying*. Rachel knew that was Jac code for: When Ares returned from routine patrol, we shagged like bunnies and didn't think about the consequences.

Deep down Jac was thrilled. There was no doubt in Rachel's mind. But her friend was still trying to get used to the idea that she was now a *mom* and not a high-powered shark of an attorney. It didn't matter that Titus was four. Jac had just never pictured herself as domesticated and she was still trying to get used to the idea. Eventually the kicking and screaming would end, but until then, they would continue to show their solidarity.

"We can get a tree from the forest," Brigit said.

"They're the size of redwoods, or hadn't you noticed?" Jac said.

Brigit's shoulders slumped. "Don't be mad at me. I didn't let your secret slip."

"That's only because you didn't know it, oh blabby one," Jac retorted.

Everyone knew that Brigit couldn't keep a secret to save her life. It was one of the things they loved about her.

"Okay, so we get a 'baby tree' from somewhere. It doesn't have to look like a pine. As long as it has leaves and branches, it'll do," Rachel said.

"We don't have any wrapping paper," Brigit said. "Or costumes."

Rachel shrugged. "We'll improvise."

"Costumes?" Jac said. "This isn't Halloween."

Brigit pouted and her eyes filled with tears once more. She scrubbed a hand over her face.

"So when do you want to throw this party?" Jac asked, ignoring her.

"In a week," Rachel said.

"A week!" Jac shouted. "Are you insane? We can't get everything together in seven days."

Brigit beamed and her tears slowed to a stop. "I think it sounds like a great time. I'm sure we can put something together in a week. Besides, it isn't like the Atlanteans or the Phantoms are super familiar with celebrating Earth's holidays. We can do anything we like...like wear costumes." She gave Jac a pointed stare and stuck out her tongue.

Persephone caught her. "Mommy says that's not nice." She indicated to Brigit's tongue.

Brigit grinned. "She's right. Don't ever do that." She winked at Persephone when she thought Rachel wasn't looking.

Rachel stood and helped Brigit to her feet. "Good, it's settled then."

"I'm going to be a dragon." Brigit brushed her belly absently.

Rachel and Jac looked at her. "It's a Christmas party."

Brigit waved their concerns off. "I know, but Orion and I have fond memories of me being a dragon."

"Fond memories, eh?" Jac snorted. "I bet."

Rachel stifled a giggle. From what Eros had told her, Brigit's husband had nearly decapitated her by accident, thinking that she was a real beast. If her false head hadn't fallen off, she might not be here.

"Wear whatever you'd like," she said, meaning it. If

nothing else, the costume would be a good conversation starter.

"There they are," a deep male voice called out from across the room.

The women turned in time to see two tall Atlantean warriors walk through the door. Unlike most Atlanteans, these men were dark in coloring. One had piercing green eyes, while the other had one blue eye and one green eye.

Separately, they were distinguishable, but side by side there was no doubt that they were related. Though their initial reunion had been tense, the brothers had quickly bonded and now were inseparable.

"Daddy!" Titus shouted and launched himself into his father's arms.

Ares caught him easily and brought him up to eye level. "Have you been behaving for your mother?"

"Yes." Titus didn't meet his gaze.

"What did you do?" Ares glanced at the women standing around the table, waiting for one of them to answer.

"He hit Loki," Jac said.

Ares' expression grew serious, but Rachel noted the sparkle in his green eyes. "Why did you hit Loki? Did he hit you first?"

Titus shook his head, sending his long black hair into his face. Ares gently brushed it back from his forehead. "No, but Persephone did."

"She hit Loki?" Ares asked, his confusion clear.

"No." This time Titus' headshake was more definitive. "She hit me. You told me never to hit a girl, so I hit Loki instead," he said as if it made complete and total sense. And to a four year old, it probably did.

Rachel turned to her daughter. "Persephone Ann, is that true?" she asked, shocked that her little girl had reverted to violence.

Her daughter looked up and smiled at her. One finger slipped into her mouth and she grinned wider. "I like him,

Momma. He's pretty."

Her gaze shot to Titus, who looked as if he'd swallowed a bug. It was everything she had not to laugh. Apparently, Ares didn't feel the same.

He roared with laughter. "I see your daughter has taken after your best friend." His gaze slid to Jac and heated.

Jac flushed as Ares approached. He shifted Titus to his other hip and wrapped one strong arm around his wife. His big hand settled lovingly over her flat belly as he nuzzled her neck. "Come, let's go home before our son is forced to defend his honor."

The women giggled.

Orion reached for Brigit's hand and squeezed it gently. "Are you feeling well today?"

"Super!" She looked into his face, her love glowing brightly for all to see. "Better now, since I get to wear my dragon costume," she said, cheerfully.

His brow furrowed. "Dragon costume?"

"I'll explain everything once we get home. Can we stop by the market on the way? I'm starving!" she said.

"Didn't you eat?" Orion glanced at the remains of the food on the table, then gently cradled her stomach in his palm.

Brigit shrugged. "Yeah, but that was like ten minutes ago."

Ares clapped him on the back. "Get used to it, little brother. Cravings are only the beginning." His gaze slipped to Jac's. "Your life is about to change in ways you never imagined."

Orion smiled. "Can't wait." There was no doubt that he meant every word, as he led his pregnant petite wife away.

"You say that now," Ares said, obviously teasing Jac.

"What do you mean by that?" Jac asked. Her tone left no doubt that she was gearing for a fight.

Before she could get too wound up, Ares kissed her. Jac appeared to melt before Rachel's eyes.

Jac's gaze moved down her husband's rock hard body, settling on the loincloth hugging his slim hips. He'd refused to change his style when they arrived at New Atlantis because he knew how much she loved it. "Something's come up," Jac said. "Got to go. I'll see you later, Rach." She was already dragging Ares across the room.

Rachel stifled another giggle. This was going to be the best Christmas party Zaron had ever seen.

*****

CHAPTER FOUR

Taylor's heart pounded so hard she was pretty sure it was about to burst through her double D's and splat onto the floor. She had never heard anything so terrifying as the roar that had come out of Hades.

When he'd told her to run, part of her...a teeny, tiny part of her that deserved a swift kick in the pants, had actually been *excited.* But her excitement quickly waned once her commonsense kicked in and she got a quick glimpse of him. Self-preservation made her run. She was still running, but she didn't know where to.

She still couldn't believe that she'd managed to escape. Hades had moved so fast. If she had blinked, she would've missed him coming off his throne. When she'd looked back all semblance of the man had been gone, replaced by a monster of a cat with fangs that would shame a saber-tooth.

He'd looked like a liger, but he was so much bigger than those huge cats. What kind of prehistoric beast was he?

The scratches and screeches coming from the other side of the door were even more frightening than the ear-splitting roar. Her ears were still ringing. At any moment, she expected him to burst through the stone. Even when the horrific noises stopped, Taylor continued on. The guards she passed didn't try to impede her, but they did follow her movements.

She turned right and stumbled down another hall. Darn cave! Everything looked the same. She continued to jog. Taylor didn't care where she ended up as long as she got far away from Hades. Maybe she should run all the way to the King of New Atlantis and turn herself in. Eros would deport her on the spot, but that was better than being eaten by a Monster Kitty.

Several of the guards watched her breasts bounce as she sprinted by. Taylor clutched her arms over her bountiful chest and kept moving. She could see the opening of the cave up ahead. She was almost out. Freedom came with the smell of fresh air.

Two huge guards stepped into her path as she reached the entrance. They didn't bother to pull the massive swords hanging at their waists. They didn't need to, not when their bodies were the size of boulders. *Gorgeous boulders*, she noted, but boulders all the same. Taylor yelped and ground to a halt, nearly running into them.

"No one is allowed past this point without an escort into the Walled City," the pale-haired giant on the right said.

Taylor looked back, but no one was following her. "Hades gave me permission to leave." The lie slipped from her full lips without her feeling an ounce of guilt. When a Monster Kitty was after you, little white lies didn't mean a whole lot.

The raven-haired man on the left stepped forward. "What is your name, little one?"

"T-taylor," she sputtered.

He smiled. "I am called Perseus." He indicated to the man next to him. "This is Kon."

It was nice to see that not all the men around here were brutes. She grinned at Perseus, whose gaze had dropped to her cleavage. "Nice to meet you," Taylor said, glancing over her shoulder once more. Maybe her luck would hold out for a little while longer.

As an exotic dancer, Taylor wasn't above using her body to get what she wanted. She inhaled deeply, causing her large breasts to quiver beneath her shirt, then cocked her jean-clad hips to draw attention to her long legs. She tangled her fingers in her red hair and twirled the long locks. "I was worried that there were no gentlemen on this planet. I'm grateful to be proven wrong."

Perseus stepped closer, his large body crowding hers. "I'm sorry that your welcome lacked warmth, but what can you expect from a Half-being?"

"Perseus! Watch your tongue!" Kon's alarmed expression made her tense.

Perseus' affable gaze slid from hers. He scowled at Kon.

Taylor didn't know what was going on, but she knew something was wrong.

"The King has not informed us that you are free to leave," Kon said.

"I'm sure it's just a miscommunication on the King's part. He was rather busy when I left him." Taylor needed to get by them. She stepped closer and saw Perseus' nostrils flare. Taylor bit her lower lip and gazed up at him from beneath her lashes. "I won't tell, if you won't," she purred.

She saw indecision in Kon's eyes, but none in Perseus'. He was more than happy to let her go.

Come on, boys, let me pass. Freedom called to her.

The warriors took a step to the side, then suddenly stopped. Their eyes widened and locked on something behind her. Perseus paled a second before they both stiffened to attention.

A low growl rumbled next to her ear. Taylor didn't have to look to know who it was. Gooseflesh broke out over her skin and trickled down her spine. If her reaction was due to fear, she could've easily ignored the sensation. But it wasn't.

"Going somewhere?" Hades' warm breath brushed her

cheek, sending a delicious shiver through her.

Taylor's nipples hardened and her back straightened. The warmth rolling off his body felt like someone had left a furnace blasting unchecked during a heat-wave. "I didn't realize that I was a prisoner," she said without looking at him. She didn't want Hades to see the affect his nearness was having on her.

"You're not." He inhaled, then slowly circled her, using his impressive height to intimidate.

Okay, so maybe he didn't need the height to be intimidating. His presence alone did the trick.

Hades' fiery gaze licked at her skin, tightening it, making Taylor hyper-aware of his maleness. She tried her best to ignore her body's reaction, ignore him, but it was like trying to ignore the sun right before it engulfs the Earth. Hades stopped in front of her, blocking sight of the two warriors with his broad shoulders.

Taylor craned her neck to look into his eyes. At five foot eight, she wasn't a slouch in the height department, but compared to the Phantoms she felt downright puny. Taylor had to clear her throat twice before she could speak. "Then why won't they let me pass?"

The King stared at her, until the intensity made her look away. This close she could smell the slight musk of his skin and see every ripple of muscle beneath his clothes. Taylor nearly swooned, when she reached his washboard abdomen. And she'd never swooned a day in her life.

"It's not safe for you to wander beyond the Keep alone," Hades said, then glared at his two guards. "Perseus and Kon know this." His words were mild, but the threat of punishment behind them was unmistakable.

"Are you saying your city is unsafe?" Taylor knew the question would prick the King's temper. She'd purposely asked to draw his attention away from the guards. As far as she was concerned, they had done nothing wrong.

As if on cue, Hades' eyes narrowed and his lips pressed

into a thin line. "My city is perfectly safe."

"Then why am I not allowed to go into it?" she asked.

"Yes, Sire," Perseus said. "Why are you keeping her a prisoner, when she is obviously *unclaimed*?"

Hades turned on the dark-haired guard. "Are you questioning my authority?"

Kon's face drained of color and he took a step back. "No, Sire," he said hurriedly before Perseus could respond. He grabbed his friend by the arm and pulled him away. "Tis time we check the perimeter." Kon's gaze pleaded with Perseus to comply.

Perseus glanced at Taylor once more. "I will act the gentleman that you believe me to be. Until we meet again." He inclined his head and strode off with Kon hurrying behind.

Hades watched them leave, his expression stony. "As Perseus so rightly stated, you are an unclaimed female. A rarity on our world. On top of that, you're from Earth and Slavers have been sighted. Even if that was not reason enough, I take my vows to other Phantoms seriously. I told Linx that I would protect you and I will...even if that means locking you inside the Keep for your own good."

Taylor snorted. She couldn't help it. Did he really think that she was buying the vow of protection crap? She glanced at him once more. This time humor replaced the simmering heat in his eyes.

Hades held out his hand. "Come," he said. "I will give you a tour of the Keep, then you need to get ready."

Taylor took his hand, before she registered what she was doing. When she did, she tried to jerk her fingers back, but Hades wouldn't let her go. "Get ready for what?" she asked, allowing him to lead her back inside.

"The Pit," he said, like that should mean something to her.

Hello! Earthling here. "What's the—"

"I'll show you to your room after we've explored the

Keep." He cut her off before she could finish the question. "Suitable clothing has been provided." He glanced at her jeans and his nose wrinkled. "If you need anything else, let my Righthand know."

Taylor glanced at his empty hand in confusion. "I have my own clothes. Thanks!" She hadn't packed much, but she had brought the essentials, day-to-day clothing, workout shorts, and a couple of costumes just in case. It would have to do until she could go shopping.

He looked at her and his sensual lips tilted into a smile. "I doubt what you packed will be fit for viewing the festivities at the Pit."

Was he implying that her clothes were trashy? Okay, so some of the things she'd brought might be considered risqué, but they weren't trashy. *Jerk!* She lifted her chin and squared her shoulders. She refused to feel ashamed about her clothing. She glanced at what Hades was wearing. For a King, he wasn't exactly the height of fashion.

Hades led her past the Great Hall. "We take meals in there and hold important meetings. If you prefer to eat in your room, notify the food preparers." He kept walking, but not before she caught a glimpse of the deep furrows marring the door. "Most of the doors you see lead to guard quarters and strategy rooms." His grip on her tightened as they passed several warriors in the hall.

Taylor was surprised by his reaction, but didn't show it. Maybe being single here really was a big deal. "Where are they going?" She used her free hand to point to the retreating guards.

"Shift change." He tracked their movements with his eyes and didn't stop until they were out of sight. "What did you do on your planet?" he asked, when they were gone.

Taylor felt her face flush. It had to be from the exertion of fleeing. No way was she embarrassed. She'd never been embarrassed about how she made a living. Sure, there'd been times in the beginning, but after the first year of dancing her nerves had passed. Maybe it was because the question was coming from a King. She thought about lying, but quickly dismissed the idea. He'd find out eventually.

"I was a dancer," she said. "An *exotic* dancer."

Hades frowned in confusion. "What does that mean?"

"Do you know what dancing is on Earth?" she asked. It would be hard to explain, if he didn't.

He nodded. "Yes, but moving to various rhythms seems quite foolish. The movements don't have meaning and cannot possibly help one in battle," he said.

Taylor sighed. This was going to be harder than she thought. "There are all kinds of dances on Earth. Some are for pleasure, some are for competition, and then there's the kind I do, which involves taking my clothes off." She swallowed hard. "For money."

Hades froze. Something akin to disappointment flashed in his eyes before he suppressed it. He didn't say a word. He just continued to stare.

She'd shocked a King. For the first time in a long time, Taylor felt...*ashamed*. She tried to explain, but every time the words came out it only seemed to make the situation worse. Hades' expression grew darker and darker, until Taylor felt her eyes burn. She would not cry. Would not cry. Not here. Not in front of him.

What kind of reaction had she expected from Hades? A King wouldn't know anything about needing to survive or fit in. His social network was built-in on the day of his birth.

"I did what I had to do. I will not apologize for my actions," she said.

Hades' granite expression didn't even crack, when he said, "Linx did not tell me that you were a sex companion."

He thought she was a whore. This was nothing new. A lot of people thought the same thing over the years, but none of the accusations hurt as bad as it had coming from Hades. Taylor gritted her teeth and tried to calm down, tried to ease the pain.

"I am not a *sex companion*. I get paid to take my clothes off and dance. That's it!" She used her hands to slash the air for emphasis. "No sex! Just dance!"

Hades didn't look like he believed her, but he didn't say anymore. He simply grabbed her hand and continued on. They strolled out a side door into a large courtyard. Wooden swords, shields, and a ton of other equipment Taylor didn't recognize hung on hooks that had been bolted to the stone. Several large poles lined the wall.

"This is where we train. One of the places anyway." He glanced at her body. It was obvious that he was thinking about what she'd just told him. "You don't really need this area."

That's right, what would a *whore* need with a workout area? Taylor glared at him. Did he think she got this body by sitting on her ass?

No, he thought she obtained it by lying on her back.

Kings were supposed to be nice, cultured, polite. This man was judgmental, bullheaded, and beyond rude. Until this moment, Taylor had thought she'd met every type of man that existed in the universe, but she'd been wrong. Hades deserved a category all his own.

His lips parted in surprise as the thought slipped through her mind.

Taylor's scowl deepened. She supposed she should be grateful that he was no longer growling.

*****

Hades fought to get his temper in check as he showed Taylor around the Keep. When he'd seen her standing next to Perseus and Kon, talking her way past them, something inside of him snapped. Not only did he want to destroy the two males for drooling over her, which was utterly out of character, but part of him was outraged that she'd attempted to escape *him*. No one tried to escape him. No one would dare...except Taylor.

He'd known better than to accept Linx's proposal. Something had told him that the Earth woman would be trouble, but Hades had ignored his instincts because he hated owing anyone, and now he was acting like a cat high on space blossoms.

The images of her dancing flashed through her mind. He hadn't been trying to read her thoughts, but they'd been impossible to ignore. Now Hades couldn't stop picturing her naked.

He was relieved that she wasn't a sex companion. More relieved than he should be. If she had been, Hades would have hired her instantly, even though part of him would've found the end of the chase unsatisfying. He wasn't sure where that left him.

"Why did you run?" he asked, to keep his mind from replaying the naked image.

Taylor's perfect brow flickered. She looked at him like he'd lost his faculties. "You told me to," she said. "Remember?"

Hades' grip on her hand tightened. He forced himself to loosen it. Earthlings were weak. He didn't want to bruise her, or worse, break her bones. "It was a temporary loss of control. It will not happen again." He sighed. What had he intended? He wasn't sure, but he knew he had to stop whatever it was. "I didn't mean to drive you away from the safety of the Keep."

She stopped walking, making him halt, too. "How was I supposed to know that? When someone tells me to run, then turns into a Monster Kitty, I don't pause and ask for clarification."

Hades couldn't seem to tear his gaze away from her full lips. The woman had a mouth made for kissing, among other things. He felt his cock rise as he wondered what she'd taste like. She was still talking, but he'd missed part of what she'd said.

What had she called him?

Taylor flushed under his regard and cleared her throat. "I thought you planned to take me to my room."

His mouth clamped shut. "Of course, this way." Hades led her down the stone corridor toward his chambers. He'd ordered her put here before he'd even met her. Now he was questioning the wisdom of that decision.

Several rooms branched off as they neared the end of the hall. He stopped before a door on the right. "You should have everything you need. I'll be by in a few hours to escort you to the Pit."

"About that," Taylor said.

"Be ready. I do not like to be kept waiting." Hades strode down the hall without a backward glance. He knew if he stayed that she'd have to be worried about more than a Monster Kitty.

Hades didn't know what had come over him. He *never* acted that way around a female. He'd nearly growled aloud when Perseus approached Taylor. He shook his head and shoved the doors to his chambers open.

The gray stone walls were punctuated by shafts of light. He'd made sure that his chamber would open to the outside. It had taken months of excavation, but it had been worth it. Emerald green fabrics draped his bed and thick furs lined his floor. He strode across them into his bathing area, which consisted of a waste disposal, a modest sink, and a deep bath. With a flick of a switch, water would cascade from a hole in the ceiling and fill the tub or he could simply stand under it to bathe.

Hades walked over to the copper basin to splash water on his face and gazed into the image reflector. Water dripped from his permanently broken nose to his chin, down the side of his scarred jaw. His blue eyes seemed to glow with a red ring surrounding them, despite the fact that he'd shackled his beast. He gripped the side of the basin and sneered. The action twisted the scar, making him appear even more menacing.

He grinned at his reflection and noticed that his teeth seemed sharper than normal. Hades ran his tongue over his incisors, nicking it on the deadly tips. Blood filled his mouth. He spit it out and shoved away from the basin in disgust.

Despite the temptation Taylor presented, he didn't have time for distractions. If Opal was correct, and he had no doubt that she was, Perseus wouldn't wait much longer to make his move. Hades snarled in frustration. He hadn't had many challenges for his throne, but the number seemed to be growing lately even though he was a fair ruler and took good care of his people.

He scrubbed a hand through his tawny hair. Phantoms were different from the genteel Atlanteans. Their beasts rode them hard to establish supremacy. They were alpha by nature, but there could be only one ruler. His father had ruled for years over the Phantom people. He was well respected and had established a treaty bond with the previous Atlantean King. That bond had kept peace within their kingdoms and remained until both rulers were killed during the last war.

Hades hadn't bothered to establish a treaty with the old King's son in New Atlantis. Forging a new treaty bond was on a very long list of things he needed to get done. If he were honest with himself, Hades might acknowledge that he'd put the treaty off. Not because he intended to start a war with the Atlanteans, far from it, but because he didn't like how the Atlantean people treated him when he began his reign.

His mixed blood had caused more than a few whispers among the royal lines. None attributed directly to King Eros, but dissension was dissension. Whether the Atlanteans and the Phantoms liked it or not, he was his parents' only child, only heir. That meant Half-being or not, sooner or later everyone had to deal with the Dark King.

The severed bond with the Atlanteans was the main reason Hades was having so much trouble now, but it wasn't the only reason. There was the little matter of him having no mate. Phantoms didn't trust mateless leaders. He understood that better than most, but he wasn't going to change his mind. Taylor was right about that, too. He was stubborn.

Hades was determined to remain unattached. He didn't want any child to have to go through what he'd gone through growing up. The constant ridicule and fights had nearly destroyed him. Any child of his would be subjected to the same things or worse. He would not, could not in good conscience do that to his heir, to his child.

Despite his perceived 'handicaps', Hades was a capable Phantom Warrior. Only two things betrayed him from passing for anything other than a Phantom: The fact that he didn't heal as quickly and his mother's blue eyes. That same Atlantean blue stared back at him every time he looked into the image reflector.

Hades walked back into his chamber and pressed a button on the wall. His wardrobe shot opened. He gazed at his clothing, trying to decide what to wear. Normally on Pit nights, he dressed for combat, but for some reason tonight was different.

His mind wandered to Taylor. Had she bathed yet? The thought of her naked body, splashing in the water caused him to tense. Had she danced that way? Dripping, gliding through the water like a Zaronian Goddess. Or had she always performed on dry land? Both would be stunning to see.

He'd had a very special wardrobe put in her room after they'd been introduced. Would she wear the revealing outfit tonight? Or would she balk at the Phantom attire? Given what she did for a living, he hoped she would think nothing of the choice of clothing.

Hades could almost picture Taylor's soft curves filling out the layers of silk to overflowing. *She's under your protection. You told her that you took your vow seriously.* Hades swallowed hard and grabbed the nearest outfit to him.

He tossed the clothes onto the bed, then undressed. His claws ripped through his uniform as he tore it off his body. His hard shaft sprung free from the confines. Hades stroked it once, then released his cock. Tonight he'd either fight in the Pit or he'd find someone willing to fuck.

*****

CHAPTER FIVE

Taylor couldn't get over the outfit that Hades had picked out for her. The dark green gauzy material barely covered her large breasts and the slits in the skirt stretched all the way up to her hipbone.

She looked as if she'd stepped out of the Arabian Nights' stories. Not that she had anything morally against the clothing. Compared to what she used to wear onstage, the dress was positively demure. But it did seem a *little* revealing for attending a royal function.

She'd decided that must be what Hades meant by the Pit. It was probably another dining hall of some kind or a gathering place. The name was off-putting, but Taylor knew names could be deceiving.

She stared at her reflection and re-adjusted the material over her breasts, when she noticed that her nipples were clearly visible through the sheer fabric. She'd pulled her long hair back in a loose braid to avoid accidentally sitting on it.

The swept back style made her normal features appear almost exotic, but now she was second-guessing her choice. If she let her long hair hang loose, she'd be able to maintain a modicum of modesty. The King already thought she was a whore. She didn't want to arrive dressed like one.

Taylor glanced longingly at her jeans and T-shirt lying on the bed, then at her reflection. She barely recognized herself in the gorgeous gown.

She should just change back into her own clothes. She'd be more comfortable that way, but Taylor didn't want to offend her host or his people. The tension between she and Hades was already thicker than it needed to be. One of them had to be the bigger person and given Hades' behavior thus far, Taylor knew it had to be her.

She stared wistfully at her jeans. She'd feel so much better if she had them on. Taylor had taken one step toward the bed, when a knock sounded on the door. Too late to change now. She took a deep breath and studied her appearance one last time, then answered the door.

*****

Hades' hand hung in mid-air as the door opened. The breath seemed to rush from his lungs as his gaze landed on the vision in green standing before him. He'd thought Taylor was appealing before, but now she was extraordinary.

The soft fabric cupped her full breasts, before gently curving in at her trim waist. The slits in the skirt played peek-a-boo with her long legs, leaving his mouth dry. She'd put on the matching slippers and pulled her long red hair back, twisting the length into a stylish knot. Hades forgot to move, forgot to breathe—forgot to think.

"I can change." Taylor crossed her arms over her chest, her fingers fluttering nervously over her skin, but not before he caught a glance of her luscious nipples brushing the front of the silky gauze.

Hades swallowed hard. The beast inside of him perked its head up to get a look at her. When he inhaled, Taylor's sweet scent filled his lungs, leaving him winded. A growl rumbled from his chest. Hades clamped down on the noise, wrestling his beast into a stranglehold. He didn't trust it or himself enough to let it go. He was afraid of what might happen if he did.

You're supposed to protect her, remember? He chastised.

"I think I should change clothes." Taylor shifted under his regard and glanced back at the clothing she'd brought from Earth.

"That won't be necessary." Hades' voice croaked as he spoke. "You look stunning."

She gave him a small smile for the compliment, then swallowed hard as her nerves returned.

Drums pounded. The thick base beat vibrated his chest as he stepped aside, so she could leave her room.

"You didn't tell me there would be music." Joy filled her face. Taylor's hips swayed as she shut the door behind her.

Did she even realize what she was doing? Hades didn't think so. He followed the sensual side-to-side movement, mesmerized by the gentle swoosh of fabric and the slight jiggle of the round globes.

Taylor cleared her throat.

Hades tore his gaze away from her lush ass to find her staring at him. "We'd better hurry." It was either that or push her back into her room and ravish her. "We don't want to be late." In truth, the Pit wouldn't start its festivities until he got there. One of the many perks of being King. And at the moment, also one of the disadvantages.

*****

He'd bathed since he had left her. Moisture still clung to his damp hair, making it appear darker. Hades had also changed clothes. He was still in black, but his pants were tighter and the collar of his shirt hung loose, giving her tantalizing glimpses of his impressive chest. Taylor hated that every time she looked at him, she had the overwhelming urge to lick him from head to shaft. He was like candy and she'd always had a sweet tooth.

Hades tripped beside her and a slash of red shadowed his cheeks.

Taylor automatically moved to steady him, but he stepped easily out of her reach. She shrugged the odd behavior off as a 'guy thing'. If he was too proud to accept her help, then so be it. Hades might act aloof, but he wasn't totally immune to her charms. She'd busted him staring at her ass. He didn't try to cover what he'd been doing, but he had quickly changed the subject.

The sound of the drums grew louder. The steady boom, boom vibrated her chest and made her want to dance. Not strip, but dance. How long had it been since she'd gone out dancing for fun? Taylor couldn't remember and that made her sad. She loved music. Loved to dance.

"I didn't realize that there'd be a band," she said. "How long will they play?"

"Not a band." Hades shook his head. "It's the call that summons everyone to the Pit."

"Oh." She heard the disappointment in her voice, but she hoped that Hades hadn't.

A different set of stone doors rose before them. Red gems twinkled from the door handles. Rubies, maybe? Taylor wasn't sure. The only real jewels she'd ever had were diamond earrings and she'd left them when she had fled Sergei. She tried to get a better look at the gems, but the doors swung open, revealing a regiment of towering Phantom guards.

"All hail the Dark King!" one of the guards shouted.

The men responded with, "Hail the Dark King!"

Taylor jumped at the thunderous sound. Rows of carved seats, resembling an amphitheater, fanned out around a caged arena with mud floors. Two men stood nose to nose in the arena dressed in loose black loincloths and leggings. Their chests were bare and their long hair had been tied back away from their faces. Growling, hissing, and snarls emanated from them as they tried to stare each other down.

Taylor tugged on Hades' arm. "This may be a stupid question, but what is going on? I thought the Pit was another place where you dined."

Hades stared at her hand until she slowly released him. Taylor flushed. *Did you need permission to touch a King?* She hadn't meant to offend him. She took a step back, not that the distance would do her much good if he became Monster Kitty again.

Amusement lit Hades' eyes, but did not fill his voice when he spoke. "Food will be served, but the Pit is where disagreements are settled."

Taylor's eyes widened. "You mean they're going to fight?" She hoped she was wrong. She'd always hated fighting, whether it was in MMA or boxing. To her the idea of a couple of guys beating the crap out of each other was frankly stupid. Most men in her opinion didn't have the brain cells to spare.

Hades looked at her like she was a child, who'd just been caught running with sharp scissors. "Come." He held out his hand for her to take and led her up several rows to a spot in the middle. Not exactly box seats, but they did give them a good view of everything in the arena.

Yippee! Lucky me.

Once they'd settled into their seats, the stadium filled up around them. It was as if everyone had been waiting for Hades to arrive. *He's the King, dummy. Of course they were waiting.* She sighed and tugged at her dress.

Taylor didn't think she was fit to be in the company of a royal, not even an unconventional royal. Her whole life had been built around survival. There'd been no time for afternoon teas, etiquette classes, or high society parties. Strippers didn't tend to be invited to the latter. And she couldn't afford the prior, not when her budget meant the difference between rent and buying noodles.

She would never admit it to her sister, but Taylor

sometimes wished she'd gone to college like Tabby. Trouble was after their parents died, there'd only been money for one of them to go to school and given Tabby's grades, the choice was obvious.

She leaned over to Hades and whispered, "I think I should go back to my room. I don't really fit in here."

Something dark crossed his face. "Nonsense. You belong here as much as anyone else."

Taylor opened her mouth to protest, but took one look at Hades' expression and changed her mind. She crossed her arms over her chest and did her best to ignore all the curious glances she was receiving from the men around her. A dark-haired beauty stepped into the room. She was the first woman Taylor had seen, though she knew there had to be others, unless breeding on this planet was *very* different from Earth.

The woman's gaze slid from hers to the King and back again, then she slowly made her way through the crowd. Taylor noticed the men gave the woman a wide berth. She wondered if it had anything to do with the wicked sword strapped to the woman's side. The woman stopped before the King.

"You're Highness." She gave him a slight bow, then took a seat on his right side.

Hades inclined his head in return, then fixed his gaze on the arena below.

"Hi! I'm Taylor." Taylor held out her hand.

The woman stared at Taylor's extended hand. She glanced at Hades, who gave her an almost imperceptible shrug.

"Opal," she said. "I am the King's Righthand." The woman reached out and took Taylor's hand in a punishing grip that made her knuckles crack.

Taylor winced and forced a smile. "Nice to meet you."

The woman didn't respond, instead, she stared at the two men in the arena. "Pitticus is finally going to do it?"

"Looks like," Hades said.

"I didn't think he'd ever make a move," Opal said.

"I, neither." Hades sat back and draped his arms on the ledge behind them.

"This should be good," Opal said.

"Or at least interesting," Hades murmured.

"Fifty credits says Cornelius takes him," Opal said.

Hades arched his brow and smiled. "You underestimate the Blood Clan or perhaps you're overestimating the Tooth Clan. Either way, I'll take your bet and your credits when you lose."

Opal's expression spoke of victory, but Hades' face harbored no doubts. If they were going by size alone, the men were fairly evenly matched from what Taylor could see. Each stood a little over six and a half feet like most of the Phantom Warriors. She wasn't sure what Blood Clan and Tooth Clan meant, but if it was anything like Scotland, Taylor figured it had to do with family bloodlines.

The warmth of Hades' hand near her back distracted Taylor, though he hadn't actually touched her. She rolled her shoulders and sat forward, but not before catching Hades' mischievous grin. His was playing with her like a cat pawing a terrified mouse. Considering what normally happened to the mouse afterwards, that didn't bode well for her.

Taylor scooted toward the empty seat beside her, but it wasn't nearly far enough. That fact was driven home, when a dark-haired warrior that she recognized instantly approached.

"Hello again," Perseus said.

"Hi." She beamed.

"I believe you're in my seat," he said.

"Sorry." She moved over just enough to allow him to sit down.

Hades frowned at them, then slowly stood. He raised his hands to quiet the crowd. The cacophonous volume dropped to silence. "Let the games begin," he shouted.

The men roared, some quite literally. Perseus louder than most, as his eyes bled red and fur sprouted on his face.

Despite her need for space, Taylor found herself scooting closer to Hades. She was pretty sure that he wouldn't let anything happen to her, since he'd sworn to Linx that he'd protect her. He also seemed to have better control over his Other half. And in a room full of shifters, that counted for a lot.

What was that old saying about the devil you know?

*****

Hades didn't think Taylor's brownish-green eyes could get any wider. As it was, they'd almost swallowed her pretty face. So confused, so frightened. She trembled as she took in the crowd around her. Sensing her discomfort, Perseus squeezed her hand and engaged her in conversation. She seemed to relax a little after that and even laughed a couple of times.

Hades didn't blame Taylor for being scared. He blamed himself. He'd done nothing to alleviate her fears. If anything, he'd fanned them so she'd want to keep her distance. He just hadn't anticipated his response to her turning to another warrior for reassurance and protection. The swift gut check was most unwelcome.

If he were being honest with himself, Hades would admit that he still wanted her. Wanted to fuck her so bad that he could almost taste it, but he'd resigned himself to the fact that it wasn't going to happen. That didn't mean he'd allow another warrior to experience what he chose to deny himself.

He glared at Perseus, who was now back in his humanoid form. The warrior seemed oblivious to the threat. He continued flirting with Taylor, trying to distract her from what was happening around them.

Had Hades not read Taylor's thoughts before she asked to return to her room, he might have taken pity on her and allowed the request. If only to get her away from Perseus. But he had read them, and her thoughts had infuriated him. Even now the beast clawed at Hades' insides. How could she think that she wasn't good enough to sit by his side? Him of all people.

Looking at her, it seemed unfathomable given her full lips, stubborn chin, and lush body. Her long, silky hair alone was a cat's wet dream. How could she be so insecure? What in Zaron had happened to her on Earth to make her think such a thing? He made a mental note to send Linx a message. Hades needed answers...*wanted* answers, which was odd in and of itself.

Had she been anyone else, Hades might've worried about deception, but since Taylor had no idea that he could read her thoughts, he'd quickly ruled manipulation out. She truly believed herself to be unworthy. It was a feeling he could *relate* to. Was that why she'd turned to Perseus?

Perseus leaned over and whispered something in Taylor's ear. She giggled and playfully swatted his arm.

Hades forced his attention back to the Pit, while he fought to get his considerable temper under control. He kept Taylor in his peripheral vision, making sure that Perseus didn't get out of line. At least that's the lie he told himself as jealousy threatened to consume him.

*****

The men in the Pit glared at each other one last time, then stepped apart. One stood on one side of the oval cage, while the other stood across from him. The fight started the second they shifted into their Other forms.

The man Opal had called Pitticus sprouted fangs and his skin took on a scaly, silver reptilian sheen. His eyes glowed red and his pupils elongated to narrow slits as he launched himself at Cornelius, landing on his fur-covered back.

Cornelius had turned into a massive bear like the man

who'd helped Linx fight the mobsters on Earth. What was his name again? Riot? Taylor didn't ask, since a large part of what had occurred on Earth that day had been 'illegal' by Phantom standards. She thought the less she knew the better.

"Not the smartest opening move," Opal commented.

Hades didn't look at her. "We'll see. If Pitticus manages to get some of his venom into Cornelius, then the fight will end quickly."

Taylor straightened. "Did you say venom?"

He nodded.

"Like a snake?" Taylor couldn't wrap her brain around what was happening. Wasn't it bad enough that the two guys were attacking each other? Did there have to be poison involved?

Hades looked at her. "Yes, but it won't kill him. Pitticus knows how to control his venom flow. Every adult Blood Clan Phantom does."

The Dark King's nonchalance scared her more than what was happening in the Pit. Taylor's thigh slammed into Perseus' leg as she tried once again to distance herself from Hades. She didn't care how attractive he was—there was no way she'd sleep with a guy who had venom dripping out of his teeth.

"Don't worry, I'll protect you." Perseus smiled encouragingly.

Taylor stared at his mouth. His teeth didn't look sharp, but neither had Pitticus' before he attacked. Was it rude to ask Perseus what he was? Before Taylor could phrase the delicate question, a low menacing growl rumbled beside her, causing the hair on her arms to rise.

Perseus' smile dropped, as a strong hand reached out and clasped Taylor's arm, pulling her back to where she'd been originally seated. Her gaze followed the muscular arm all the way to Hades' glowering face. His incisors had lengthened and his aqua eyes were ringed in red.

Taylor gulped, even though the Dark King's anger and

aggression weren't directed at her. These men were looking for any excuse to fight. And like a fool, she'd just given them one.

The tension between the King and Perseus felt like a physical weight pressing upon her. It was so heavy that it nearly squished her in her seat. In an attempt to diffuse the situation, Taylor turned her attention back to the fight.

Blood covered both fighters. Cornelius's ear seemed to be pointing in the wrong direction and he was swaying on his feet. Pitticus circled him like a Tiger shark, sensing an easy meal. His fangs were bared as he searched for another opening to attack.

The stare down between Hades and Perseus continued until the Dark King growled again. The deep rumble promised pain. Perseus finally broke eye contact and both men went back to watching the fight.

The bear bellowed, then rushed whatever Pitticus had become. The blow threw Pitticus onto the dirt floor, but he rolled out of the way before Cornelius mauled him. Taylor screamed. Opal and Hades turned as one to look at her. Heat flooded her face. Taylor didn't think her queasy stomach could take much more violence. She'd never been good around blood. After her sister Tabby's torture, her aversion had been even worse.

"Can't you end this?" she asked, the question turning into a plea. "Make them stop and declare one a winner."

Hades gaped at her. "Why would I do that?"

"Because they're going to kill each other," she said. There was so much blood. Cornelius's fur was slick from the various wounds on his body.

Hades glanced at the men. "It's possible that one will die."

"How can you be so casual about death?" she spat. "What is wrong with you?"

He looked at her. "I forget that you're human."

Hades made it sound like an insult. Perhaps it was.

Perhaps to these 'civilized' beings Earthlings were nothing more than talking chimps.

"I've been told that you have strange rituals when it comes to dealing with loss. You fight what is natural. Death is a part of our society that's accepted as normal. You'd do best to remember that before you try to disrupt a sanctioned fight." Hades turned his attention back to the men in the Pit.

Disrupt a fight? She wasn't trying to disrupt anything. Taylor just wanted Hades to declare a winner so that she could return to her room. She crossed her legs and hugged herself.

The bear's claws swiped across the side of Pitticus, ripping deep furrows into his flesh. The warrior grunted, then ran his hand over the raw wound and brought the blood to his mouth. He sucked on his fingers, slurping the crimson, then snarled. The next blows were too fast for Taylor to follow. She could no longer tell who was winning. In her eyes, they were both losers.

Suddenly, Cornelius swayed and fell over. The crowd hushed and everyone waited. Pitticus nodded to someone standing outside the Pit. The warrior tossed in a sword that was nearly as tall as Taylor. Pitticus caught the hilt with one bloody hand, then slowly approached Cornelius.

"Get up!" He demanded.

The bear grunted, but didn't move.

"I said, get up!" Pitticus kicked him in the ribs.

The bear groaned and rolled over onto his back. A swirl of light surrounded him. When the light faded, Cornelius was in his human form and the wounds he'd suffered in the fight had sealed. His jaw clenched as he glared at Pitticus, then he slowly struggled to his feet.

Taylor's heart was in her throat. She couldn't seem to take a deep breath without choking on it. She had no idea what was about to happen, but it didn't look good.

Cornelius swayed, but somehow managed to keep his feet under him. Pitticus pointed the sword tip at Cornelius's bloody chest. "Move!" he shouted.

Cornelius hesitated.

Pitticus drove the tip of the sword in just enough to draw fresh blood. "I said, move!" This time when he pushed the bear-shifter with the blade, Cornelius backed toward the fence surrounding the Pit.

"That's far enough," Pitticus said. "Now turn."

Cornelius looked as if he was about to resist, but the warning look he received from Pitticus seemed to change his mind. He slowly turned, leaving his back vulnerable to the Pitticus.

"Grab the fence," Pitticus said. He reached into a strange pouch attached to his loincloth and pulled out two lengths of rope.

Cornelius grasped the fence, his muscles flexing convulsively as he forced himself to hang on. Pitticus quickly secured his wrists to the fence.

Was he going to bind him and then kill him? The thought horrified Taylor. Hades had already unjustly accused her of trying to disrupt the fight. Well this time he'd have just cause. There was no way she would sit back and watch one man slaughter another. Taylor started to rise, but Hades quickly pulled her back down and gave her a quick jerk of his head to silence her.

The stench of the Phantoms' depravity thickened the air. The smell of blood, sweat, and desperation gagged her. Taylor curled in upon herself unable to watch the carnage to come. She covered her eyes with her hands and waited for it to be over. Everyone around her seemed oblivious.

The crowd shouted, "Do it!" Their thunderous voices drowned out reason. They were barbarians, each and every one of them. Beasts in both their human and their Other form.

Taylor peeked between her clenched fingers. Perhaps watching with one eye would make what was about to occur somehow less horrifying, but she didn't think so. Pittacus slowly approached Cornelius with the sword in his hand. Taylor's heart lurched.

All the while the crowd droned on, hammering her eardrums with their ceaseless chants. Her stomach churned with acid threatening to ruin her new shoes. Beside her, Hades watched in eager anticipation.

Part of her was disappointed that he could be so blood thirsty, while another part was grateful that she was seeing him for who he truly was. It would make resisting her attraction to the King much easier.

Pitticus raised his sword. Taylor's stomach recoiled. With two quick slashes that seemed to arc like heat lightning, Cornelius's loincloth dropped to the ground, leaving him naked. The crowd roared in approval.

Taylor refused to voice her confusion. She'd already caused enough trouble in the stands. She had no idea what was going on. Was it tradition to strip someone of their clothes before you killed them? To humiliate the loser even more? If so, then this society was as messed up as Earth's and Taylor wasn't sure she wanted permission to stay.

Death awaited her, if she returned to Earth. The Russian mob would kill her on sight, but Taylor was beginning to think her chances of survival were greater with the mobsters. They may torture, but they didn't tend to humiliate their victims in the process.

Cornelius's muscled ass twitched from side-to-side as he tried to pull his hands free. Pitticus took his time loosening the ties of his own loincloth. He kept glancing at the crowd and grinning maniacally, which only seemed to urge them on.

The material finally slid down his long legs, revealing his hardening shaft. The crowd's applause became deafening and their chants turned into roars of encouragement. Everyone seemed glued to what was happening in the Pit. Taylor couldn't blame them. She couldn't seem to look away either.

Pitticus grasped his erect cock and began to stroke it.

Juices pearled on the tip, but not enough to lubricate his thick length. He opened his mouth, revealing his fangs. Liquid shot out from the tips of his incisors, covering his shaft in shimmering moisture.

What was that?

"Venom," Hades answered her unvoiced question.

Taylor glanced at him, but he wasn't looking at her. He appeared to be speaking to Opal. Something twinged in her chest at the obvious intimacy the two shared. Taylor steadfastly ignored the unpleasant sensation and turned back to the spectacle before her.

Pitticus was an impressive man, in no way small and he seemed to be growing larger by the second. Taylor crossed and uncrossed her legs, shifting restlessly in her seat. She tried not to think about the venom or his dripping shaft.

When his cock couldn't get any harder, Pitticus approached Cornelius. "You led me on a merry chase, but now I have won fairly. You will surrender your ass to me and your body from this day forth."

His words carried over the din of the crowd. A slight tremor ran down Cornelius's spine and the muscles in his thighs twitched. Pitticus kicked Cornelius's legs wider, then positioned the head of his cock against the man's straining backside. He stroked a bloody hand over Cornelius's flank, leaving a streak of blood behind, then reached around and grasped Cornelius's balls, rolling them in his palm.

Cornelius jerked and his shaft grew. The strain on his face took on a look of eager anticipation. Pitticus cupped him roughly and Cornelius groaned. He wanted this. Wanted him. This wasn't an act of rape or humiliation. This wasn't punishment for losing. This was seduction, pure, simple and raw at its core. One man staking a carnal claim on another.

A flush of heat swallowed Taylor's body in one insatiable gulp. She squeezed her thighs together to ease the sudden ache. Despite the prior carnage, she found herself growing wet and aroused. She glanced at Hades to make sure that he hadn't noticed. Fortunately, his eyes remained locked on the men. She cleared her throat and shifted again.

Pitticus gave Cornelius one final squeeze, which rung a moan from the bound man's throat, then rocked back and plunged his cock inside the warrior's tight butt. The ring of muscles gave way by force and determination. Cornelius's back bowed and he cried out, his legs giving way beneath him.

Before he fell, Pitticus caught him around the waist, holding him in place. His hips continued to rock, driving him deeper and deeper inside of Cornelius's willing body. Taylor's nipples hardened. Her breath sawed in and out of her lungs as the warriors fucked.

Her gaze strayed once more to Hades. Instead of watching the spectacle, his red-ringed eyes were now locked on her. His breathing had also deepened and a slight flush covered his cheeks. He inhaled and his nostrils flared as the musk from her arousal reached him.

Lust struck her hard and fast. Taylor's body responded automatically. Her eyes drifted down of their own volition. A massive bulge filled the front of Hades' tight pants and seemed to grow under her perusal. Her gaze shot back to his face and she froze.

It was a purely instinctive action on her part. Something told Taylor if she moved, he'd be on her doing exactly what Pitticus was doing to Cornelius. And she wasn't altogether certain that she would stop him.

A bellow came from the Pit, echoing around the room. All eyes turned back in time to see Cornelius spill his seed onto the ground. Sweat covered their bodies, the strain showing in every fiber. Pitticus leaned his head back and his fangs appeared to grow even longer than before. His strong hands locked onto Cornelius's trim hips. He thrust twice more, then roared a second before he plunged his fangs into the bound man's neck.

His whole body shuddered as his hips cradled Cornelius's

ass. Pitticus jerked once, his mouth still locked and sucking hard, then he slowly released the warrior and pulled out, his spent cock dripping with their shared juices. Pitticus reached for his sword and slashed the bindings holding Cornelius in place. The other man fell to his knees.

"Come." Pitticus wiped his bloody mouth with the back of his hand. "I am not nearly finished with you yet."

Cornelius looked shattered and...*besotted.*

Pitticus turned to the King. "I claim Cornelius as my mate from this day forth."

Hades glanced at Cornelius. "Any objections?"

The man slowly shook his head.

"Then your claim is accepted," Hades said. "Go forth and be happy."

Taylor really wanted to go back to her room now. She needed to be alone, so she could seek her own release. She didn't think she could take anymore 'fights' like this one without embarrassing herself.

"I don't understand," she said in way of a question.

Hades glanced at her. "It's simple. In the Pit everyone has a choice to either fuck the loser or kill them. Most fights end in death. In this case, Pitticus and Cornelius have been harboring a 'not-so-secret' attraction for each other, but were both too dominant and stubborn to act upon it. So Pitticus finally sent out a challenge. The fight took care of the dominant question and gave the men the relief they've been wanting for months."

"What about the venom?" Taylor asked.

"If used properly, it can work as a numbing agent," Hades said. "Did you think Pitticus fucked him to punish him?"

"I—" It was about the only syllable she could handle at present. Taylor had thought that and worse. She glanced over at Opal, whose small nipples were showing through her uniform. At least she and Hades weren't the only ones turned on. She was afraid to look in Perseus' direction. The tension in the room changed. Several of the warriors rushed out. She had a pretty good idea what they intended to do.

"I need to fuck," Hades said like someone saying 'I need a drink'. He looked at Taylor and waited.

Hades was temptation incarnate. Taylor had thought so the moment she had laid eyes on him. Her body thrummed with the need to say yes. But she couldn't act upon those instincts. Taylor had made many mistakes in her life. Almost all had started with her falling into bed with men too quickly. It gave them the wrong impression. Hell, it gave her the wrong impression.

There'd already been so many misunderstandings between her and Hades, which had to be a record of some kind, since she'd only arrived a few hours ago. If she accepted the King's unspoken invitation, it would just complicate matters. Worst yet, it would confirm his earlier beliefs about her. And contrary to what he might truly believe, she wasn't a whore.

She couldn't do it. No matter how badly she wanted to.

Taylor shook her head, not trusting herself to speak. The definitive movement ended the internal argument she'd been having and gave Hades his answer. This was her chance to start over, begin again, even if that meant giving up something she dearly desired.

Something dangerous flashed in Hades' eyes before it was carefully suppressed. Without a word, he reached over and grabbed Opal, pulling her to her feet.

"Come!" He hesitated, then glanced at Taylor as if she were an afterthought. "You, too." He glared at Perseus over her shoulder, all but daring him to speak, and waited for her to rise.

What did he mean by 'her too'? She'd told him no. Okay, so she hadn't actually said the word aloud, but she'd been clear. If he thought she was going to have a threesome with him, he was going to be a very disappointed King. Taylor wasn't sure how it worked here in Monster Kitty land. Just because she was a stripper didn't mean she was a *sharer*.

Hades walked away before she could set him straight. Taylor said her goodbyes to Perseus, and reluctantly followed the Dark King into one of the halls leading out of the Pit seating area. They weren't in plain view of the crowd, but they were by no means hidden. Anyone strolling down the hall would come upon them.

The King pushed Opal against the wall and stripped the lower half of her body bare. She made no move to stop him. Instead she eagerly spread her legs. Hades loosened his pants and pulled his cock out.

Taylor's mouth dropped open. No wonder Opal spread her legs so quickly. And like a fool, she'd turned him down. Taylor had been with men who were well endowed, but Hades made them seem inconsequential by comparison. He stroked himself, making his shaft harder and longer. She could do nothing but stare in envy.

There were no prelims. Hades simply positioned the head of his shaft at Opal's opening and parted her with one hard thrust. Taylor froze, suddenly unsure of what to do. A myriad of emotions churned inside of her. None of which were pleasant.

Why had he asked her to come along? Was he some kind of exhibitionist? Did he get off on other people watching him? Or had he asked her to follow so he could keep an eye on her?

Another thought struck, this one far more insidious. Was Hades punishing her because she'd said no?

Taylor didn't need a babysitter and she certainly wasn't about to volunteer to be an audience of one. If Hades' intent was to punish her, then he had succeeded. She'd seen enough to know that he'd haunt her dreams for the rest of her life. And worst yet, she still wanted the sexy bastard. There had to be something wrong with her.

She gave the rutting couple one final envious glance, intending to leave. She couldn't watch this, couldn't watch him. Not like this. Their eyes met. Hades' blue gaze trapped her. By sheer force of will, he kept Taylor from moving while he continued to fuck Opal. Taylor felt every thrust, every glide, every brush of his chest. And she hated him for making her want him even more.

*****

Hades locked gazes with Taylor as he ripped open Opal's clothes to get quick access to her moist sex. And there was no doubt that she was wet. He could smell her ripening. Opal's aroma wasn't nearly as sweet as the lush scent emanating from Taylor, but the female Earthling had turned him down.

Him, the King of the Phantoms.

Despite her rejection, Hades couldn't let Taylor go. He demanded she stay without a word spoken. He wanted Taylor to feel every inch of him filling *her*. See the need burning inside of him. Taste the raw hunger driving him to fuck another, when all he wanted to do was reach for her.

It was that shocking realization that had driven him to act rashly. The powerful emotion Taylor had stirred inside of him had felt like a maelstrom, threatening his mooring, tearing apart his carefully constructed foundations. His body had quaked as the beast fought for release and nearly won.

Panic over the implications of the emotional onslaught coupled with the sting from her rejection had made him choose Opal as a surrogate. It was either that or throw Taylor down in front of the entire arena. Hades knew if he did that, he wouldn't stop until he'd claimed her. And that was something he could not allow. Would not allow. Even with Perseus sniffing around.

His beast roared inside of him, angry at what he was doing. He told his Other half to shut the fuck up and drove his cock deeper into Opal, hoping to ease the yearning desire. He knew in his hearts that any attempt would be futile. But he didn't stop. Couldn't stop.

Opal moaned in his ear and clung to him, wrapping one long leg around his hip so she could grind against him, but it wasn't her velvet sheath that he needed.

Hades growled in frustration, his gaze searing a path down the front of Taylor's curvy body. Her rigid nipples tented the front of her dress. They were so hard that he could see every dimple. His mouth watered to taste them, feast upon their rich bounty. He bit down, tasting his own blood instead and redoubled his efforts.

He'd always been able to forget women easily. Taylor should be no different. If he just let himself fuck her, then it would end his torment. But she was under his protection. In a matter of days, she would be gone. Months from now Taylor Shelley would be just a memory. Until that day came, she was a threat to his sanity.

Hades thrust harder, grunting animalistically as he reached between their bodies to find the sensitive nerve endings that would send Opal into ecstatic convulsions. Taylor's wide eyes glazed with desire as she watched him. Her body swayed toward them, though he was sure she was unaware of the fact.

He felt himself growing impossibly harder. Taylor's need was palpable. Her mind may have rejected him, but her body wanted him. All Hades had to do was reach out and she would be his.

Instead, he acted the bastard that he was.

Hades teased her, tortured her, made Taylor want as much as he did with no intention of fulfilling her...just like she'd done to him. Her need perfumed the air. The spicy musk tempted the beast within him.

The plan had worked beautifully...and failed miserably. Hades now wanted Taylor more than she wanted him. And thanks to his petulance and impulsiveness, she would probably never let him touch her.

Hades felt his sac rise against his body. His gaze dropped to Taylor's parted mouth. She licked her lips, whether by instinct or to torment him, he'd never know, but the tentative movement sent him over the edge. Hades snarled, then came, but not before he pinched Opal, taking her with him.

When his vision cleared, Taylor's shattered expression registered and proceeded to rip his two hearts in half. He closed his eyes so he wouldn't have to gaze upon her and cursed viciously under his breath.

What in Zaron's fires was he doing? Opal remained trapped in his arms, her languid body draped against him. Hades was many things, but he'd never been cruel...until now.

*****

By the time Hades spent himself, Taylor's ache had turned into an inferno and she was ready to scream. Her whole body felt as if one touch would send her spiraling into space, burning up before she ever made it out of the atmosphere. She knew when she met Hades that he'd be a great lay. Too bad he was such a dick.

The knowing smirk Opal sent her way only made the awkward situation worse. Taylor couldn't really blame the woman for feeling superior. She'd gloat too if their positions were reversed.

The need to go to her room became a cloying desperation. Taylor did not understand all the reasons why Hades had put on this performance, but there was no doubt that at least part of it had been to punish her. She'd been right about that.

If he wanted her to think about what she was missing, he needn't have bothered. Taylor had thought of little else, since watching the men in the Pit have sex. Tonight made it more than clear to her that she didn't understand Phantom society. And she definitely didn't 'get' the King.

She wondered if it was too late to find Perseus and take him back to her room? At the thought, Hades' eyes flew open and the red ring returned. A low growl rumbled from his chest.

Okay, maybe not.

No matter what his ultimate reason for behaving the way that he had, Hades had been rude. According to her mother—God rest her soul—there was only one way to handle that kind of rudeness. Taylor straightened her shoulders, lifted her chin, and adopted a decidedly bored expression. She'd faced down an abusive boyfriend and the Russian mob. Taking on one Monster Kitty was no problem.

"If you're finished," she glanced at his dick, which was still semi-hard, then crinkled her nose like she'd smelled something bad. "I'd like to go back to my room now." Taylor laid on a thick coma-inducing sweet tone to make the jab go even deeper.

Hades' jaw clenched and his muscles tightened. His ice blue eyes flooded with red, flashing back and forth in color like a caution stoplight. Taylor thought his head might explode—*wishful thinking on her part*—but in the end he acquiesced.

"Thank you for the performance, your Royal Highness," she said, making sure the 'highness' part sounded an awful lot like asshole.

Taylor continued her unaffected act until she got back to her room. Once there, she walked inside and slammed her door, then stomped her anger out until her knees hurt. How dare that arrogant jerk treat her like a common whore lining up to watch him fuck!

He asked you first. You turned him down, remember?

Didn't matter. He could've handled the rejection better. Hades was a grown man, not a deprived five year old.

He's a King, the insidious voice whispered.

Again, not an excuse as far as Taylor was concerned. He didn't have to grab the nearest woman and take her instead.

The thought made Taylor stop pacing. Oh my God! Was that why she was so mad? She'd only known him for a day.

The 'old Taylor' was stupid enough to fall for someone that fast, but not the 'new Taylor'. The 'new Taylor' knew better. *Didn't she?*

No matter how many ways she turned the scenario over in her mind, there was no denying the anger churning inside of her, or the hurt. Only one thing could cause that. Damn it all to hell, she was *jealous*.

The truth smacked Taylor upside the head, leaving her rattled.

She *had* wanted to fuck Hades when he asked, but she'd come to her senses before she said yes. *And look where that got you, a one-way trip to voyeur land.* She growled in frustration.

Taylor needed to get out of this place, away from these people. Away from Monster Kitty before she acted on the urge to neuter him. She was pretty sure that neutering Hades would get her arrested, but it might be worth it.

Did Zaronians arrest people or did they just toss them into the Pit?

This line of thinking wasn't helping. She glanced at the pebble-shaped communicator Linx had left her. He'd said to call if there were any problems. Right now, she had problems. Before Taylor could change her mind, she pressed the contact button.

"Hello?" The communicator made several bleeps and blurps, then went silent. Was it broken? She tried again. "Hello! Testing one, two, three. Linx, can you hear me? I need you to come back." There had to be someplace else she could stay. A tent? Another windowless storage container? Hades' Keep wasn't working out.

A computerized voice came on the line. "Message sent," it said, then the device powered down.

Taylor dropped the communicator back onto the carved bench. Now all she had to do was wait. She glanced around her empty room. Her body still ached...for *Hades,* which only fueled her anger. There had to be something she could do. She glanced around the room. Nothing leapt out. On Earth, she'd never had time for hobbies.

She strode into the bathroom, searching for something to throw or at least shred into little pieces. Something with the King's strong face on it would do nicely. Taylor spotted the tub instead. Not her first choice, but a nice soak would go a long way toward calming her down.

Who needed a man or a King, when they had a tub full of steaming water, naughty fingers, and an active imagination? Not her. Definitely not her. Hades could fuck Opal until he went blind for all she cared and Taylor planned to tell him so the next time she saw him. She turned on the water, blasting the hot until steam rose in the air, then yanked her dress off and climbed in.

She closed her eyes and stewed. Was it wrong of her to wish for Hades' dick to fall off?

Taylor didn't think so under the circumstances. Even if said 'dick' had been *mouthwateringly impressive.* She growled again and slammed her hands onto the surface of the water, sending waves splashing over the sides. It was definitely time to leave.

*****

Opal's body ached in all the right ways. The King had left shortly after the Earthling, but that didn't matter. He'd proven once and for all that the woman meant nothing to him. And he'd done so with her. Opal's smile spread across her face.

It was more than apparent that the Earth woman was attracted to the King. Who wouldn't be, given his power? The woman hadn't even bothered to hide her desire, especially after Hades had expressed interest.

The stench of Taylor's arousal had nearly choked Opal. Had it not been rude, she would've asked the woman to bathe or at least cover the offending odor. But in the end, the King made the request unnecessary. The woman could now hold no illusions about her future with Hades. He had chosen.

Her.

A warrior. A woman. His equal.

How long before he made a formal announcement to the Phantom people? After that performance, she knew the declaration was coming soon. The King didn't grab random females and fuck them in front of an audience. He'd never been one to share his passions with multiple partners, though he'd had many opportunities to do so. In that respect, the King had been a little staid for Opal's tastes, but she'd learned to make due.

Soon Opal would be Queen of the Phantoms. She just had to be patient.

She rearranged her torn clothing. The material wouldn't stay together. Perseus and a couple of other warriors passed her and snickered under their breath. No doubt they could smell the King on her skin.

Perseus stopped walking. "Where's your Sire now?"

"I'd remind you that he is your Sire, too." She tugged at her clothes.

Perseus shrugged. "For now, but that may change very soon. I am not alone in believing that the Phantom people need a leader who can protect them from alien threats. Actions against such things should be swift and merciless. The fact that he hasn't acted yet makes me think that the Slavers were *invited*."

"Bite your tongue, warrior!" she snapped. "Hades will deal with the Slavers once he locates them."

"From what I've seen, the King has done nothing but chase his tail." He paused. "That is, when he isn't pursuing the Earth woman."

"Hades doesn't need you or anyone else to tell him how to run his Kingdom. The Slavers were just spotted. Even you couldn't act that quickly."

"We'll see," he said.

"If you have something to say to the King, then you can

find him in his chambers," she hissed. "I'm done listening to your treasonous drivel."

"Are you sure that's where he is right now?" Perseus asked. "I wouldn't be surprised if the King was outside Taylor's door, scratching on the stone as we speak. She is a rather irresistible specimen, don't you think?"

It was a rhetorical question, so Opal didn't answer.

"If Taylor is an example of the type of women to be found, no wonder so many Atlanteans and Phantoms go to the Earth to seek a mate," Perseus said as if musing to himself. "I wouldn't be surprised if the King suddenly had second thoughts on the matter, especially after she gives him a *taste*."

"She wouldn't! He wouldn't! Not after..." her voice trailed off.

Perseus laughed viciously. "You obviously don't know males well, if you think this little tryst will satisfy all his needs." He inhaled and his eyelids fluttered shut momentarily. "Not when a female that ripe is available. Her heat calls to every male in this arena." Perseus' eyes were blood red, when he opened them again and his cock was hard.

Opal's body vibrated with anger. She knew what Perseus and the other guards thought. They thought she was the King's private sex companion, to be used and tossed aside whenever someone new came along, but they were wrong. She was destined to be Queen. Nothing and no one would come between her and her rightful place. Opal glared at Perseus. The day she was crowned Queen, he and the other warriors would regret every moment they had laughed at her. She'd make sure of it.

"You are wrong," she spat. Hair sprouted from her arms and her claws extended.

Perseus gave her pitying look. "What if I'm not?" He let the question hang in the air between them for a moment, then walked on.

Opal tried to calm herself. She wasn't wrong. She knew she wasn't mistaken. Her plans were right on schedule, more or less. If it weren't for Hades' stubbornness, they'd already be mated.

She inhaled. The King's scent filled her lungs, along with Taylor's cloying sweetness. There was only one way to get rid of the odors until she got back to her chamber. Opal called to her Other half and shifted the rest of the way into her cat form. She was smaller than all the males, but she was a fierce fighter.

She may give her body to the King, whenever he wanted, but Opal had earned the position of Righthand. *Another thing the warriors would do well to remember*, she thought as she slinked down the corridor toward her room, her tail slashing violently from side-to-side.

*****

Hades found himself outside of Taylor's chamber. He raised his hand to knock upon her door, then stopped short when he realized what he'd been about to do. Phantoms rarely apologized for their behavior. And Kings *never* did. He stared at his clenched fist inches away from her door, then turned and slammed his knuckles into the stone wall behind him.

The rock cracked beneath his fist and crumbled to the floor. He leaned forward until his forehead rested against the cool stone. What was she doing to him? How had she gotten so far under his skin in such a short period of time? Despite his determination to keep his distance from Taylor, Hades' mind sought hers. What he found only made his 'condition' worse.

Taylor's fingers were entwined in the soft curls between her legs. He couldn't *feel* them, but he could 'see' them in her mind. That was bad enough, but the worst part was she wasn't thinking about her fingers. She was thinking about *his* tongue, dipping between her folds, lapping at her growing moisture, and nibbling on her engorged clit.

His claws slowly extended from his splayed fingers. He'd been semi-soft after leaving Opal, but now he was rock hard again. Taylor's body undulated, causing the warm water to lap at her nipples.

Hades mouth watered and his claws scraped the rock. Two fingers plunged inside her and he heard Taylor's internal gasp. Now she was picturing his cock, entering her, filling her, fucking her.

Hades growled, the sound vibrated his chest. The beast watched as the Atlantean part of him sought a stronger connection. His shaft bowed under the weight of his erection as he focused on Taylor. He'd never allowed himself to merge his mind with anyone before. He'd read thoughts when it was necessary...or he was curious, but he didn't go around randomly invading Other's minds and he'd always kept his distance during sex for fear of the intimacy it brought.

For Taylor, he'd make an exception. His body shook as he forced his mind into hers, forging a bond he never thought to feel in his lifetime. Never thought possible. The merge was tenuous, but it held. When he was sure that she wasn't going to toss him out, Hades began to explore. What he found shocked him. Taylor kept much hidden behind that smart mouth of hers.

There was a softness, a vulnerability that he hadn't sensed. One she kept hidden from the outside world. There was also fear, loneliness, and a deep-seated yearning to belong. He shied away from the latter thoughts before they could latch onto him and magnify his own insecurities, but not before something powerful rose inside of him. Something that demanded he protect her from any who would do her harm.

A new wave of fear struck, this one his own. Hades quickly retreated to the carnal section of her mind. This was what he'd been searching for. The only thing he needed from Taylor. The only thing he'd ever need. He observed her actions for a few seconds, then carefully joined into her fantasy.

With invisible hands, he grasped her breasts, palming their heavy weight. He groaned as her nipples hardened even more. He concentrated. His 'lips' latched onto her breast and his tongue circled the turgid flesh. Hades wished that he could taste her, but at least he could sense her reaction. Taylor gasped and her back arched out of the water, offering him more. Her fingers slipped from her channel as he continued to feast.

Put them back inside, he willed, sending the message deep into her mind.

She stilled.

Hades had no doubt that she was looking around, trying to figure out if she'd imagined his voice. At least she'd heard him. He'd been in doubt until that moment, since they didn't have a true bond. Hades held his breath and waited, trying to ignore the maelstrom of emotions swirling around him, inside of him, inside of her. The intimacy of the moment was nearly overwhelming. Thank the Goddess that he didn't have to wait long for Taylor to make her decision.

She slipped her fingers back inside her moist entrance.

Let me fuck you. It was a dark request, especially given what he'd just done to punish her, but Hades couldn't resist. If he could not have her body beneath his, this would have to be the next best thing. His beast growled its dissension.

She didn't answer with words, but Taylor did move her fingers out of the way. Hades focused hard, while his shaft threatened to burst. He sent the image of his cock sliding through her folds, filling her, stretching her, until she could feel nothing but him surrounding her. The surge of satisfaction he received when she relaxed was palpable.

He rocked his hips, slowly at first as he imagined the feel of her tight channel gripping him. Taylor's little moans filled his mind. Hades closed his eyes and tried not to think about the feel of the real woman or he'd lose himself. Instead, he focused on her pleasure. His claws retracted and he reached out to the air as he imagined swirling his fingers around her clit, teasing her, drawing out her need.

Taylor's body quivered and Hades rocked faster. Her breathing was coming in gasps now. He could hear the sound echoing inside his head and feel her tightening around him. She was so close to release that he could taste it. His tongue swirled around his lower lip as he latched onto her nipple and drove himself deeper 'inside' of her.

He felt the beginnings of a shudder. His breath caught. The shudder was followed by a low keening cry as Taylor fell apart. Hades' body jerked as she came, the physical reaction yanked him out of her mind, leaving him momentarily dazed. He tried to get back in, but her mind was closed off. He longed to feel the connection they'd shared, even if it were only for a minute more. Blackness met him.

"No!" He cursed as the stone hall came back into focus. The expletive was followed by a groan of frustration as he glanced down at his straining shaft. He hit the wall once more, punishing rock, punishing himself for being so stupid, then he grasped his cock and shoved it back into his pants.

*****

Chapter Six

Hades spent a restless night reliving his moments with Taylor in her bath. Eventually he'd grown tired of his wayward thoughts and gotten up. If sleep wasn't an option, then he might as well work. He was peering over his Kingdom's ledgers, when a knock sounded on his chamber door at dawn.

He scrubbed a hand over his tired face and slowly rose to his feet. "Enter," he said.

A guard stepped inside his chambers. "Sorry to disturb you so early, Your Highness, but Phantom Warrior Linx is here. He's being quite insistent that he see you immediately."

Hades frowned. What was Linx doing here? He wasn't supposed to return for another six days. Had he already gotten King Eros' permission for Taylor to stay? It seemed unlikely given the amount of trouble the cat went through to secure her a spot in the Keep, but why else would Linx be here other than to take her back to New Atlantis with him?

The thought nearly caused a blood vessel to burst inside Hades' skull. A sudden surge of panic nipped on its heels. Both reactions were unexpected and entirely unwelcome.

He sighed. Wasn't he just telling himself last night that

the sooner she was out of his care the better? Hades should want Taylor gone. And he did. Really. She'd managed to engage him, enrage him, tempt him and shame him, and it had only been twenty-four hours. He wasn't sure he would survive a whole week with her.

Let the cat take her and be done with her distracting ways.

Even as the thought slipped through his mind, Hades knew he couldn't let Taylor go. Not yet. Not after the intimacy their minds had shared last night. He needed *more*. Hades braced himself. "Show him in."

Linx stepped through the door and gave the guard a knowing smirk. "Told you he'd see me." The cocky cat strolled into the room with not a care in the moons.

"What do you want?" Hades made sure his face displayed a mask of boredom. He didn't want the unease churning inside of him to show.

Linx arched a brow. "What do you mean what do I want? I came here as fast as I could."

What in Zaron's stars was he talking about? Hades took a deep breath and mentally counted to five. "I have no time for your games, Linx," he said. "State your business and be gone."

Linx's eyes widened in surprise. "You don't know why I'm here. Do you?" Amusement laced his words.

Hades' gaze narrowed, his temper made short through lack of sleep. "If I knew, then I wouldn't have asked."

"Interesting…" The damn cat looked as if he were ready to burst out laughing.

If he did, Hades' claws would be around his throat before he could gasp for air.

Linx must've sensed the danger he was in because he hurriedly added, "I'm here to retrieve Taylor. She sent word last night to come and get her. I have to admit that I'm surprised. I thought she'd at least make it a few days with the Dark King." He shrugged. "But if she's calling for help after one day, then staying here is really not an option. I'll have to see if I can find her a Phantom to bunk with in New Atlantis. I'm sure one of the warriors wouldn't mind sharing his bed with her." It was a deliberate taunt. One Hades should ignore, but couldn't.

He felt heat building inside of him. The room went red a second before his beast struck. Claws sprang from his fingertips and he heard his shirt rip as his Other burst through his skin.

Linx ignored the sudden change like it was something that happened to him every day and scanned the shelves that held Hades' favorite reading material. "I'd assumed that you had told her to call," he said absently, then glanced at Hades, before going back to perusing. "I see now that Taylor didn't tell you." Had Linx been in his Other form his tail would've twitched. As it was, he grinned knowingly.

Hades' gnashed his teeth. "You assumed wrong."

Linx looked deceptively innocent. "I told her not to call unless things weren't working out between you two." He tapped his chin. "I believe I used the word 'emergency'."

What had Taylor told him? What had she shared?

The events from last night flashed through his mind. Hades felt the color drain from his face as he fell into a well of shame. He'd acted like a brute, giving Taylor multiple reasons to run. His beast receded, its sudden silence confirming his misdeeds.

If she was truly upset, she should've come to him. Confronted him. Railed at him, before contacting Linx. Taylor had more fire than that. She was a fighter. He'd sensed it inside of her. So why hadn't she? Hades flushed with newfound anger, determined to find out. Wait until he got his hands on that little minx.

When Hades could speak without anger sharpening his words, he said, "I believe you've been misinformed. I told you that I would keep her for seven days to pay back my debt to you. My mind has not changed." His knuckles cracked as he clenched his fists, but at least his claws were gone. "You may come back and retrieve her at that point, if King Eros wishes."

"And what if he doesn't?" Linx asked. "What if he orders her to return to Earth?"

Hades ignored the questions because he wasn't ready to confront the answers. He continued on as if Linx hadn't spoken. "Until then, Taylor shall remain under my protection. Are we clear?"

Linx beamed. "Oh, I understand your motivations completely," he said. "The question is, do you?"

"Get out!" Hades bellowed.

The guard threw open the door and rushed inside, sword drawn.

Linx held up his hands, but his grin never wavered. "I was just leaving. Don't get your uniform in a twist," he said. "See you in a few days, Your Majesty." He bowed. Hades heard him chuckle on his way out the door.

The Dark King glared at Linx's back until the cat was out of sight. Despite what he'd said to Linx, Taylor wasn't going anywhere until he deemed it so. Hades knew he was being unreasonable and abusing his power, but he couldn't seem to stop himself. "Bring me the Earth woman!"

"What if she's not awake?" the guard asked.

"Then wake her! I want her brought to me immediately!"

"Right away, Sire!" The guard bowed and swept from the room.

*****

Taylor stared at the communication device. From what she could tell, there hadn't been any messages left. Why hadn't Linx called her back? She'd expected to hear from him last night or at the very least first thing this morning. Did she somehow mess up the call? Maybe the device didn't work.

What do you expect from something shaped like a rock?

Taylor had checked the device before she'd jumped in the shower, and checked it again when she got out. Nothing. No sound. No chirp. No message. Her towel was still wrapped snugly around her, when someone knocked on the door.

"One minute, I'll be right there." Maybe Linx hadn't bothered to call back. Maybe he just came instead.

She rushed to her closet, but before she reached it a guard she didn't recognize pushed the door open and entered her room. Taylor screamed and grasped her towel.

The guard flustered and looked around. When he spotted no enemy, he said, "You need to come with me." His gaze caressed the bare skin sticking out beneath her short towel, but his grim expression never changed.

"Let me get dressed first," she said.

He shook his head. "No! Now!" He grabbed her arm and led her out the door.

Taylor barely caught her towel before it hit the floor. "Where are we going that is so important that I couldn't get dressed first?"

The guard glanced at her, but didn't slow his pace. "The King demands your presence."

Taylor's heart jumped in panic. After his performance at the Pit and the daydream she'd had last night in her bathtub, the last thing she wanted was to face the Dark King.

"Then I definitely need to get dressed first." No way was she facing Hades wearing nothing but a towel.

Taylor dug in her heels, but the guard didn't seem to notice. She might as well have been trying to stop a rhino with a butterfly net. The guard was on a mission and her wants and needs were not part of his vocabulary.

They stopped in front of a massive set of double doors. The guard raised his fist and knocked.

"Enter!" a booming voice called out.

The guard pushed the doors open and shoved Taylor inside. She turned to follow him back out, but he closed the doors in her face. "This is ridiculous! If you need someone to watch you screw your girlfriend again, pick someone else."

"Why in the Goddess did you contact Linx?" Hades bellowed, trampling her words.

Had Linx called Hades first? Why would he do that?

Taylor swung around to answer the King, only to discover that the corner of her towel was wedged in the door. The move ripped the towel away from her body, before she could catch it, leaving her *naked*.

Hades' expression morphed from outrage to shock to desire in less time than it took her to gasp. Taylor turned and lunged for her towel. She tugged hard, but the material wouldn't budge. She covered herself with her hand, while she attempted to open the door. She hadn't heard Hades move, but she sensed the instant he was standing behind her. The raw heat from his body hit her like a volcanic eruption, making her melt inside.

"Please leave it," he murmured in her ear. His warm breath teased the shell-like flesh and she quivered.

Taylor didn't think the word 'please' left the Dark King's mouth often. That more than anything else stopped her.

Hades' hands shook as they gently touched her bare shoulders and slowly turned her to face him. The red rings had returned to his eyes, nearly swallowing the blue. "I tried." He sounded ashamed. "You have no idea how hard I tried not to touch you." His mouth nuzzled her neck. "But I'm not strong enough. I need…I want..."

She wanted, too.

Taylor closed her eyes as the heat of his lips scorched her, leaving gooseflesh in its wake. Her traitorous body responded despite her resolve to change old behaviors. The release she'd found while fantasizing about Hades last night was still fresh in her mind. What would it feel like to really have his hands exploring her body? His mouth tasting her hidden places? His shaft touching her soul?

She rose onto her toes, seeking his warmth, wanting his kiss, even though he'd never belong to her. Their lips met tentatively, a quick touch, an exchange of breaths. It wasn't enough. Not nearly enough. His sensuous mouth tempted her, demanded that she take more.

Taylor reached for his neck and sank her hands into his thick hair. The strands were soft as silk as she threaded her fingers deeper, so she could pull him closer. The first press of his muscles made her weak in the knees. Hades groaned and his grip on her tightened. The embrace went from innocent exploration to inferno. Their tongues greeted, then began to dance.

Taylor's body went up in flames as Hades yanked her against his hard length. One hand rose, winding its way into her long, red hair. His fingers tangled, then pulled gently. He held her exactly where he wanted her and deepened the kiss. This time Taylor moaned.

The Dark King could kiss. She'd give him that.

He explored her mouth with an expertise that only made her long for more. Taylor pulled at his clothing. How did this darn thing open? Last night, he'd made it look so easy. The thought gave rise to bitter memories. Taylor jerked her head back. They shouldn't be doing this.

"No! Do not pull away." Hades refused to let her go. He growled and sought her lips once more. By the time he finished kissing her, Taylor was boneless and he'd managed to change her mind, but only because she'd let him.

"Take this off," she said, weakly tugging at his clothes.

Hades complied instantly. One second his clothes were there, the next they were gone.

"How did you?" She glanced at the floor, but his clothing was nowhere in sight.

"Later." Hades took her hand and led her into another room that held a massive bed made up of a pile of furs that would've given animal right's activists an apoplexy. The furs were stacked over three feet high and ten feet wide and took up most of the room. Hades didn't give Taylor time to look around. He picked her up and carried her over to the furs and gently laid her down.

Taylor expected him to follow, to immediately thrust inside of her like he had Opal, but he didn't. He simply stared at her like he'd never seen a woman before. The intensity of his gaze made her nervous. "Hades?"

"Let me look at you. Smell your delicious fragrance. Savor this moment." The Dark King looked pained as he stared down at her. The longing in his eyes seared her soul.

A dangerous feeling rose inside of Taylor, it was that same emotion she'd vowed to ignore for a while. She couldn't go down this road again. She'd promised herself that she wouldn't fall for another bad boy. This was just sex. This *had* to be just sex.

"I imagined what you'd look like lying amongst my furs, but my fantasies paled by comparison to the real thing," Hades said. "You are exquisite."

Taylor didn't think her body could get any hotter, but she was wrong. Hades reached for her foot and gently kissed the bottom of her sole. A shiver tracked through her leg, settling at the juncture between her thighs. He kissed her again and ran his tongue along her arch. Taylor giggled and tried to pull away, but he wouldn't let her.

"I need to taste you. Every inch of you." Hades nibbled on her ankle, then rained kisses upon her leg. He worked his way up one leg and down the other. He was patient, attentive, and far too thorough a lover for her piece of mind. Yet he avoided the places that needed him most.

Oh he was good, so very good.

That careful avoidance only ratcheted up her need, driving her into frenzy. When Taylor thought she couldn't take another second, Hades flipped her onto her belly and kissed his way up the back of her legs. Her sex grew moist as he neared her bottom. He had to smell her. Heck, she could smell the musk rising from her skin and she wasn't even down there.

*****

Hades leaned over her and inhaled. Taylor smelled so rich, ripe, and sensual. He'd never tasted skin like hers and he doubted he ever would again. The round globes of her bottom jiggled beneath him. Hades couldn't resist taking a small bite, careful not to break the skin. She squealed as his sharp teeth latched onto her, then burst into laughter.

"Stop that." She swatted at him, but he easily avoided her half-hearted blow.

"A King doesn't take orders," he said. "Besides, I needed to see if you tasted as good as you smelled."

She glanced over her shoulder. "And do I?"

"Better," he said, meaning it. Hades continued his journey, this time exploring her back.

The Dark King never realized how much restraint he had until this moment. All he wanted to do was bury his nose in her moist sex and lap up her juices for hours. He longed to taste her release on his tongue, feel her clit swell beneath his teeth, and plunge into her depths. But he wouldn't. Not yet. Taylor was the type of woman meant to be savored.

He kissed her shoulder blades, then nibbled on her fragile neck, licking and sucking on the tender flesh. The tendon jumped when he touched it. Hades focused on the taut muscle, feeling it flex beneath his mouth. One bite would be all it would take. One bite would change both their destinies. He felt his incisors grow along with the urge to mark her, and quickly jerked his head away. What was he doing?

Hades stared at the small purple blemish marring the base of her pale throat and shuddered at how close he'd come to sealing their fates.

He shook his head to clear it and slowly kissed his way down Taylor's supple spine, away from temptation. "Spread your thighs for me. Your delicious scent is driving me crazy. I want to taste you. I want to bury my face in the dew dripping from your soft curls."

Taylor reacted in an instant. Her legs parted so wide that at first he was shocked, then Hades remembered that she was a dancer. He'd researched the meaning after she'd explained what she did. He'd seen her 'dancing' in her thoughts, but for some reason he couldn't believe it, even when faced with the facts. Hades was still angry over the idea of other men staring at her naked body. He didn't think that would ever change, but looking at her now he realized her *skills* held a lot of possibilities.

Hades positioned his wide shoulders between Taylor's trim thighs, then leaned over and inhaled. Her glorious scent washed over him, drowning him and he didn't even try to save himself. Instead, Hades scooted forward and stuck out his tongue—*his very long Atlantean tongue*—and licked her from end to end.

Taylor's sharp flavor burst inside his mouth. Hades closed his eyes and groaned. She tasted even better than he'd imagined. He swirled his tongue around her back entrance until she squirmed upon the bed and her bottom rose up to meet him. The new position brought her dripping sex up to eye level.

"Don't move!" He growled, latching onto her hips to hold her in place. Hades extended his tongue to its full seven inches and slowly entered her tight channel. Taylor's body gripped him as he continued his journey deeper inside of her. When he was fully seated, Hades curled his tongue, undulating the thick muscle, then purred.

*****

Taylor's breath rushed out of her body as vibrations shook her from the inside out. She knew what she was feeling though her mind wrestled with the truth. No one's tongue was that long and flexible. It wasn't possible.

His purr deepened and the vibrations increased. When Hades swirled his tongue inside of her, he stroked a bundle of nerves that she never knew existed. Taylor cried out as an unexpected orgasm hit her, sending her spiraling. She tried to stay still, but she couldn't. Her back bowed and her hips convulsed a second before her channel clamped down on him.

She dropped onto the bed. Her breath came out in loud pants, as her body continued to twitch and jerk. Hades flicked and swirled his tongue inside of her and a new wave of tremors shook her, extending her pleasure.

When the shudders finally slowed to a waning pulse, Hades withdrew his raspy tongue and lapped at her nether lips, greedily devouring the dripping juices from her release.

"You taste like nothing I've ever experienced. I could eat you for days and never grow tired," he murmured between licks. "My Kingdom could fall down around us and I would not notice because I'd be so drunk on your sweet nectar."

Taylor tried not to picture a lifetime of having Hades' head buried between her thighs and failed miserably. Her whole body shook with emotion. She chastised herself again for letting the Dark King get under her skin.

"There are other places I need to taste before this day is through." Hades rose onto his knees and carefully turned her over. His eyes locked onto her nipples and seemed to dilate. He slowly licked his lips. "And I know just where to start."

The second his body came down upon hers, Taylor knew she was in trouble. They were a perfect fit. There was no shuffling for position or readjusting. It was like they'd been made for each other.

Sure, she'd thought the same thing in the past, but she'd had to *make* her exes into the perfect fit. It took a lot of imagination. Not so with Hades. His massive body seemed to slot right into hers.

He leaned over and latched onto her nipple. It felt so much like her daydream last night that she had momentary déjà vu. Reality erased the hazy vision, as Hades swirled his rough tongue around her, teasing her flesh into tight kernels.

Taylor found herself growing moist once more as he sucked her deep into his mouth and bit down. There was a flash of pain, which was quickly eased by a gentle swipe of his tongue and a press of his sensual lips.

His hard shaft rested against her belly. It throbbed in time to the strong pulls of his mouth. Taylor's skin tightened and she couldn't seem to hold still. She writhed beneath him, her body feeling empty, wanting. Her need grew palpable. She could taste it on her tongue. But Hades wasn't taking the hint. He continued to suck on her nipples until they ached and turned bright red, flushed with blood. He buried his face between her breasts and inhaled.

"You smell sweet here, too. Like one of your earth desserts," he murmured. "I was brought one years ago. I have not forgotten the sugary aroma."

"I need you." Taylor nibbled on his shoulder, before trailing her lips over his skin and nuzzling his neck.

Hades ignored her and continued to feast.

Taylor rocked her hips, trying to rub her clit along his shaft. He was driving her crazy. She needed him inside of her. Hades shifted, preventing her from reaching his glorious cock. She growled in frustration and bit down hard on the spot where his shoulder met his neck. Her blunt teeth sank into his skin, leaving white marks behind.

Hades released her instantly and reared back. His face was flushed and he was breathing hard. His eyes turned dark crimson, erasing all trace of the aqua blue. "Why did you do that?" A snarled demand for an answer.

"Because you weren't paying attention," she grit out. There was only so much teasing a girl could take.

"Oh, but I was." His voice lowered to dangerous levels, but she noticed his cock grew even harder. "Don't ever bite me again unless you mean it."

Taylor wasn't sure what he meant by that, but she'd agree to anything as long as he stopped messing around and gave her what she wanted.

"You want me to fuck you?" he asked, trailing a thick finger along her moist opening.

It galled her to answer, but Taylor was desperate. "Yes!" she hissed. "If it's not too much trouble."

"No trouble at all." Hades positioned the head of his shaft at her entrance. "Human anatomy is smaller than that of the Phantoms."

She writhed. "What does that mean?"

"It means that since I'm your first, it may hurt when I take you," he said, looking far too pleased by the fact.

The warning made her hesitant, but she wasn't going to change her mind. Taylor was way beyond caring about a little pain. She braced her heels on the furs and prepared for him to plunge inside of her.

Once again Hades surprised her. He entered her slowly, inch by glorious inch until she felt stuffed, packed, overflowing with his maleness. Even then, it wasn't enough. Taylor needed more.

"Hades." A cry and a plea for mercy. She lifted her hips and a few more inches slipped inside. He was so achingly big. For a moment she worried that he wasn't going to fit. He moved again and Taylor's eyes rolled back in her head.

"I'm not finished yet." Hades reached between them and adjusted her body until her hips tilted even more.

Taylor felt him go even deeper.

"Almost there." Hades pulled back and thrust.

If it weren't for her cervix stopping him, Hades would've hit the bottom of her heart. He was so hard, so long, and so incredibly thick that Taylor didn't think she'd be able to move once they were done. Not that she'd want to. Not that she'd care. She'd always been a greedy lover, but prided herself on being able to give as good as she received.

Hades thrust again, rolling his hips.

Taylor bit her lip to keep from crying out in pain and ecstasy.

"Don't hold back," he murmured. "Let me hear you."

He moved again and she mewed.

Taylor had heard of women being 'whipped', but she had never understood the saying until this moment. Hades was a master at making love. It was like he'd been made for the act. Taylor could see how that would make the Dark King highly *addictive*. And like any addiction, exposure needed to be limited.

But how could she walk away from the best sex of her life?

Easy…if sex was all that was between them. Unfortunately, the chances of that being the case were now slim.

Taylor had felt the moment a tenuous connection formed. It hadn't been there before. Of that she had no doubt. The fragile web now stretched between them and was as tangible as the hard muscles of Hades' back, flexing beneath her fingertips. The intensity of the friable bond scared her to death.

She hadn't wanted a deeper connection with the Dark King. Definitely wasn't looking for one. She was sure Hades wasn't either, but it was there nonetheless. Taylor was smart enough to keep the information to herself. No need to mess up an otherwise perfect moment. She'd deal with the emotional fallout when she got back to her room.

*****

Taylor's tight channel had a death grip on Hades' shaft. He could barely breathe from the pleasure of it. He'd never felt anything so wonderful in his life. Thrusting inside her had been like coming home, except he'd never really had this connection to home or to anything else for that matter. Only to Taylor. The urge to share minds rode him hard.

He kept still for a few seconds as his hearts thundered inside of his chest. He used the sparse time to fight the need to connect. It was dangerous to try to re-experience the intimacy they'd shared last night. Repeated mind melds would only make the separation harder when she left.

"Relax." The request was meant for both of them. Hades' breath brushed the hair on her forehead. Taylor's body softened beneath him and he slowly began to move.

Each thrust felt like the first. Their bodies glided together in perfect synchronicity. Velvet heat surrounded him, cradling him, as he drove them toward completion. Taylor's whimpers of pleasure turned to passionate cries. The joyous sound rang in his ears, filling him with pride and satisfaction…and a longing so deep and dark that for a moment Hades was overwhelmed.

Taylor tensed beneath him and her sheath fluttered. She was close, so very close. Hades brushed her hair from her face and marveled at her beauty. Her lips were swollen from his kisses, yet remained ripe and welcoming. So much so, he couldn't resist another taste.

He latched onto her mouth. The kiss deepened as their bodies rocked in unison. Without conscious thought, Hades' mind entered hers. The instantaneous connection knocked the air from his lungs. He could feel what Taylor felt, hear what she heard, and taste himself on her full lips. The intimacy of the merge was bliss and sheer agony in equal measures. How could he live without this? Tingles prickled his spine and his sac rose. He wouldn't last much longer.

Still Hades couldn't let go. He drank from her, swallowing Taylor's cries as she fell apart in his arms. With one final clasp, she pulled him under, milking his body until he was but a shell of his former self. Lost to the world, Hades felt contentment for the first time in his existence. It was an odd sensation, but one he could easily get used to. He gazed down at Taylor's flushed face. She was the epitome of a well-pleasured woman. Pride surged through him. He'd been her first Phantom.

Her only Phantom, a darker voice whispered. Fear's icy fingers squeezed Hades, until the only option left to him was to run.

Taylor may not know it yet, but she held the power to bring the Dark King to his knees.

*****

Blissfully sated, Taylor had never felt this dreadful in her life. She'd made a lot of bad decisions over the years, but sleeping with the Phantom King had to be the worst. She shook her head. What was she thinking? Last night she'd been so disgusted by Hades' behavior that she'd called Linx to come and get her.

What a difference a morning made.

She couldn't even blame her poor judgment on alcohol. This one was all on her. Hades, and his great sex, had just ruined her for all mankind. She snorted. Like that was her biggest concern.

No, what truly made this lapse in judgment a monumental disaster was that Taylor had fallen for him. A King. A Phantom. A stranger, who in a few days time she'd probably never see again. She sighed and stared at the ceiling.

"I am such an idiot," she muttered, knowing she couldn't hide in his chambers forever.

Hades had been unusually quiet when he slipped out of bed an hour ago. There'd been no bantering, not even a quick exchange of teasing smiles. The only thing he'd asked before he left the room was that she notify him prior to contacting Linx again. The request had been all business and had left her feeling cold.

Still, Taylor had readily agreed, since he'd seemed genuinely hurt that she'd gone behind his back. That hadn't been her intention when she'd used the device, but he didn't give her time to explain. He simply inclined his head and left. Hades hadn't returned since their awkward exchange. She could hear him working in the other room, which somehow made the situation worse.

Was he waiting for her to leave?

Taylor flushed with embarrassment. She'd done several 'walks of shame' over the years, but this one by far was shaping up to be the most humiliating. Despite all her proclamations to the contrary, she hadn't changed a bit. Taylor was still the ditsy stripper, who fell into bed with the wrong men and gave her heart away too easily. She had let her sister, Tabby down. Worst of all, she'd let herself down.

Hades had probably realized that he'd screwed up, too. That would explain the uncomfortable silence. Or maybe he was over her now that they'd had sex. The depressing thought hurt more than it should. Taylor took a deep breath. She'd delayed the inevitable for as long as she could.

She swung her long legs over the side of the bed and surveyed the room. Taylor didn't immediately spot anything that she could wear. Her gaze landed on the closet door. No way was she going to rifle through the Dark King's clothes. She glanced down at the mound of furs beneath her. Surely he wouldn't miss one. It wasn't like she planned to keep it.

Taylor hopped off the bed and grabbed the smallest fur she could find. She draped the hide around her body, then searched for something to hold it in place. A scarf of some kind had been tossed over the back of a chair. That would have to do. Taylor wrapped the scarf around her waist, then jumped up and down to make sure the whole outfit stayed in place. Confident that the fur would remain where it should, at least until she got back to her room, she marched out of the bedroom.

She didn't look at Hades, though she sensed him seated behind the desk, watching her. Instead, she walked directly to his chamber door and opened it. He didn't try to stop her. In fact, Hades didn't say a word. Taylor fought back tears as she picked up her towel and stepped into the hall. She kept her head down as she passed the guard, which was why she didn't see Opal until she ran into her.

"Sorry." She glanced up long enough to catch Opal's

shocked expression, then rushed on. Her shame over being caught coming out of the King's chambers was magnified by her lack of clothing. It's hard to be dignified, when you're dressed like an X-rated, prehistoric cartoon character.

*****

CHAPTER SEVEN

Opal couldn't hide her shock at seeing Taylor slip from the King's chambers. Her curvy body had been draped in furs that barely covered it. Frozen in place and her mouth gaping, she watched the human female rush down the hall.

It wasn't until the King's guard cleared his throat that Opal realized what she'd been doing. If she'd harbored any doubt of what had occurred inside of Hades' living quarters, it was quickly squashed by the guard's taunting smile.

"Looks like you've been replaced," he said.

"You don't know what you're talking about, now move aside," she hissed. "I have a report for the King that cannot wait."

The guard didn't budge. "I'll check to see if the King is *available*."

"Did you not hear me?" she asked.

The guard stared at her. "I heard you, but the Dark King has been *busy* this morning. He may not be prepared to receive anyone at this time."

"I'm not just anyone," Opal said through gritted teeth. "I am the Dark King's Righthand. Now move."

The guard hesitated, loyalties clearly torn. He finally took a deep breath and stepped to his left.

Opal pulled herself together and knocked on the door.

"Enter," Hades called out after a moment's hesitation.

She wasn't sure what she'd find, when she walked through the door, but Opal was determined to keep her emotions in check. Maybe Taylor had been there for innocent reasons? Maybe the guard was goading her to see her reaction. It wasn't like he'd been inside the room with the pair. There was no way to know exactly what had happened.

Opal took a long look at Hades as he sat behind his desk. Had the King finally succumbed to his desire and got Taylor out of his system? From the sated look on his face that seemed the most likely scenario, but there was no telling with Hades.

She stepped deeper into the room. Hades glanced up in eager anticipation. When he saw her, the expectation faded into disappointment. Jealousy twisted Opal's gut. She inhaled to calm herself, but the move backfired. The smell of sex permeated the room, mocking her.

It was as she suspected. The King had lain with the Earthling. Taylor's cloying scent still clung to his lightly tanned skin. That in itself wasn't alarming, but the King's reaction to seeing her certainly was.

Hades wasn't the type to brood. After a conquest, he tended to be jovial and self-satisfied. He loved the hunt, the seduction, and ultimately the capitulation. It wasn't unusual for him to start planning his next pursuit hours after bedding his latest conquest. He always had someone in mind. But it didn't look like that was the case today. If anything, the Dark King looked *troubled*.

"Sorry to interrupt your…" Opal cleared her throat. "Sorry to interrupt, Sire, but I thought you'd like to know that we shot down one of the Slaver ships."

"Where?" Hades' gaze sharpened. "Any survivors?"

"The Rydon Ravine," she said. "It was difficult to reach the crash site. By the time the scouts did, they only found one body. It was obvious that he'd died on impact. There was a blood trail leading deeper into the woods. The scouts are following it now."

Hades nodded. "Let me know what they find."

She bowed. "Right away, Sire."

Opal left the room feeling sick to her stomach. Taylor's musky stench had covered every inch of the King. Even now her scent saturated the air, leaving a sickly sweet odor behind.

If it were just sex, then Opal wouldn't be bothered by what had occurred. Hades had sex with a lot of women. They meant nothing to her—meant nothing to him. Or hadn't before...

She squeezed her eyes shut. No matter how hard she tried, Opal couldn't stop seeing the look on the King's face, when she'd walked into the room. There'd been hope there and *longing*. She had never seen anything like it, and certainly not on Hades' handsome face. What had the Earthling done to him? Had she somehow bewitched the Dark King? That more than anything frightened Opal. How could she compete with *magic*?

*****

Sometime over the last few hours while Taylor was soaking in the bathtub, feeling sorry for herself, trying to wash away the memories of this morning and scrub Hades' scent off her skin, clothing had been delivered to her room. She found the neat stack sitting on the edge of her bed.

No doubt the King was behind the new wardrobe. Had he bought her the clothes out of guilt? Or was he like Sergei, thinking that nice shiny things would keep her pacified, while he went off and did whatever he wanted? Both ideas hurt, but not as much as the possibility that he might be 'paying her' with new clothes for the sex. That thought made Taylor nauseous.

She wasn't a whore.

Even if Hades did this for every woman he slept with, Taylor wanted no part of it. He didn't *owe* her anything. And she certainly didn't want any kind of *compensation* for sex, even if it came in a roundabout way. Time to tell him so before she lost her nerve.

Taylor ignored the beautiful fabrics and dug out her pair of jeans from the back of the closet. Someone other than her had put them there, burying them with the tote she'd packed before they'd left Earth. She slipped the denims on, pairing them with a sweater and pumps.

Some people wore body armor to battle. Taylor wore her high heels. If she were going to face Hades again, she'd need all the 'armor' she could get.

Taylor opened her door and instantly recognized a familiar face, standing guard outside her room. "Hi, Kon," she said.

"Good day to you." He replied politely, but Taylor noticed his gaze didn't linger this time. That was a first. Every Phantom she'd encountered stared at her chest. It was the one constant she'd been able to count on, since she'd arrived.

Had word of her indiscretion already spread through the Keep? A wave of fresh humiliation struck, but Taylor forced it aside, replacing it with anger. She had a King to beard.

"Do you happen to know if the Dark King is still in his chambers?" Her face heated at the question, but Taylor forced her chin up. "I need to speak with him." She needed to clear the air before things between them got worse.

"He is with the warriors in training," Kon said.

Taylor shoved her hands into her back pockets. "I don't want to disturb him, but it is important that we talk."

She wanted answers. If she were mistaken about Hades' intentions, Taylor would apologize. But if it turned out that she was right about the clothes and that Hades now wanted nothing to do with her, then she'd set the Dark King straight and move on.

His rejection would hurt, but Taylor was done hiding from her mistakes. And there was no doubt that sleeping with Hades had been a major mistake. A mistake that she planned to remedy right now.

"I'll take you to him," Kon said.

"Thank you." Taylor glanced back at the new clothes. Her anger returned. She wrapped the destructive emotion around her like a cloak. It would protect her. Keep her focused. Prevent her from doing something embarrassing like—cry.

Kon led her down another hall and out what amounted to a side door that had been carved out of part of the mountain. There was a huge courtyard full of training equipment to one side. Taylor recognized the space instantly. Hades had brought her here.

Was it only yesterday? Ugh! That made her feel even worse, but she had to be strong. She was about to take on the Dark King.

On the other side of the courtyard, fifty or so warriors had gathered. Taylor did a double-take. Make that fifty *kids*, ranging in age from about five years old to mid-teens. They stood in a circle around Hades as he raised a sword and swiped the air, making circle eights with the blade.

From the looks on their upturned faces, he entranced them. Taylor's righteous fury deflated and uncertainty returned. She quickly stepped into the shadow of the doorway, before Hades spotted her. The position allowed her to watch unimpeded.

Hades looked so comfortable around the children. He bellowed an order and they all raised their sword-shaped 'sticks'. When he moved, they moved. It was like watching a mirroring game. He made a lunge, then approached a little dark-haired boy.

"Keep your arm straight, Marcus. You don't want to give your enemy an easy target." He tapped the boy's chest for emphasis, then lifted his arm higher. "Now try it again."

The child thrust the stick sword forward, nearly toppling himself in the process.

It must've weighed more than it appeared, Taylor thought.

"Much better." Hades mussed the boy's hair and smiled. "Keep practicing and someday you'll be as good a warrior as your father."

Kon straightened beside her.

"Is he yours?" she asked.

He nodded. "So is that one." He pointed to another, this one a girl with thick blonde braids and a determined expression. "She looks soft," he said, eyeing Taylor instead of his daughter. "But she is tougher than all of them combined." The pride was evident in Kon's voice as he returned his attention to the children.

"Are any of them Hades'?" Taylor asked, even though it pained her to do so. She knew so little about the man that she'd fallen into bed with. It was a pattern that she wasn't proud of.

Kon looked at her as if she'd shot unicorns out of her nose. "No! He's vowed never to take a mate."

She frowned. Taylor wasn't sure what that had to do with having children, but it did make her curious. "Why would he do that?"

She had to be misunderstanding him. Surely, Kon didn't mean 'never' in the strictest sense of the word. Never was a long time. But if he was right, what did that mean for Hades and Opal? She thought for sure that they had a thing going. They'd seemed pretty cozy at the Pit.

And yet, you still slept with him, a little voice admonished. Her stomach twisted. Taylor wasn't a whore, but she'd stepped ankle deep into slut territory.

Kon shifted, looking decidedly uncomfortable. "It's not for me to say."

"But what about children? It's obvious that he adores the kids. Doesn't he need an heir to take over the throne?"

Wasn't that a King thing? And why was it so easy for her to imagine a bunch of little Hades running around?

"He's vowed never to have any." This time Kon appeared genuinely sad. "He's a good ruler, but a ruler needs a mate and heirs."

"Is there something wrong with him? Is that why he's vowed to abstain from both?" Fear filled Taylor. Was Hades sick? And if so, was it catching? The blood drained from her face.

Kon's red eyes widened in horror at her implication. "Of course not! The King is fit to lead. Like all Phantoms, he's never been ill a day in his life."

Relief flooded her. That answered one question, but created several others. Taylor glanced back at Hades. If he wasn't ill, then why didn't he want a mate or at least children?

She watched him work with the budding warriors. There was no doubt in her mind that he liked being around the kids. She could see the joy on his face, the love. "If he's physically fit, then remaining mateless doesn't make any sense." She shook her head. "Kings need heirs." Everybody knew that.

Kon shifted on his feet and glanced up at the light green sky. "The Dark King can do whatever he desires. It's not my place to question his reasons nor is it yours. And for Goddess sake, do not bring up his handicap."

Taylor's gaze swung around, pinning him in place. "What handicap?"

As far as she could tell, there wasn't a thing wrong with the King. She'd explored every inch of him *thoroughly*. Taylor would be willing to look again, but she didn't think she'd find much beyond perfection.

"Earthlings," Kon muttered under his breath, his disbelief clear. "Must I point out the obvious?"

Taylor glared at him. "Yeah, you must."

"He has blue eyes." His jaw clenched, but he somehow squeezed the words through. "Are you visually impaired?"

No, she wasn't blind. Taylor had noticed Hades' sexy blue eyes. She just wasn't getting the connection. "What about them?" She hadn't seen any other Phantoms with aqua blue eyes, but Taylor hadn't thought much of it since she hadn't been around many people outside the Keep.

Hades' eyes were gorgeous, especially when they were staring up at her from beneath his obscenely long lashes.

Kon tsked. "You are lovely, but no brighter than your nearest relative, the monkey," he said.

Suddenly bearding Hades wasn't nearly as important as defending him. Taylor's temper flared anew and her voice rose unchecked. "That's rich coming from a shape-shifter! At least this *primate* doesn't view a change of eye color as a handicap! What's the matter with you people? You can build ships, fly across the universe, and yet you get hung up over a slight variation in appearance." She snorted. "I may be dumb, but even I know that as your King, Hades deserves your respect, not your pity over something he has no control over." Taylor was so angry that she totally missed the fact that Kon seemed pleased by her tirade.

She stepped out of the shadows into the courtyard to find the Dark King staring at her. Hades had an odd expression on his face that she couldn't read. The children had stopped their exercises and were now gaping in her direction. Taylor opened her mouth to explain her outburst, but Opal rushed into the training courtyard before she could utter a sound.

"The Slavers have been spotted again," Opal said. "Two more ships. That brings the total up to three. We think the downed vessel was able to send out a distress signal before it crashed."

"So they're here to pick up their shipmates?" he asked, scrubbing a hand over his face. "Is it possible that they called for re-enforcements to launch an attack?"

Opal's brow creased. "Slavers are unpredictable, but I believe it's a retrieval mission. The survivors took everything of value out of the cargo compartment. As far as we know, Slavers don't have the numbers to go to war," she said.

"Not against the Phantoms anyway," he said.

Opal nodded. "We believe we have them cornered near my family's old homestead. The two trackers are continuing to call in with more details."

"I want more guards around the fortress and the Walled City," he said, then turned to Taylor. "You're not allowed to go outside or into the city."

Taylor raised a brow and glanced at the sky for emphasis.

Hades took an exasperated breath. "Without an escort."

She hesitated, then gave her assent. She wasn't about to contradict him in front of his guards or the kids, especially after the argument she'd just had with Kon. Besides, Taylor knew how to pick her battles.

"I can find the men, Sire, and the other Slaver ships," Opal said, drawing his attention away from Taylor.

Hades shook his head. "No! I need you to guard Taylor."

Opal looked aghast. "But, Sire, I'm more help in the field."

Taylor had to agree. The last thing she wanted was to be shadowed by the woman, who'd had sex with Hades and hated her guts.

"You have your orders." Hades strode off to meet the scouts.

Opal glowered at her.

"If it makes you feel any better, I'm not crazy about having a babysitter either," Taylor said.

Opal's scowl only deepened.

Taylor approached her. "Listen, we got off to a bad start." *Understatement of the century.* "I'd like to begin again. I'm Taylor Shelley." She held out her hand for Opal to shake.

Opal glared at it. "Not this again. I know who you are."

"Then you also know that I won't be here for much longer. Five days at the most. Our short time together doesn't have to be drudgery."

Opal's expression hadn't changed, but she did appear to be listening. That was a start. "What would you suggest?" she asked.

Taylor studied the various pieces of equipment. "Since we have to hang out together today, you could teach me how to use this stuff, how to fight."

"Have you ever been in battle?" Opal asked.

"No." Taylor shook her head. She'd never even been in a fight. Oh sure, she and Tabby had argued as kids. There may of been some hair pulling and a few tears, but she wouldn't exactly call it a fight. And it certainly wasn't a battle.

Opal circled her, examining every inch of her. "You're well defined, but you're too soft to be a warrior," she said with more than a little disgust in her voice. "What did you do on Earth?" She crossed her arms over her chest and stared at Taylor like she was an annoying piece of earwax stuck on her finger.

Taylor glanced at the poles. It would be easier to show her than to tell her. Not that she thought a demonstration would change Opal's poor opinion of her. That wasn't going to happen, not after they'd slept with the same man. "Will those hold my weight?"

Opal looked to where she pointed. "They're made for Phantoms. What do you think?"

You don't have to be such a bitch, Taylor thought, but didn't say so.

She was trying to make the best of a bad situation. For that alone, she decided not to take the bait. Opal was already in a bad mood because of this morning. It wouldn't take much to provoke her.

"Will I get splinters?" Taylor asked.

"The wood has been hardened and sealed," Opal said impatiently. "Get on with whatever you're about to do. We don't have all day for this foolishness. There are Slavers in the area."

"Sure," Taylor said. "But before I show you, I have a

quick question."

Opal glared at her.

Taylor took her silence as permission to proceed. "What's the deal with Hades' eyes? The other guard called them a handicap." Maybe the word had a different meaning here on Zaron. She was trying to give the Phantoms the benefit of the doubt.

Opal's expression hardened. "The King does not like his weaknesses pointed out!" she chastised. "Particularly from a non-Zaronian."

"Weaknesses? Can he not see properly?" That made more sense than a problem with the eye color. Maybe that had been what Kon was trying to explain and she'd just misunderstood.

Opal glanced around to ensure they wouldn't be overheard. "He's a Phantom. Of course he can see."

"Then I really don't understand," Taylor said. "How can an eye color make such a difference?"

Opal bared her teeth and she growled. "The King's blue eyes show his mixed blood heritage. They bring attention to his Half-being status. I don't personally mind his *handicap*, but there are others who are not so understanding," she said.

Taylor smiled to keep from punching Opal in the mouth for being so condescending. She hadn't misunderstood Kon. She'd been right all along. The fact that Opal was claiming not to care about Hades' status was laughable.

How dare these people look down upon the Dark King because he was different! So what if he didn't quite fit in. She knew all about being a social outcast. Taylor had been one for years. Because of her job, she'd been on the receiving end of a lot of derogatory language. Taylor recognized disdain when she heard it, even when it was 'prettied' up. She had dealt with the pain of not being accepted, of being thought of as 'less than', but it had taken its toll on her psyche. The last thing Taylor expected was for that type of vitriol to be directed toward a King. And not just any King, but one of their own.

Opal may have feelings for Hades, but the emotion wasn't love. Love wouldn't have allowed her to say such a thing.

The Dark King deserved better. Hades deserved someone who would appreciate his differences, not point them out as deficiencies.

"There's nothing wrong with being different," Taylor said, then walked over to the dual poles. "As a woman of rank among a legion of men, you of all people should know that." She searched for any indication that her words had sank in.

Opal didn't even flinch.

How sad. Phantoms weren't so different from Earthlings after all.

Taylor shook her head and swallowed her disappointment, then began her demonstration. "This is what I did for a living. It's hard to dance without music, but I'll do my best." She hummed a quiet tune and slowly twirled around the pole, holding it with one hand.

"Aren't you going to use the other pole?" Opal interrupted.

Taylor stopped moving. "Why?"

"The point is to climb them." Opal motioned with both arms to show her what she meant.

"I only need one," Taylor said, then started dancing again.

Taylor's anger slipped away and her body went liquid as she circled the pole once more. She hooked her knee around it and let gravity take her, slowly spinning until she came to a stop.

She ground her hips against the pole, undulating, then spun, gripping the pole behind her back. Taylor slid down the pole, then quickly turned and jumped onto it, spreading her legs wide in a perfect 'V'. She held the pose for several seconds, then clamped the pole tight with her thighs and hung upside down, arching her back to make her large breasts thrust out. She shimmied some more, weaving her hands in the air, humming a little louder, then grabbed the pole and slowly flipped her body over, landing softly on the ground.

Opal looked both fascinated and confused. "What use is that?"

"I'm sure to you it doesn't seem like much, but where I'm from," Taylor said, "men pay money to see me do that. Of course, I'm normally topless at the time."

Opal blinked, then blinked again. "You do that unclothed?"

Taylor shrugged. "I slowly strip my clothes off as I'm dancing until I am down to a thong and heels." She glanced down at her feet and tapped her toes for emphasis.

"Those shoes are impractical for everything, including a fight."

Taylor cocked her head and slipped off one heel. "I wouldn't say that," she said, showing Opal the business end of the stiletto. "It hurts if you put this," she pointed to the tip, "through a man's foot."

"A sword works better," Opal muttered.

"Yeah, well, there aren't a lot of those lying around on Earth," Taylor said. They'd moved onto guns long ago.

Opal frowned as Taylor put her shoe back on. "You said you dance in those and a thong."

"That's right," she said.

"What is a thong?" Opal asked.

"A small piece of clothing that goes here." Taylor pointed. "It's not much, but it's better than nothing at all. I know some girls from a totally nude revue. The level of clientele drops considerably."

"Clientele? I know this earth word. Are you a sex companion?" Opal took a step back as if Taylor were contagious.

"No! Why does everybody keep thinking that?" *Probably*

because you came running out of Hades' chamber this morning wearing nothing but a fur. Taylor huffed.

"It would explain what you were doing in the King's quarters earlier," Opal said.

"So you don't think I'd sleep with Hades unless he paid me to, is that it?" Taylor didn't think Opal's opinion of her could drop any lower, but she'd been wrong.

Opal seemed oblivious to her distress. "You don't have a proper position here on Zaron or any obvious means of obtaining credits. Becoming a sex companion would be your best option given your skill set. There are enough warriors here to keep you busy and provide you with a comfortable life. Who knows," she shrugged, "the King might even hire you on occasion."

Heat flooded Taylor's face. She tried to imagine having Hades as one of her *many clients*, but her brain shut down. "You know what, I was wrong. This isn't going to work out." She'd taken a few steps toward the door, when Opal called out.

"Do you think that you could show me how to do that?"

Taylor stilled, questioning whether she'd heard her correctly. First the woman insults her, then she wants her help. She spun around, planning to blister Opal's ears with expletives.

Opal was holding one of the poles, rocking from side-to-side, trying to imitate Taylor's moves. Her face flushed, when she caught Taylor watching her. "Forget it," she hissed and walked off.

"Wait!" Taylor said. No doubt she was going to regret this. "I'll show you how to dance…if you teach me how to fight." It was a generous offer on her part. If Opal were smart she'd take it.

Opal switched direction at the last second and grabbed a couple of practice swords. She tossed one to Taylor. The wooden handle hit her fingernail and she immediately dropped it. Not the best way to impress the warrior woman.

"Pick that up and we'll get started."

*****

Hades stood in the shadows entranced by Taylor's 'performance'. He'd never seen anything so seductive in his life and she hadn't even been trying. Watching her twirl around the pole only made him want her again. It was one thing to see her dance in her mind, quite another to experience the movements firsthand.

He adjusted his hard cock inside his uniform, but it did little to ease his discomfort. He stared longingly at the woman, who only hours ago had cradled him within her body. The heaviness in his groin increased. There was no chance of obtaining relief anytime soon.

Hades watched Taylor and Opal spar. It was obvious the Earthling had never handled a weapon, yet she moved with grace and speed as she attempted to thwart Opal's repeated attacks. Given enough time and adequate practice, she might even become proficient one day.

Taylor's wooden sword clamored to the ground with a loud thud. Or maybe not. He grinned, admiring her round bottom as she bent over to pick up her practice weapon. Suddenly, it wasn't that *sword* he wanted in her hand.

Hades had heard what Taylor said about him—both times. It shouldn't thrill him that she'd stuck up for him, but it did. He didn't care what his people thought about him personally. All he cared about was that they respected his position and his power. Their hushed whispers didn't make a difference, but Taylor's opinion did. Why? Why now? Why her of all people, a hapless, helpless human female who couldn't survive a day on her own?

What was it about this woman that distracted him so? He'd had her writhing beneath him only hours ago. Hades thought bedding her once would be enough to get her out of his system, out of his mind, but still she *lingered*.

Taylor made him want in ways he never thought possible. Her presence was a danger to him, to his carefully constructed world, yet Hades couldn't bring himself to send her away.

"Sire, we have the coordinates. Are you sure that you want to go out and see the area?" The guard's words brought him out of his musings. He was holding a holomap in his hand, circling a location with his finger.

"Yes, now show me what you've found." Hades turned away from the one thing, the one woman that could make him break his vows.

*****

CHAPTER EIGHT

The next morning, Opal was waiting for Taylor in the Pit. They'd agreed to meet before Opal reported for duty, so they could continue their lessons. The warrior woman had brought several practice swords and had two poles placed at the far end. She was dressed in loose leggings and a snug shirt.

"I see you're ready to go." Taylor entered the caged arena in her workout shorts. She'd thrown them into her bag, along with a couple of T-shirts just in case. She'd hung the clothes Hades had given her, deciding they were unimportant in contrast to what she'd learned yesterday.

"I warmed up, while I waited for you," Opal said.

Taylor bent over and stretched, then picked up her wooden sword. The women faced each other.

"Begin." Opal struck immediately.

Taylor danced back, moving lightly on her toes to avoid the blow. She thrust the wooden sword forward like Opal had taught her yesterday and nearly made contact with the warrior. With a little more practice, she just might be able to hit her someday.

They sparred steadily. A rhythmic thud, crack, thud

sounded as the swords met and parted. Sweat dripped from Taylor's body from the exertion, while Opal wasn't even winded.

"Nearly got you there." Taylor lunged to the side and missed again.

A slow clap sounded from within the Pit, startling them. Taylor and Opal looked up to find Hades leaning against the opening, avidly watching them. She hadn't seen him after he'd left yesterday afternoon.

When evening rolled around, Taylor had chosen to eat in her room, instead of joining the warriors in the Great Hall. Hades wasn't gone long, eight hours at the most. There hadn't been time to miss him. Yet Taylor couldn't deny the lurch of her heart or the sudden thrill zinging its way through her body upon seeing him again.

She grinned at Hades as he approached. "Soon I'll be good enough to challenge someone in the Pit." Taylor swung her wooden sword for emphasis. It slipped from her hands and she fumbled to catch it.

"After a day and a half?" Opal balked. "Doubtful."

Hades' gaze flicked to his Righthand, then quickly returned to Taylor. Heat scorched her as he continued to stare. "If you want fucked that bad, I'd be more than happy to oblige. Fighting in the Pit isn't necessary." The bulge in his pants attested to the fact that he was ready to go, but his tone said something altogether different. Hades' words were cool, detached, despite the smolder she'd glimpsed in his eyes.

Taylor shivered from the sudden chill. This was the Dark King she'd met on her first day at the Keep, not the man she'd slept with yesterday.

Before she could come up with a pithy response, Hades turned to Opal. "When you're finished here, we need to debrief. I require your expertise on the area the Slavers chose to hide in. We were unable to locate them, despite having a blood trail. I suspect the blood was planted to throw us off. The Slavers have not only cloaked their ships, they've somehow cloaked their scents. Either that or..."

"Or what?" Taylor asked.

Opal stared at her, this time with distrust. "Or someone is feeding them information on where our scouts will be."

Why would somebody do that? It didn't make sense. By all accounts, the Slavers were extremely dangerous. "Are you saying that you have a traitor in your midst?"

They didn't immediately reply.

"I find it odd that all this started when you arrived," Opal said.

"Me?" Taylor gulped and looked at Hades. His expression remained stony. "You think I'm your traitor." She pressed a hand to her chest. "I'd never betray the Dark—the Phantom people." She stumbled over the words, already admitting more than she liked. Taylor didn't even know how to send a message from the Keep. The fact that she'd had so much trouble contacting Linx proved it. But she knew it would take more than her word to convince Opal and the Dark King.

"We shall see," Opal said.

Hades left as silently as he'd arrived. They both watched him go. It was hard not to, when his pants lovingly gripped his sexy ass as he strutted off.

"You do know that the King is only interested in sex, right?" Opal asked.

Pain slashed Taylor's heart, but she made sure it didn't show on her face. The woman could sense weakness and she'd all but accused her of being a spying prostitute.

"He doesn't *care* about anything, but a willing quim." The look Opal sent her way told Taylor that she knew all about how willing she'd been. "And even those he tires of quickly."

Taylor's first thought was to apologize, though she didn't know for what, but something stopped her. Why should she say that she was sorry, when she'd done nothing wrong? Having sex with Hades might not have been the smartest move and it may have been bad timing on her part, but she no longer regretted it. Not after everything that she'd learned.

It was more than great sex and you know it, a little voice in her head whispered, but Taylor wasn't ready to acknowledge that yet—if ever!

She steadied herself, then glanced at Opal. "If all Hades is interested in is a warm, willing female to fuck, then why do you hang around waiting for him?" Opal opened her mouth to vehemently deny the accusation, but Taylor raised her hand to stop her. "Save it for the other guards!" she said. "It's not exactly a secret. Anyone with eyes can tell that's what you're doing."

Opal's mouth snapped shut with an audible click and black fur bristled under her skin.

Taylor watched, fascinated by the display of emotion. Opal quickly got her beast under control.

"According to the guards I've spoken to, Hades doesn't want a mate and he isn't interested in producing an heir. You knew this going in, so why waste your time?"

"I could ask you the same thing," Opal spat. She swung her sword.

Taylor barely got her sword up in time to block the strike. "I'm not looking for a mate," she said with a calmness she did not feel.

"Then you are a fool." Anger suffused Opal's face. "And so are the guards you've been speaking to. They do not know the King as I do," she said. "The truth is Hades isn't interested in a *weak* mate." She glared at her. "His handicap makes him hesitant, but the right woman, the right *warrior* will change his mind...and make up for his shortcomings."

Shortcomings? Was she serious?

Opal's determined expression said that she was.

"I wouldn't count on it," she said under her breath. It didn't escape Taylor that Hades and his powerful position were interchangeable in Opal's mind. She wondered how many other women the Dark King had slept with felt the same.

Hades was a royal ass. There was no reason to feel sorry for him, yet Taylor still found herself pitying the King. He must feel so alone surrounded by these types of subjects. No wonder he walked around like he didn't care. It was the only way to survive.

They dropped their swords and walked over to the poles. She stood by one and waited for Opal to take her position beside the other. Taylor had seen many women over the years, herself included, set out to change a man. More often than not, the journey ended in heartbreak for the woman. "I take it that you think you're strong enough to tame the King?"

"Isn't it obvious?" Opal asked. "I am the only person fit to claim the position of Queen."

The only thing obvious to Taylor was that Opal was clueless when it came to men.

"Have you ever dated anyone else?" she asked.

Opal's brow creased. "Dated?"

"Gone out with any other warriors besides Hades?"

Opal's face flushed.

That answered that question. It also explained a lot.

Taylor knew men well. She may not have the best track record when it came to choosing them, but she knew there was no changing men's minds or habits once they were set. She knew something else, too. If Hades hadn't claimed Opal by now, he never would. But Taylor didn't think Opal wanted to hear the truth. No one liked hearing that they were wrong.

*****

Opal reported to Hades' quarters after Taylor showed her a few moves on the poles. She was nowhere near good enough to perform for the Dark King, but she was

116

determined to try. Unfortunately, the dancing would have to wait until they finished their briefing. Perseus had taken advantage of the Slavers arrival and finally made his move.

She'd expected him to wait, but he hadn't. Opal had found his third official challenge sitting on her desk, when she returned to her quarters and had brought it directly to Hades. She laid the challenge onto the King's desk and stepped back. He didn't need this right now. Not with his Kingdom under threat.

Hades lifted the missive and sneered.

"This is Perseus' third challenge, Sire. You cannot toss it aside like you've done all the others," she said. "I told you rumors are beginning to spread."

His expression turned mutinous.

Opal rushed on. "Most people don't believe them, Sire."

Hades ran a hand through his hair, leaving it disheveled.

"Perseus has convinced some that you are unable to protect your Kingdom. He uses the Slavers as an example. He has told everyone who will listen that you've rejected his challenges because you fear him."

Hades scowled. "That's ridiculous. I've rejected all his previous challenges because I know the fool will die, if I accept. Doesn't he realize that?"

Opal shook her head. "No, Sire. He truly believes he has a chance at taking the throne. He's so confident that he's already picked out a mate to rule by his side."

"Really?" Hades snorted. "And just who would his future widow be?"

Opal kept her expression blank. "The Earth woman of course. Surely you noticed Taylor's *interest* in the warrior two nights ago at the Pit? It was rather hard to miss."

"I believe things have changed since then." Hades sounded like his usual cocky self.

"Hmm..." Opal reined in her anger before jealousy sealed her throat. "That wasn't the impression Perseus gave me when we last spoke. Are you sure that things have changed?"

She glanced at the King. "Just this morning before you arrived, Taylor was telling me how impressed she was by Perseus' manners. I wouldn't be at all surprised if she sought him out upon her return to New Atlantis." It was a lie, but it needed to be said. Anything to snap the King out of his foolishness and get him to focus on what was important.

Red bled into Hades' blue eyes and his face hardened. "No one will take my throne from me." His words sliced the air, making it hard to breathe. "Tell Perseus that I accept. As for claiming a *mate*," he ground the words with his teeth, gnashing them to dust, "he lost that privilege when he sent me the challenge. He should use his remaining hours to make peace with the Goddess for tomorrow he dies in the Pit."

"As you wish, Sire." Opal bowed and finished her report. "I have looked at all the data. Analyzed it closely. I believe I've located the Slavers' hiding place. It was as I suspected. They are near my old homestead, hiding in Rydon Ravine not far from the crash site. You should've spotted them."

"They weren't there. We checked entire area," he said.

"Perhaps they're there now," she said.

"They would be foolish to return to the same location."

"I know, but if we have a leak as we suspect, they will not anticipate our next move," Opal said. "Especially if we do not announce the outing ahead of time."

"Taylor is not our traitor," Hades said.

"We do not know that for sure, Sire," Opal said.

"I do." Hades voice held such firm conviction that there could be no doubt in his mind.

"Do not allow your feelings for this woman to cloud your judgment," she pleaded. "We know nothing about her other than what Linx has told you. It could all be a lie."

Hades' gaze darkened. "I never allow emotions to interfere with my command. Now choose two warriors that you trust and give them the information you've uncovered. If we send them out immediately, then there's a very good chance that we can detain the Slavers before they know that we're upon them."

"But Sire, it was my idea. I should be allowed to lead the raid," Opal stuttered.

She wanted to be the one to capture the Slavers. If she brought them in, her achievement might take the King's thoughts off that useless Earth woman and put them back where they belonged.

On her.

"That's an order." Hades glanced up from the discarded challenge on his desk. "I want you to continue to guard the Earthling."

"Guard her from what?" Opal asked, directly questioning a command from the King for the first time. "She should be perfectly safe in the Keep."

Hades stared at her. "Can you guarantee her safety?"

"No, of course not," Opal said. "No place is impenetrable."

"Then you have your answer," Hades said. "You will continue to guard Taylor until the threat to the Kingdom is over. Are we clear?"

"Yes, Sire." It was an order that Opal planned to disobey. The first order from Hades that she'd ever disobeyed, but she was determined to do what was best for the Kingdom, best for herself. Ultimately, if she succeeded, it would also be best for the King.

All she had to do now was locate the Slavers, capture them, and bring them to Hades. Should be easy enough. She was a Phantom Warrior after all. Guarding a useless female, who liked to dance on poles, was a waste of her skills. Opal had no intention of wasting a minute more.

"If you have no further need for me?" Her voice automatically dropped to a seductive purr. It was a tone she'd used many times on Hades. One he'd responded to repeatedly. Given his earlier 'condition', she expected him to take advantage of the offer, proving once and for all that

Taylor meant nothing to him. Opal waited for her pheromones to reach the King.

Hades' nose twitched, but his eyes remained Atlantean blue. He didn't even look up, when he said, "You're dismissed."

His reaction, or lack thereof, only reaffirmed to Opal that her decision to lie had been the right one.

*****

Rage bubbled within Hades. He'd barely contained it, when Opal shared Perseus' plans. How dare Perseus try to claim Taylor, when she was under his protection! No one was allowed to touch her.

You did.

He growled. Angry at himself. Angry at Perseus. Angry with Taylor for somehow getting to him, when no one had been able to reach inside. What was he going to do? He couldn't claim her, but there was no way in Fury's fires he'd let Perseus do so.

What if Taylor petitioned him on behalf of Perseus?

Hades' chest clenched, squeezing his two hearts. He rubbed the spot to ease the ache. Taylor had given herself to him. She had surrendered her body to the Dark King. Surely that meant something to her. It did to him. Even though afterwards he'd gone out of his way not to show it.

His furs still held her delicious scent. The sumptuous aroma had made sleeping in them nearly impossible. Hades had been hard all night and had eventually taken himself in hand to relieve the pressure, when all he'd wanted to do was send for Taylor. Keeping his distance had been a mistake.

Hades had half a mind to hunt the flame-haired Earthling down and remind her again that she was *his*. His to pleasure, his to fuck, his to keep, for as long as she remained in his Kingdom. He could almost picture the shocked expression on Taylor's face if he did so. Hades would've smiled if the situation weren't so serious.

Just the thought of another warrior laying his hands upon Taylor brought out his Beast, his Other. The Beast would fight Perseus or any other warrior stupid enough to try to take her from him. Hades refused to look too closely at why the thought of her with another bothered him so. Or why he'd so easily ignored Opal's sexual invitation.

His gaze strayed back to the challenge. If Perseus was in a hurry to die, then he was done trying to save him.

*****

Opal left the King's chambers, still stinging from his rejection. She strode down the hall and stopped outside of Taylor's door. She knocked and impatiently waited for a response. Taylor opened the door, her hair wet from a recent cleansing.

"I need to go out for a while. Do you think you can stay out of trouble until I return?" Opal asked.

Taylor cocked her hip. "I didn't realize that I'd been in any trouble," she said. "Did I miss something?"

Opal projected patience she did not feel. "It is my duty to keep you safe. King's orders, remember? But I have something that I need to do. I should be back in a few hours."

Taylor's expression lightened. "So you want me to cover for you, is that it?"

"Yes," she said through tight lips.

They stared at each other for a few more seconds, then Taylor shrugged. "Sure, why not? If I run into Hades, which I doubt, I'll make an excuse for why you're not there."

Opal inclined her head. "Thank you."

"No problem." Taylor shut the door.

Opal rushed off, making her way out the side of the Keep, past the courtyard training area. Perseus and another warrior were working on their sword skills. He was both precise and deadly, when he struck. For a second, Opal felt doubt creep into her mind. Could Hades beat Perseus in the Pit?

Perseus spotted her and stopped sparring. "Where are you going in such a hurry?" he asked.

"That is none of your concern," Opal said.

"Aren't you supposed to be guarding the Earth woman that the King is so fond of?" he asked.

Opal hesitated. "She means nothing to him. Another distraction. He'll tire of her soon enough."

Perseus' brow rose. "Is that what you think?"

"Yes, why wouldn't I? The King is nothing if not a creature of habit." Opal tried to move past him, but he stepped in her way. "I told Hades about your mutual interest in Taylor. Fortunately for you, the Dark King isn't one to fight over a female."

Perseus frowned. "You told Hades that I was interested in Taylor? You shouldn't have done that." An odd expression flashed across his face.

"It's the truth, isn't it?" Opal asked.

"Yes, I suppose it is," Perseus said. "But I don't think your plan is going to work."

Opal's face paled. Did he know that she was going in search of the Slavers? "W-what plan?"

Perseus snorted. "The one to drive Hades and Taylor apart. That is what you're trying to do, right?"

Relief warred with surprise. "I don't know what you're talking about," Opal said.

"Yes, you do." Perseus shook his head and gave her a commiserative look. "You've noticed the way the Dark King looks at Taylor. He practically salivates every time she enters the room. Not that I blame him, Taylor is rather luscious." Perseus grinned in remembrance, then his sharp gaze speared Opal. "Honestly, I'm surprised he hasn't marked her yet."

"You know not of what you speak." Opal denied his

accusations vehemently, but she couldn't shake the doubt that crept into her mind. She'd invited Hades to take her and he'd refused. The Dark King *never* turned down a chance to fuck.

Perseus' mouth curved. "Don't I? If I had the opportunity to bed Taylor, she'd be wearing my mark right now. Too bad she only has eyes for the Dark King."

"She is a foolish human who will leave here soon enough," she said. "Besides, everyone knows that Hades has no intention of taking a mate."

"Yet you still live in hope," Perseus said with a laugh.

"Watch your tongue, warrior, or I might just cut it out," Opal spat.

His expression hardened. "Righthand, do not think that your current position intimidates me. I am not like the other guards. Speaking of which, did you deliver my challenge to the King?"

Opal snorted. "You're a fool!"

"Did you?" he repeated, this time with more force.

"Yes!" she snapped. "The King said that you should make peace with the Goddess before tomorrow night."

Something flared behind Perseus' eyes, but he quickly banked the emotion. Whether it was doubt, fear, or triumph, Opal would never know.

"You side with the wrong warrior, Righthand," he said. "Perhaps if you'd come to me first, before spreading your thighs for the King, then you would be marked and mated by now."

"I would never allow you to touch me." Opal's chin rose. "You know I side with the King."

Perseus shrugged. "And what if I am King after tomorrow night? What then? Where will your allegiance lie?"

"Wherever it needs to," she said.

He smiled, but there was no warmth behind it. "Perhaps you should come to my chambers tonight, I just might be able to sway you in my favor ahead of time."

Opal looked him up and down. "That is doubtful. Now I must go." She hurried out the side doors.

Before she slipped through, Perseus added, "Watch out for the Slavers. They're turning out to be quite a challenge for the King. Who knew they could be so useful?"

Opal paused to look at him, but Perseus had already gone back to sparring. What did he mean by *useful*? It was an odd phrase that continued to eat at her as she made her way down the mountain, along the stone-covered path that wound its way into the Walled City.

She paused at the bottom of the rough trail to review her calculations. Opal skirted along the city's east wall, slipping behind the various merchant stalls that lined the streets during the day. At sundown most of the stalls would fold up shop and return home. A few of the food vendors stayed open for longer hours to take advantage of late night strollers and shift changes at the Keep.

She caught a whiff of delicious spiced bread wafting on the air. Opal's stomach growled at the thought of biting into the aromatic dough. When had she last eaten? She couldn't recall. Opal ignored her hunger and kept moving. She didn't know how long it would take to reach the search area, so there was no time to waste. She needed to be in and out before Hades noticed.

Thanks to Perseus' formal challenge to the King, that might be a while.

She reached the transport loaner station near the great doors that marked the entrance to the Walled City. The hover transports had been tethered to various poles, their engines running. The soft puttering sound barely registered over the loud voices haggling in nearby clothing stalls.

Opal flashed her credentials, then handed the man a fist full of credits. He pointed to a transport hovering three feet in the air. "Bring it back the way that you found it," he said. "The last time one of the King's guards checked out one of my hovers they brought it back in pieces."

She didn't answer because she couldn't make that kind of promise. Opal had no idea what she would encounter in the ravines. She grabbed the tether and pulled the machine to her. The hover sputtered, threatening to rise in the air. Opal hopped on before it succeeded and strapped herself onto the narrow seat. Once secured, she unfastened the tether. The transport rose into the air. She adjusted the altitude setting, then shouted, "Open the gates!"

The sentry guards held fast until she flashed her ID. Upon seeing the symbol of the Righthand, they pressed a button and the gates dematerialized. Opal gunned the hover's engine and zipped out into the Ruggeds.

Most people in Hades' Kingdom lived within the Walled City. Some, like her parents, had chosen to homestead in the valleys between the mountains, aptly known as the Ruggeds, since life there was difficult and survival was questionable.

Opal knew this land like the back of her sword. She'd grown up here, played here. She knew every place to hide, every spot to hunt, and every water source. If the Slavers were still on Zaron, she would find them.

*****

Four hours later, Opal was ready to give up. She'd searched the three ravines that scarred the land near her old homestead. Other than the crash debris in Rydon Ravine, she hadn't spotted any sign of the Slavers or their ships. Since she'd told no one of her mission, there wasn't a chance that the Slavers could've been forewarned.

Given the lack of supplies at the crash site, it was more than obvious some of the crew had survived. Solo pilots didn't man slaver ships and there'd only been one body. She thought about all the places she explored as a child. There were so many. She'd covered the most obvious locations and was slowly making her way through her secret spots.

The sun was sinking fast. Soon she'd have to return to the

safety of the Keep. Opal turned the transport in a wide arc, scanning the land and the woods in the distance. As she was doing so, something sparkled amongst the dark purple leaves, then quickly vanished.

It could be nothing, she thought, but she needed to be sure.

Opal turned the hover once more, watching the tree line closely. The flash came again, this time more definite. Not natural. Alien tech. Reflective camouflage. She cut the power on her transport and it slowly floated to the ground. With a flick of a button, she hid the vehicle, using less sophisticated tech than the Slavers had.

She couldn't afford for them to hear her approach. Opal shuddered at the thought of being captured by the vicious Slavers. She'd seen what they'd done to imprisoned females firsthand, when she'd participated in a rescue mission three years ago. They'd only found five of the eight women alive. The rest had been dissected, their parts distributed to exotic shops around the galaxy.

Opal couldn't fathom that there were sentient beings in the galaxy that still believed that ground up humanoid organs worked as aphrodisiacs and had healing properties, but she'd seen the stalls with her own eyes and she'd helped unpack the body parts of the women they'd been unable to save.

Slavers didn't always kill and dissect their captives. Sometimes they took them to Slave markets and sold them to the highest bidder. From that point, the women could be used for sex or for hard labor, sometimes both. Neither fate was one any woman wanted to experience. Opal had even heard rumors that on very rare occasions Slavers claimed the women for themselves. But as far as she could tell, those stories were only rumors, since she'd never seen any proof.

Opal crept through the woods, keeping downwind. Slavers weren't like Phantoms, but it wasn't uncommon for them to have 'enhanced' their senses with nanotech. She stayed low to the ground. When she couldn't get any closer without betraying her position and the rugged terrain became too difficult to navigate, Opal shifted into her cat form.

She launched herself into a tree, using her sharp claws to gain purchase, then worked her way from limb to limb until she had a clear view of the area. Opal froze, her tail flicking dangerously behind her as she stared at the crude campsite.

It was larger than she'd expected. Large enough that it should've easily been discovered. No way could they have remained hidden without help. Their tech wasn't that good.

A whoosh sound came from her right. Opal crouched low on the branch as a leather clad Slaver with black, braided hair stepped out into what seemed to be thin air. Instead of crashing to the ground, he appeared to float on invisible currents. Given his broad shoulders and muscle packed body that should've been impossible.

The craft was completely camouflaged, but she could tell he was standing in an entrance door. He was far above the treetops, situated much higher than what an average-sized Slaver ship was designed for. They'd somehow managed to interlock all three ships together, turning it into one massive craft.

The Slaver's blue skin held a tinted hue that indicated he'd spent a lot of time on one of the water planets. Since Slavers were nomadic by nature, there was no way to narrow down the location. Without warning, he looked in her direction, his golden eyes glowing against the setting sun.

Opal didn't move. Didn't breathe.

His gaze held for longer than it should have, then slowly drifted on. Opal could still feel that molten gold searing her fur. She waited for him to sound the alarm, but he didn't. He simply continued to survey the area. Had the purple leaves somehow hidden her?

"Captain Hawk!" someone shouted. "See anything?"

The leather-clad man turned his head, his unerring gaze skimming over her feline form once more. "Nothing to worry about," he said in a deep reverberating voice that made Opal's fur bristle.

More men filed out behind him. They jumped, dropping over thirty feet, landing easily on the ground.

Definitely enhanced, Opal thought, especially the one they'd called 'Hawk'.

He'd *seen* her. Of that there was no doubt. She'd felt his gaze. Could still feel it. Why hadn't the captain informed anyone of her presence? Opal scented the air, but she smelled nothing of the men or their ship.

Fear and something unidentifiable worked its way through her, raising the fur on her back. She'd never encountered Slavers this cunning. Maybe they weren't receiving help from the inside. Maybe they were simply far more advanced than the Phantom world. What did that mean for Zaron and its people?

Opal silently counted their numbers. She wanted to make sure that her report to Hades was as accurate as possible. Twenty-five exited the massive ship, which meant there were probably another ten or so still onboard.

She watched them closely, while maintaining her position amongst the trees. The men stood around a holomap, pointing at various locations. From this distance, Opal could only make out a few of the areas, but it was more than obvious from the ones that she did identify that they had somehow gotten their hands on classified material.

Her thoughts flashed to Taylor. Hades thought she was innocent, but Opal wasn't so sure. Was Taylor a spy? Was she helping the Slavers? Did she know the one called Hawk? Her stomach soured at the thought. First Hawk, now Hades. It was time to confront the Earth woman.

*****

Taylor woke with a start, her hair tangled in her face. What was that sound? The banging came again, this time louder. It took her a minute to figure out that it was coming

128

from her door.

She stumbled out of bed and stubbed her toe. She yelped and hopped the rest of the way. Taylor opened the door with a yawn to find Opal standing on the other side, glaring at her.

She blinked, trying to clear some of the sleep away. "What's up?"

Opal shoved her back inside the room and followed her in, shutting the door behind her. "I want the truth!" she demanded.

"What?" Taylor yawned again. "Why are you shouting?"

This time when Opal shoved her, Taylor fell. She dropped onto her bottom and bounced. The jolt woke her addled brain. "What is your problem?"

Opal glared at her and her hand moved to the pommel of her sword.

Taylor jumped to her feet and backed away. She quickly searched her room for a weapon, but the only sharp object in sight was the heel of her stiletto. She picked up the pump and pointed it at Opal, though there was little chance of doing any damage against a sword.

"Do you want to explain what's going on?" Taylor held the spiked heel between them.

"Tell me how you contacted them and I will make sure that your death is merciful," Opal said.

Taylor shoved her hair back. "Uh, who are you talking about?"

"The Slavers! Do not try to lie, I have seen evidence of their presence with my own eyes."

She held up one hand. "Listen, I don't know what you've seen, but I assure you that I have had no part in helping your invaders," Taylor said.

"Slavers!" Opal screeched.

"Whatever." Taylor rolled her eyes. "I had never heard of those guys, until you brought them up."

Opal's red gaze narrowed and seemed to glow in the low

lighting. "Hawk!" she shouted.

"Squirrel!" Taylor countered.

Opal took a menacing step forward. "Who is Squirrel?" she grit out between clenched teeth.

Taylor shrugged. "How should I know? I thought we were playing a word association game."

"You do not know a squirrel?" Opal asked.

Her brow tilted. "A squirrel is a what, not a *who*. Furry rodent, bushy tail, likes nuts, kind of cute. Ring any bells?"

Opal snorted in disgust and her hand dropped from the pommel of her sword. "You really are an underdeveloped species." She shook her head. "I do not understand what our warriors see in you. A fertile womb and plentiful numbers do not make up for the loss in aptitude. We would've been better off facing our extinction with dignity than to lower ourselves by breeding with dimwitted humans."

"Okay..." Taylor drew the word out. "I think someone needs a nap." She had no idea what Opal was going on about, but she was awake enough now to know that she'd been insulted. Again. She hiked her thumb over her shoulder and pointed at the furs. "I'm going to go back to bed now. I suggest that you do the same." Taylor walked Opal to the door. "Glad we had this talk."

Opal stepped over the threshold.

"Oh," Taylor said, stopping Opal before she left. "The next time you need somebody to dump on or to cover for you, don't bother coming to me."

The warrior opened her mouth to speak, but Taylor didn't want to hear it. She shut the door in her face. "That was fun," she muttered under her breath and went back to bed.

*****

Opal's body ached from the hover ride back to the Walled City. The whole time it had felt as if Hawk's gold eyes were boring into her spine. She'd never ridden so fast or so recklessly in her life. She rolled her tense shoulders.

She shouldn't have confronted Taylor tonight. She knew that now. But she'd been so stressed out by what she had discovered that she'd needed to find out the truth. The talk hadn't gone as she'd planned. Opal thought that by catching Taylor off guard that the human would slip up and confess, but that hadn't been the case. The woman had been her usual clueless self.

Fortunately, she had kept most of the information she'd uncovered private, so there was little chance of Taylor talking about things that she should not. Tomorrow, Opal would approach Hades and share her intel, but not until after the Pit challenge. She didn't want anything distracting the Dark King from the upcoming fight. Not when his life and throne were on the line.

Hades would have to eventually hear her report. He wouldn't be happy when he realized that she'd disobeyed a direct order. That was something the Dark King would not overlook. She'd have to face the consequences for her behavior. Opal would be punished severely, possibly stripped of her rank, but she hoped that what she'd learned would be taken into consideration before Hades did so.

What if Perseus was the one standing after the challenge?

Opal would cross that valley when she got to it.

She tried not to think about what would happen if she were no longer the King's Righthand. The other guards would never let her live down the demotion. She'd have to leave the Keep, unless Hades claimed her for his Queen. The whole situation didn't bear thinking about.

Hawk's shimmering gold eyes flashed in her mind. Opal shivered.

"Who are you?" she whispered. "And why are you here?"

*****

CHAPTER NINE

The Keep was unusually quiet the next day. Taylor awoke late because Opal hadn't shown up to rouse her for practice. After last night's unexpected visit, she wasn't surprised. Maybe the King's Righthand was embarrassed by her behavior.

If she wasn't, then she darn well should be, Taylor thought.

She got dressed and worked out on her own. It was nice to practice without fear of being struck. Taylor worked on her swordsmanship against wooden and stone enemies, slashing at them until her arms hurt. Sweat dripped from her body as she repeated the moves Opal had taught her. She was getting better. She could tell.

"Do you need some help?" a deep male voice called out.

Taylor turned expecting to see Hades. Perseus stood at the edge of the Pit instead. She kept her disappointment hidden behind a smile. Ever since they'd slept together, Hades had gone out of his way to limit their contact. Taylor tried not to take it personally, but hadn't entirely succeeded.

"Sure." She motioned Perseus over. "I can use all the help that I can get."

He grinned. "Happy to oblige."

At least one man seemed to enjoy her company.

Perseus was a handsome warrior with raven hair, dancing eyes, and a playful demeanor. He was a shameless flirt, but he'd extended her friendship, when no one else had. For that kindness alone, Taylor would be forever grateful to him. Perhaps if she'd never met the Dark King things would be different between them. They might've had a chance. But she had met Hades, and he was a hard act to follow.

Perseus picked up a wooden sword as he passed the rack. He swung it smoothly like it was a part of his limb. She thought about how young some of the kids in Hades' class had been. No wonder Perseus was so proficient. He'd been holding a sword since he could walk.

"You need to extend your arm more. You don't want your enemies to get too close." Perseus demonstrated. "When you arc wildly, you leave your torso open to attack. That's not a problem for a Phantom because we have two hearts, but for a human a direct strike can be fatal."

Taylor shuddered in mock horror. "We wouldn't want that." She snorted, then followed his lead.

They sparred for an hour or so, laughing and joking the whole time. Perseus concentrated on teaching her defensive moves. Stuff that would keep her alive in a fight until help could arrive. His optimism was catching.

"You are beginning to get the hang of it," he said.

"I have a good teacher." Taylor winked. Flirting was as natural as breathing to her. She did it without thought, but she was well aware it didn't mean anything.

Perseus grinned. "I could do more than teach, if you'd let me." He lowered his wooden sword and slowly approached her. The mirth in his eyes changed to liquid heat.

Taylor's heart hammered and not just from the workout. "Um..." She glanced around, but they were still alone.

Perseus ran a finger over her cheek, grazing the side of her mouth before following the gentle slope of her neck.

"You are so soft, so lush," He glanced down, admiring her curves. "So very beautiful. If I were Hades, I would claim you before another gets the chance."

Taylor's face flushed and warmth spread throughout her body. "The King isn't looking for a wife."

Perseus leaned forward until they were but a breath apart. "Then Hades is an imbecile. If I ruled the Phantoms, the first thing I would do is make you my Queen."

Like any little girl, Taylor had dreamed about being a Princess. It wasn't until she'd gotten older and life had kicked her in the gut that she realized the fantasy in no way matched the reality of the title. Royalty in general never had a life of their own. She couldn't live like that, not that she'd ever get the chance. Taylor knew her position in the world. She was comfortable with it, which was good, since her situation was unlikely to change on Zaron.

Before she could reply, Perseus stopped her with a gentle press of his finger to her lips.

"Only a fool would allow one such as you to remain unattached. With a quick bite, I could change that." He ran the pad of his callused thumb over the spot where her neck met her shoulder, where Hades had left a love bite. "I wonder, would you let me?"

What did he mean by *bite*? Was he being literal or figurative? She could tell that Perseus was asking her something important. But Taylor didn't know enough about the Phantom culture to ascertain the significance of the question. How did Phantoms mate? Was there a ceremony involved? Or was it a 'with this bite, I thee wed' sort of thing?

Taylor wished that she'd thought to ask Tabby. Her sister would know, since she was mated to Linx. Was Perseus proposing? She didn't want to hurt his feelings, but she also didn't want to encourage him if that were the case.

"I can't make any big decisions," she said, going for diplomacy. "Not with my future on Zaron being so precarious. Do you understand?"

"I suppose," he said tightly. Perseus' hand dropped to his side and he stepped back. "Perhaps after tonight you will have a change of heart."

"What's tonight?" she asked, totally confused. Was it a Phantom holiday of some kind?

"The dawn of a new Phantom realm," he said.

Okay, whatever that meant. Perseus was making even less sense than Opal. And that was saying something. Soon Taylor would need a decoder ring and a map to figure out what the Phantoms were talking about. Maybe speaking in riddles was just a Zaronian thing? Either that, or she'd been here too long and her mind had finally gone bye-bye. Taylor hiked a thumb over her shoulder. "I need to shower, so I'm going to head back to my room."

He gave her a slight bow. "Please think about what I've said. Honor me by seriously considering my offer."

Was he talking about the proposed bite? That didn't seem like a good offer to Taylor. In fact, it sounded painful. But she couldn't exactly say that because it was obvious that it meant a lot to him.

"All right," she said, even though she'd already made up her mind. Whatever Perseus was asking her, the answer was no.

Heaviness settled around them. There was nothing left to say.

Taylor walked to the entrance of the Pit, then stopped. She glanced back. Perseus hadn't moved. He was still standing in the center of the cage, this time lost in thought. "Thanks again for your help."

He blinked in surprise and looked at her, as if he'd forgotten that she was there. "Anytime," he said, but seemed distracted.

"Is everything okay?" she asked.

His expression softened. "Yes, thank you for inquiring."

"Can't wait to show Opal all my new moves." She waved

her sword in the air dramatically, pretending to slay an invisible enemy. Anything to lighten the mood.

Perseus chuckled. "I'm not sure that she'll appreciate that I've interfered."

Taylor snickered. "Maybe not, but I sure do."

"Until tomorrow, sweet Taylor," Perseus said, then slowly walked away.

Taylor lowered her sword. Her buoyant mood was gone, replaced by sadness. The worst part was that she didn't know why.

*****

Hades entered the stands surrounding the Pit at the precise moment Perseus touched Taylor's cheek, then slid his finger down her neck. He brushed the fading purple spot that Hades had left, as if to erase it.

The sight stopped the Dark King in his tracks. His beast bristled. Perseus slowly closed the distance between them and Hades' hearts clenched. He ducked into the shadows before they spotted him and continued to watch the intimate exchange.

Snippets of the conversation reached Hades' ears, each word more painful than the last. There was no doubt that Perseus intended to claim Taylor and from her reaction she didn't seem opposed to the idea.

What if Perseus bit her right here in front of him?

Panic struck, leaving him winded. It was followed by blind rage. Hades couldn't let Perseus claim Taylor. He couldn't let anyone claim her.

The realization sobered him. He'd done his best to stay away from her, avoid further temptation. Doing so had cost Hades dearly. It was obvious that his evasion didn't affect her the same way.

Taylor smiled at Perseus.

Hades looked away, as something inside of him

136

crumbled.

Tonight he would meet Perseus in the Pit and they would do battle. Perseus wanted his throne—his *woman*. Hades could not let him live, not even for Taylor. Fueled by pain, he forced himself to watch their playful exchange, no longer hearing what was being said. They parted a few minutes later.

Taylor would hate him after tonight. Of that, Hades had no doubt. Whatever chance he had of keeping her would end, when he was standing over Perseus' dead body.

*****

Taylor was eating dinner in her room, when the drums sounded. She thought she was hearing things, until the rhythmic boom, boom, boom came again. She poked her head outside her door to see what was going on. Kon stood guard in the hall.

"What's happening?" she asked.

His grim expression told her it wasn't anything good. "A challenge is to take place."

She frowned. "A challenge? I never heard anything about there being a challenge tonight." The Phantoms who'd brought her food hadn't mentioned it. "Was it a last minute thing?"

He nodded.

"Is Hades going to be there?" Taylor groaned inwardly. Why had she asked that question? It made her sound like a lovesick teen.

Kon paled. "Yes, the King will be present."

Okay, that was weird. What was going on? "Will Opal be there?"

He hesitated, then said, "Yes. I believe the entire Kingdom will be watching this particular challenge. A holofeed has been set up for those outside the Keep."

Taylor stared at him. If the fight was so important, then

why hadn't she heard about it? Had Hades asked that she not be invited? Was his need to avoid her so great that he didn't even want to sit next to her? The idea hurt more than it should. She hadn't behaved that badly at the last challenge. All things considered, Taylor thought she'd handled the situation at the Pit well. "You said everyone would be watching. So is this some kind of prizefight?"

Kon shook his head. "There will be no prizes given after this battle."

"No, I didn't mean." She waved her hand to say never mind. "Who is fighting tonight?" Taylor wasn't sure why she asked. It wasn't like she knew many people here. Kon could name the two biggest, baddest fighters in the land and their names would mean nothing to her.

She recalled the challenge between Pitticus and Cornelius. That fight had been one of the hottest things she'd ever witnessed in her life. If tonight's challenge was like that one, Hades wouldn't have to ask her to sleep with him. She'd volunteer.

Kon shifted from foot to foot, his discomfort growing.

Unease replaced Taylor's excitement. "Kon, who is participating in this challenge?" she asked.

He hesitated.

"Please tell me," she pleaded.

"The Dark King," Kon said finally.

Taylor's mind closed down. She had to have misunderstood. Hades was rarely challenged. Hadn't he said that on the first day they met? So Kon's statement didn't make sense.

"The Dark King what?" she asked being purposely obtuse. Taylor's heart was pounding so hard she could hardly breathe.

Kon's solemn expression turned to one of impatience. "Hades is fighting," he said in a hushed tone.

Challenges to the King were to the death. Taylor remembered that part clearly. Cold enveloped her and she shivered. Kon had to be wrong. "He can't be," she said, refusing to accept what she was being told.

"He is," he said.

Who was dumb enough to challenge the King? Taylor's heart dropped to her knees, then shot back to her stomach. She clenched her abdomen as a wave of dizziness struck. She stumbled to the side and caught the doorframe to steady herself.

"The King had no choice, but to accept the challenge," he said.

"What do you mean that he had no choice?" Her voice quivered. "Everybody has a choice." This was horrible. This was worse than horrible. What if Hades died? The room spun again, but this time Taylor was ready. She held fast to the stone to keep from collapsing.

Kon sighed. "This was the third challenge he'd received. Hades had already ignored the first two. If he'd disregarded this one, then the Phantom people would begin to question his ability to lead."

He sounded sad. Or perhaps resigned. Taylor couldn't tell which and it really didn't matter. Not right now. Not when Hades' life was in danger. "Who is the King fighting?" she asked.

Was he bigger than Hades? Did his teeth hold poisonous venom? Pitticus' fangs flashed in her mind and her heart nearly stopped beating. There was only one reason for the King to enter the Pit and that was to defend his throne. *It couldn't be.*

Taylor's stomach soured and threatened to dump her dinner on Kon's feet. She closed her eyes to block out the truth. *Please let me be wrong.*

"Perseus has challenged the Dark King for his throne." His chin dropped to his chest.

This couldn't be happening. Perseus' words from this afternoon came crashing down upon her. Now everything made sense. She'd thought he was just trying to impress her.

Isn't that what men did, when they liked someone? Taylor hadn't thought for a moment that Perseus was serious—at least not about making her his Queen.

This was crazy. She had to stop the fight. "You need to take me to the Pit," Taylor said. "I have to talk to Hades and Perseus before this goes any further."

Kon shook his head. "The King does not want you there."

Bile rose in her throat, as worry wound its way around her spine, squeezing her tight. "Why?"

Kon didn't answer.

Taylor's hand rose to her mouth. "Oh my God, he thinks he's going to die."

"No," Kon said softly. "He doesn't want you to see him kill."

All this talk of death had Taylor gulping for air. She couldn't breathe. Nothing was going in. She grabbed her throat and gasped.

Kon shoved her head down, until it was level with her knees. "Inhale," he said.

"I'm trying." Stars burst behind her eyelids.

Kon thumped her on the back.

Taylor took a stuttering breath, filling her greedy lungs with air. She had to get out of here. She had to get to the Pit. She spun away from Kon and grabbed her practice sword. "If you don't get out of my way, I swear I'm going to hit you."

Kon looked at her face, then at her wooden sword and raised an eyebrow. "That's not even sharp," he said.

"Maybe not, but it'll leave one hell of a bruise. You might even get a splinter. Now move aside! I have a fight to stop."

He crossed his arms over his chest. "And I have my orders," he said.

She dropped her sword. "I thought Perseus was your friend."

"He is!" His big body shook with unchecked emotion and his expression turned bleak.

"Then how can you just stand by and let him die?" she

asked.

"I have done everything in my power to try to change his mind. Nothing I said made any difference." His shoulders dropped. "All Perseus cares about is ascending to the throne."

There had to be something they could do. She felt so helpless. Tears filled Taylor's eyes.

Kon's gaze widened in alarm. "Do not do that." He pointed at her face.

"Do what?" She sniffled.

"Cry." Kon took another step back.

"I won't if you take me to the Pit." It was an empty threat, since she didn't have control over her tears at the moment. The thought of Hades dying in the Pit was too much for her to bear. It felt as if something was ripping her heart in half. Taylor sobbed.

"Fine!" Kon said. "But your presence may distract Perseus and Hades."

"That's what I'm counting on." Taylor ran a hand over her eyes, smearing the tears across her cheeks. "Now let's go."

They reached the Pit in time to see Hades step into the caged arena. His massive chest was bare to the waist and he wore loose leggings that would give him lots of freedom to move. Not that he'd need the clothes once he shifted into his Other form. Taylor spotted Opal in the stands. She was seated in her usual spot, but this time her body was tense as she watched Perseus follow the King into the Pit.

The drums continued to pound, the steady thrum threatened to shatter nerve and bone. Taylor pushed her way through the crowd and rushed over to Opal. "Make them stop!"

Opal glared at her as if she were insane. "Sit down!" she hissed.

He could die... "You can't let him do this," Taylor said.

"What makes you think that the Dark King would listen to me? Do you have any idea what would happen to me, if I tried to stop this challenge?"

Taylor didn't. It hadn't even occurred to her that there might be repercussions. "I thought you wanted to be Queen."

"I do," she ground out between clenched teeth. "That's why I'm seated, showing my respect for the King's decision."

Respect could be earned back. Death was forever. "What if I stop them?" She was a stranger. Someone unfamiliar with their customs. Taylor could claim ignorance and it wouldn't be a lie.

Opal stared at her, unblinking. "If you try to do that, I will cut you down." She touched her sword. "Do you understand me?"

Taylor swallowed hard. "Yes." She understood perfectly. Opal might be worried, but she'd do nothing to save the Dark King.

"Now sit down. The last thing we need is for Hades to be distracted by you," she said with so much distaste and venom that it startled Taylor into sitting.

Taylor didn't think seeing her in the stands would make a difference to Hades. His actions as of late spoke far louder than anything he could've uttered. She knew exactly where she stood with the Dark King.

Nowhere.

She glanced at Opal. Her cool regal demeanor screamed power and control. She'd make a great Queen. Taylor looked at Hades. They were perfect for each other. Why hadn't she seen it before?

The warriors around her were silent. There was no chanting, no growls, and no roars, only the incessant drumming. Everyone stared solemnly at the Pit. Unlike the first fight, there was no posturing. Neither Hades nor Perseus felt the need to do so.

Hades dropped to his knees and grabbed a handful of dirt. He held the soil in his palm, then raised the dirt toward the ceiling and slowly let it slip through his fingertips.

"What is he doing?" Taylor asked.

Opal didn't look her way, but said, "He's offering a prayer to the Goddess."

Taylor sent a quick one to God just in case. She glanced to Opal. "One of them is going to die tonight. Aren't they?"

Her rigid expression remained unchanged. "It's a pity they do not fight for the throne alone."

"What else is there to fight for?" Taylor asked. Was she referring to the Kingdom? Did Hades own something else that Perseus wanted?

Opal glared at her. "You." The word came out as a curse.

Taylor shook her head in denial. Opal was wrong. They couldn't be fighting over her. Hades didn't want a mate. And Perseus… She didn't really know what he wanted. This was insane! "You need to make them stop or at least let me try."

She didn't want either of them to die. Not over of her. Perseus seemed like a really nice guy. And the thought of losing Hades made her ill. What would she do if he died? Pain crushed her, making her body tremble. If she'd doubted her developing feelings for the Dark King before, she didn't doubt them now.

"No!" Taylor shot to her feet. "You have to stop!" Hades' gaze locked with hers a second before Opal jerked her back down on the seat.

"This is your last warning," she snarled. "If you cannot sit here without interfering, then I will have you escorted out of the Pit." And from the look on her face, she would make good on the threat.

Taylor's fingers curled into tight fists. She couldn't stop it. She couldn't stop them. One of them was going to die. The room seemed to close in around her. She put her head between her knees and prayed for a miracle.

Opal stood and slowly raised her arms. The drums ceased. "A challenge for the throne has been put forth by Phantom Warrior Perseus. The Dark King has accepted. It will be a fight to the death."

A hushed murmur worked its way through the capacity crowd.

"Let the challenge begin!" Opal shouted.

Hades walked to one end of the Pit and Perseus walked to the other. When they reached the far ends, the warriors turned to face each other.

"Perseus, this is your last chance," Hades yelled. "Do you yield?"

"Nay!" He shook his head. "I intend to become the next Phantom King."

Hades acknowledged him. "So be it." The last word had barely left his lips when his body started to morph and grow. Tawny fur bristled over the Dark King's skin, along with several faint black stripes. Claws shot from his fingertips. Tusk-length teeth sprouted in his mouth. Within seconds, Hades was gone, replaced by a monstrous cat that was three times the size of the ligers on Earth.

Taylor had only gotten a glimpse of Hades' Other on the day she'd arrived. Looking at him now, Hades was even more terrifying...and impressive. It was hard to see the man she'd made love to as she stared at the snarling beast. If it weren't for his aqua blue eyes, she wouldn't have recognized him at all.

Perseus shifted, too, his muscles growing and reshaping. Gone was the handsome dark-haired warrior. In his place stood a mutated lion with dark fur and a thick ruff. Pound for pound they appeared evenly matched, but there was no way of telling who was the better fighter.

Taylor's nails dug into her palms until they bled.

Hades roared. The ferocious sound echoed throughout the room, drawing every eye. Perseus answered the roar with one of his own, then launched himself at the Dark King.

The two cats collided in a flurry of teeth and claws. Scratching and biting, yowling and growling, they tore into each other. The fight was vicious and terrifying. Nothing at all like the one between Pitticus and Cornelius.

Perseus sank his claws deep in Hades' side, leaving crimson furrows and torn sinew behind. The Dark King hissed as fresh blood darkened his pale fur, turning it to rust.

Hades buried his teeth into Perseus' shoulder, ripping away a chunk of flesh. His mouth and whiskers dripped with carnage as he spat the meat out and attacked again. Perseus roared in fury and jerked out of Hades' deadly grasp.

The beasts circled each other, hair raised, tails whipping violently from side-to-side as they searched for another opening. Perseus' muscles bunched, then he pounced. His sharp claws sought Hades' face. The Dark King jerked his head to the side. He barely avoided being blinded.

Perseus twisted in mid-air and struck Hades in the chest with his back legs. The warrior's claws raked the Dark King, taking him to the ground. Hades' back hit with a loud thud. Dust plumed around their bodies, rising high into the air. Perseus' lunged. His jaws snapped repeatedly, as he struggled to latch onto Hades' neck.

Taylor's heart lodged in her throat. Cold enveloped her, until her whole body was numb. She trembled as fear threatened to overwhelm her. Hades was going to die. She glanced at Opal for reassurance, but a gleam of excitement filled her eyes.

Oh god, she was looking forward to seeing the death of the Dark King. Talk about a fickle, bloodthirsty bitch.

Hades struggled beneath Perseus, his legs straining to keep the cat from landing a killing blow. Triumph filled Perseus' blood red eyes. Taylor stared at the King, willing him to rise, but all he seemed to be able to do was hold Perseus at bay. Hades' muscles quivered under the pressure as Perseus bore down upon him.

"Get up," Taylor whispered. "You have to get up." *I need you.*

Perseus *grinned* at the crowd, confident of his victory. He was so busy gloating that he accidentally loosened his grip. Without warning, Hades struck. He latched onto the thatch of hair around Perseus' neck and rolled them both. One second Perseus was on top, the next he was sprawled beneath the Dark King.

Never turn your back on a liger.

Perseus twisted and managed to stand, but not for long. Hades' deadly claws clamped onto Perseus' flank, dragging his back legs out from under him.

Taylor had seen lions do that when they took down zebras in Africa. It was one thing to watch it on a nature channel, quite another to witness the move in person. Her gorge rose.

Hades jumped onto Perseus' back. His massive jaws fastened onto the warrior's vulnerable neck. Perseus squirmed out of the hold, but Hades' bulk kept him pinned to the dirt.

The Dark King growled, then violently jerked his head to the right. His sharp tusk-like teeth sliced open Perseus' abdomen, spilling the warrior's intestines onto the ground. Perseus wailed and clawed at the dirt in panic, struggling to escape. Hades clung to his back, his claws continuing to shred the black cat as blood pooled around them. Powerful jaws unerringly found Perseus' neck once more.

The Dark King squeezed.

Perseus gasped for breath.

Taylor hugged herself, as the color drained from her face.

Hades didn't let up. He continued putting pressure on Perseus' neck until the warrior's life force dimmed. Twitching, the lion collapsed beneath the Dark King. Perseus took one last shuddering breath, then died.

Hades remained on top of him, his sharp teeth digging into Perseus' dead flesh. After what felt like an eternity to Taylor, the Dark King jumped off the deceased warrior's back and slowly circled the Pit. His gaze touched everyone in the stands. Hades paused when he reached Taylor and appeared to grin, flashing blood-covered incisors.

Taylor's stomach flipped. Before she knew what was

happening, she threw up on Opal's shoes.

Opal jumped to her feet and took a step to the side. Her lip curled in disgust. "You are weak," she huffed.

As if confirming her assessment, Taylor dry heaved, then threw up some more.

Hades continued to circle the Pit. When he'd made his third pass, he raised his head and roared. He was still roaring when he shifted into his humanoid form. His wounds had stopped bleeding, but remained raw from the fight. Blood covered his body from head to foot. He looked like something out of a nightmare. Taylor's nightmares.

"All hail the Dark King," Opal shouted.

The room erupted in roars and applause.

Taylor staggered to her feet, her emotions battered. She was grateful that Hades had survived, but beyond that she didn't know what to think or how to feel. Seeing the Dark King like this drove home once again just how far away from Earth she was. How could she ever fit in on this planet? She glanced at the warriors celebrating around her. She'd never be like them. Never be like Hades. No matter how much she cared for him.

Opal was right. Hades needed a warrior for a mate. Someone who could balance out his Monster Kitty. She wasn't that woman. No amount of fight lessons would change that. Taylor suddenly had newfound respect for her twin, Tabby. Not only had she adapted to the planet, but she'd adjusted to being a mate to one of these creatures.

Taylor stumbled out of the stands and ran to her room. She stopped twice along the way to dry heave, but eventually made it to her quarters. She slipped through the door and rested her back against the stone. The coolness of the rock felt good. It soothed her nausea, but did little to settle Taylor's nerves. She'd now seen Hades at his worst and wasn't altogether certain she could handle it.

You only have to last a few more days, she told herself. But the idea held no comfort.

Taylor made it to her bathroom and managed to brush her teeth. Food of any kind was out of the question until her stomach forgave her. When she finished, she returned to her bedroom and dropped onto the bed. It was only when she sat down that Taylor started to cry.

*****

Hades left Perseus lying on the Pit floor and returned to his chamber. He couldn't stop replaying the look on Taylor's face. She'd been horrified and repulsed by what had occurred. He'd seen it in her eyes. He turned on the cleansing unit and stepped under the spray. Pain seared him as the water struck his raw side.

He'd managed to heal some of his injuries when he shifted back, but he hadn't healed all of them. Once again, his Atlantean blood interfered. If only he'd inherited his mother's ability to heal with her hands...

Hades bathed quickly and slipped into loose pants, leaving his chest bare. The furrows in his side would be gone in a few days, until then he'd just have to make sure that he didn't tear them open again.

A knock sounded on his door as he stepped out of his bedroom. A cautious hope filled him. Had Taylor gotten over her initial reaction and come to check on him? His hearts kicked up a beat as he hurried to the door. When he opened it, instead of the fire-haired beauty that haunted his every waking moment, Opal stood on the other side. Hades stared at her, unable to hide his disappointment.

"May I come in, Sire?" she asked. "I have news."

He stepped aside, so she could enter. "Has there been another Slaver sighting?"

Opal paused, then said, "No, nothing like that. How do you feel?"

Hades walked deeper into the room with Opal trailing behind him. "I am fine. Thank you for your concern."

She reached out. Her cool fingers danced over his bare skin, near his healing wounds. "I felt every scratch, when Perseus grabbed you. My two hearts feared for your safety."

Hades watched her closely, unsure where Opal was going with this impromptu visit. "It was a good strike. I deserved it for not protecting my sides."

"Yes, it was an honorable blow. It was the only time I allowed doubt to enter my mind." Opal continued to stroke him tenderly. "Forgive me."

"There is nothing to forgive," Hades said, stepping out of reach. "I did not mean to worry you or the Phantom people."

She brushed off the mention of the others and followed him. "I don't know what I would do if I lost you."

Hades tensed. He'd always been honest with Opal when it came to their relationship. He had never given her any reason to think that it extended beyond the physical. "You are a capable Righthand," he said, hoping to construct a mental boundary between them. "I have no doubt you would easily find a position that pleased you under the new ruler."

Opal shook her head and met his gaze. "You, *my* Dark King, are not so easily replaced."

Hades' nerves jumped. This time there was no mistaking the intimacy of her words. "There will always be challenges. Eventually, I will lose one, but until that day comes we do not have to worry about replacing me."

"You're right." She grinned. "Tonight we should be celebrating your victory." Opal hummed under her breath and slowly rock her hips. She approached one of the chairs by his desk and grasped the back of it. She ground her body against the furniture, humming louder as she went.

"What are you doing?" Hades asked, confused by her odd behavior.

*****

"I am dancing for you," she murmured, rocking

awkwardly. This was harder than it appeared. She'd practiced with Taylor. Thought she had a pretty good grasp of the basics. But here in front of the King when it mattered the most, Opal's body refused to follow her lead.

Red streaked his cheeks and Hades stiffened to attention. "That is not necessary. I'm in no mood to celebrate. Tonight I took a warrior's life," he said. "There is no victory in Perseus' death."

Opal flailed her arms spasmodically and gyrated. She was determined to use her new skills to seduce the Dark King. He just needed to pay attention.

"Stop that!" Hades said. "You look ridiculous."

Opal froze. "What?"

His expression shuttered. "I appreciate what you're trying to do. Truly. But you have a long way to go before you reach Taylor Shelley's level of expertise in..." He waved his hand. "Dance."

Opal's face flushed and anger seared her gut. "I thought we could lay together tonight. We haven't managed to do so since the day of the human's arrival." She swallowed her pride and approached Hades, making her hips swing like Taylor taught her. Opal stood on her toes and pressed her lips to his, waiting for some kind of spark, some kind of reaction.

There was none. Not even the usual heat that came from their lovemaking. The Dark King remained as cold as his glacial eyes. Something inside Opal broke.

Hades grasped her arms and gently moved her away. "I'm sorry, Opal. I cannot do this."

"Cannot? Or will not?" she asked, her temper flaring.

"Cannot, and will not," he said, slowly releasing her.

"You have vowed never to take a mate." She needed to remind him. Remind herself. "She is weak. Did you not see her in the stands? She could not even hold her food down. What use is a woman like that?"

"There are many kinds of strength. You of all people

should know that. It's why I made you my Righthand," Hades said. "I do not need you or anyone else reminding me of my vows. I am fully aware of what I have said."

It wasn't exactly an admission, but it did cause the muscles in her face to relax. "I apologize, Sire. It's just that I have need for you after coming so close to losing you." Opal had risked too much to turn back now. She ran her hand over her modest chest, lingering on her rigid nipples. Surely he could sense her body's heat, hear the truth in her confession. He couldn't reject her. The King needed her. He just didn't realize it yet.

Hades' jaw clenched. "You said you had news."

The abrupt change of subject ended their discussion and dashed the last of her hopes. Pain blossomed inside her hearts, nearly driving Opal to her knees. She'd been so blind. All this time she'd thought if she waited long enough that Hades would eventually choose her for his mate. Now it was clear that there was only one woman he cared about, one woman he *loved*.

Oh Goddess, he *was* in love with the Earthling.

Acknowledging the emotion drove a sword through Opal's hearts, severing her feelings. How dare he dismiss her for a human! She stared at the Dark King in disbelief, but the truth was there shining in his aqua eyes.

She thought about Taylor. How weak she was. How she would hurt the kingdom. Opal pictured the Slaver they'd called Hawk and shivered. He was exactly what she needed to help her get Hades back. And he didn't even know it. She had to get rid of the Earth woman. New Atlantis wasn't far enough away. Taylor must leave the planet. And Opal knew just how to do it.

"The news I have can wait until you are healed, Sire. Sleep well." Opal slipped out the door, feeling the sting of humiliation nipping at her, but at least now she had a purpose. And that purpose was going to take her straight to the communications' room. If she succeeded in making contact, then she'd pay Taylor a quick visit. Opal had a lot to do and only one night to get everything arranged. Fortunately, she was motivated.

*****

CHAPTER TEN

Resentment roiled inside Opal as she hurried down the hall. How dare a Half-being turn down an offer of sex from a pureblooded Phantom! Tonight she'd lost Hades, but tomorrow she'd win him back.

Taylor had corrupted the Dark King's mind with her sensual ways. Opal couldn't allow that to continue. Wouldn't allow it. There was only one woman meant to rule the Phantom people and that was her. She was convinced if she got rid of Taylor, then things would return to normal and Hades would find his way back to her bed.

Opal made her way to the communications room. She hid in the shadows and waited for the guards coming on duty to take their place outside the door. As soon as they were in position, she stepped out. "The King wants to see you in his chambers immediately. He needs an updated report on the most recent Slaver communications."

"Right now?" the guard on the left said.

"Yes, now," she said.

"We're supposed to maintain our post until morning," the Phantom on the right said.

"I'll watch the room until you get back. Now hurry!" she

shouted. "Hades is in no mood for excuses."

They rushed off.

Opal waited until they were out of sight, then slipped into the room. It wouldn't be unattended for long, but she didn't need a lot of time to do what she came here to accomplish.

The crystals glowed in ebbs and flows, indicating that they were active. Opal checked the halls, then sealed the door. She sat down in front of the crystals and hit a button on her wrist, highlighting the location of the Slavers' ships. She quickly rearranged the crystals and hailed the Slavers, then did her best to wait patiently for a response. They'd be hesitant, expecting a trap. That couldn't be helped. Hopefully their curiosity would outweigh their self-preservation.

It took five minutes before she received a scrambled message from the coordinates. The response was short, sweet, and held an oddly *familiar* tone, as if they'd been expecting to hear from her. But that wasn't possible. There was no way they could've anticipated her contacting them. Opal made a mental note to look into the situation further once her mission was complete.

I have a rare female to offer you, her message said. *She is called an Earthling.*

We have heard of such creatures, but did not believe that they existed.

Opal couldn't hear his response, but her gut told her that she was speaking with Captain Hawk. Her stomach fluttered as she entered the next message.

I will gladly give her to you, if you take her and leave Zaron.

Why would we do that, when we haven't recovered what we've come for?

I know not what you seek, but she is worth more than fifty Zaronian women. Her rarity alone will fetch you more credits than you can possibly spend in a lifetime.

There was a pause. *You know nothing about my appetites, so there is no way you can guarantee such a thing. Besides, how do I know that you're not setting a trap? The Dark King's fierce reputation is known throughout the galaxy. He is cunning and should never be underestimated.*

You don't. Opal let the full import of her words sink in before continuing. *But if I'd wanted to trap you, I would've simply sent the guards to your current location.*

How will we acquire this magical creature?

I will bring her to you at the far wall of the city, where the moons align.

You will be there yourself?

Opal flushed. And was grateful that he couldn't see her. *Don't get any ideas. I will have a means to summon reinforcements.*

Don't worry, Little Cat. I will honor our agreement...for now. Communications ceased.

Little Cat? Opal stared at the screen, her hearts pounding. He knew who she was, which meant he *had* seen her that day in the trees.

*****

Taylor ignored the first two knocks on her door. She thought about ignoring the third, but knew that she was only delaying the inevitable. She rolled out of bed and padded across the furs. Taylor pulled the door open as Opal raised her fist to knock again.

"What?" she asked, in no mood for more of the woman's hostility.

Opal hesitated. "Sorry to wake you."

You couldn't wake someone who hadn't been to sleep, she thought.

"I came here to apologize for earlier at the Pit," Opal said. "I keep forgetting that you're human and not used to our ways."

Taylor blinked. She couldn't have heard her right. Opal was apologizing. She glanced behind her and expected to see ice forming on the ceiling and the walls. Did they have hell here? Whatever the Zaronian equivalent was it had just frozen over.

"I wouldn't have really hurt you," Opal rushed on. "I shouldn't have even threatened to, but I couldn't risk the King's life."

Something softened inside of Taylor at the mention of Hades. "Do you want to come in?" she asked. She hadn't exactly behaved rationally, but there was nothing sane about a Pit battle.

Opal shook her head. "I can't. It's late, and I have things to do before I can seek my rest."

"Sorry I threw up on your shoes." Taylor blanched at the memory. "I'm just not used to seeing things like that."

"I understand." This time her tone held an edge. "To make it up to you, I came here to invite you to go shopping in the Walled City with me tomorrow. Thought maybe you could use a little time away from the Keep. Get your head clear. What do you say?"

Taylor's heart leapt. She hadn't been outside of Hades' stronghold since she'd arrived. The thought of fresh air, open spaces, and sunshine was too tempting to resist. "You're sure we won't get in trouble?"

Opal arched a brow. "You are not a prisoner. You are allowed in the city as long as you have an escort. I'll be with you every step of the way."

She hesitated.

"I did say that shopping would be involved, right?" Opal asked.

"Yes, you did." Taylor grinned. "What time do you want to meet?" They quickly settled on a time, and then Opal was on her way.

The thought of shopping shouldn't cheer her up, but for some reason it did. Taylor spun toward her bed and had barely taken a step, when another knock sounded on the door.

"Did you forget something?" She threw open the door, expecting to see Opal. Instead, Hades was leaning in the doorway.

Her breath caught at the sight of him. Loose leggings covered him from the waist down, but from the waist up, he remained bare...and beautiful in a purely masculine way. Taylor couldn't seem to tear her gaze away, as she drank in every inch of him, confirming to herself once more that he was truly alive.

"May I come in?" he asked, glancing back at her guard. Kon kept a granite-like expression on his face, but Taylor noticed his eyes widen. "We need to talk."

Taylor stepped aside, shocked to her toes. Hades never asked permission for anything that she could recall. Not when they were alone and certainly not in front of any of his men.

She waited for him to enter, then quietly shut the door behind him. "What are you doing here?" she asked.

"Claiming what is rightfully mine," Hades said.

"Claiming?" Taylor's eyes widened as his narrowed.

"Not in that way," he said, though the vehement tone he'd had when they'd first met was gone.

"Of course not. Everyone knows that you have no intention of ever taking a mate." She was not disappointed. She was *not* disappointed. Taylor moved away from the door. "Hades, why are you really here?"

A muscle ticced in the Dark King's jaw. "I told you. I am here because of my victory."

Taylor watched him closely. She recognized the lie for what it was. "There were no winners tonight," she said.

Surprise bloomed in his aqua eyes. "No, there were not." He took a deep breath. "I am sorry if I caused you pain," he said quietly.

What did he mean by that? "Are you saying that you came here to apologize for killing Perseus?"

Their eyes met and held. "No, I am not sorry that I slayed

Perseus. It would've happened sooner or later. He was ambitious, but he never thought beyond his need for power."

"Then why are you here?" Taylor refused to let him off the hook. He'd avoided her for days, could've died in the Pit, and now he was here, claiming that they needed to talk. Uh-huh, he'd have to do better than that.

Hades scrubbed a hand over his face and she noticed how tired he appeared to be. She looked closer. No, not tired. *Weary.*

"It's a simple question, Hades," she said.

He sighed. "Taylor, nothing about you is simple." Hades walked over to her bed and sat down. "I came here because...I needed...I thought if I saw...I wanted to...Damn it! Kings don't beg."

Taylor tilted her head. "Nobody asked you to."

"Then what must I do?" he asked in frustration. "What must I give up in order to have you in my arms once more?"

"I'm not interested in your kingdom or your crown, Your Majesty."

Hades' lips twitched. "Good thing. Because I don't have one."

A King without a crown. Now why didn't that surprise her?

He glanced up and looked so lost, so desperate, so lonely.

It wasn't his words that swayed Taylor, though they did touch her deeply. It was the desperation, the need to connect—his need to be loved that moved her across the floor and into his arms.

Hades didn't try to kiss her. He waited for her to make the first move. Feeling empowered, Taylor straddled his lap and softly pressed her lips to his forehead. Her mouth moved to his eyes, where she gently kissed each lid. Her lips glided over his stubbled jaw before settling on his firm mouth.

There she deepened the embrace. It took a moment or two of exploration, but Hades finally kissed her back. He made no move to touch her, which only made Taylor hotter.

She set the pace. She controlled the rhythm. By the time her tongue teased its way into Hades' mouth, they were both ravenous for more.

His callused hands brushed her thighs as they journeyed toward her hips. Instead of gripping them, he bypassed them and went straight for her ass. Hades' large hands cupped her bottom and squeezed, then kneaded the flesh. Taylor's head fell back, exposing her neck. Within seconds, his lips were upon her. His teeth grazed the side of her bare throat as he sucked and licked his way from her ear to her shoulder and back again.

She moaned and scooted closer until her moist sex met his hard shaft. Too many layers of clothing separated them, which was good because Taylor wanted to play. This might be the last time she got to sleep with the Dark King and she planned to enjoy every minute of it. She rolled her hips and kicked her leg up over his head, until she was facing the door.

She ground her bottom into his erection. Hades hissed and his hands clamped down on her hips, keeping her in place before she could pull away again.

"What are you doing?" he asked.

"Dancing." Taylor gasped as sharp teeth latched on her butt cheek.

"I like it," he said.

She tossed her hair back and looked over her shoulder at him. "Most men do."

Hades' blue eyes flashed red. "I am *not* most men."

Taylor smiled. "No, you most certainly are not."

He seemed satisfied by her answer, but he didn't let her go. "Take your pants off. I want you to *dance* without them."

His raspy voice made her shiver in a good way. "You'll have to let me go a minute."

Hades did so reluctantly.

Taylor reached for the front clasp and undid her pants. She stuck her thumbs into the waistband and slowly shimmied out of them, making sure she had the King's undivided attention. She bent over in order to give Hades a clear view of her thong-covered bottom. Her long hair fell down her back and over her shoulders.

He growled low in his throat, then reached out and ripped the material off her. "That's better," he said, flicking the thong from his claws. "Now come here."

Taylor turned slowly, but instead of going straight to him, she performed a short bump and grind. Her hands stroked her chest, before sliding over her thighs. By the time she finished the dance, Hades' cock looked as if it would split his pants open.

The King's body trembled, his control barely tethered. His claws were buried in the furs on her bed. She noticed several holes where there'd been none before. His teeth had grown sharper and he stared at her through cat's eyes.

To have such command over one of the most powerful beings she'd ever met was...*intoxicating*. Taylor smiled to herself, determined to enjoy it while it lasted. She allowed her hips to sway as she walked over and climbed back onto his lap. "Once again, you have far too many clothes on."

Hades grabbed her, crushing her to his chest. He didn't stop kissing her until Taylor was breathless.

"I've missed you," he murmured, brushing the hair away from her face.

His admission tore at her heart and strangely gave her *hope*.

Hades caught the bottom of her shirt and pulled it over her head. Taylor had removed her bra earlier, so she was bare to his hungry gaze. His eyes seemed to glow the longer he stared at her.

"I cannot seem to get enough of you. I stayed away, but I couldn't stop thinking about you, remembering the feel of you beneath me. You haunt my nights and occupy my thoughts during the day."

Taylor felt the same way, but there was no way she'd ever

tell him. He already had far too much control over her.

Hades grinned knowingly, then leaned forward and latched onto one pink nipple. His sharp teeth caused a delicious pleasure-pain each time he sucked.

Taylor arched her back encouragingly. She didn't want him to stop. He hadn't touched her where she needed it most, but she already felt her body going molten. Her fingers threaded through his silken hair, then brushed over his shoulders. It wasn't until she reached his waist and Hades flinched that she remembered that he was injured. She tried to pull back, but his hands tightened.

"You're hurt," she said. The man required bed rest. He might think he was invincible, but he wasn't. He bled like everyone else. The last thing he needed was to make love.

It's just sex. Don't ever forget that, she chastised, but it was far too late to walk away unscathed.

Hades looked up, his handsome face harsh with desire. Somehow he managed to do so without releasing her nipple. His cat's eyes were almost solid red now with only a single circle of blue around the outer ring. Without a word, he let her know that he wasn't about to stop.

*****

Hades spun Taylor until she was lying flat on her back. He hadn't released her breast, couldn't release her. She tasted too delicious. He inhaled. She was in heat. If he marked her now, she'd carry his heir. His beast clawed at his insides, demanding to be released. Hades shackled it and kept sucking. Her sweet scent filled his nostrils, making him even harder. He was still amazed he'd kept his hands to himself for as long as he did. Her dance alone nearly unmanned him.

He reluctantly released her nipple in order to feast upon the other. Her puckered flesh was flushed with blood and hard as Zaronian pebbles. With a thought, Hades willed his clothes away. From the moans coming from Taylor's throat, he didn't think she'd noticed.

Her lush thighs parted, leaving her sex open and ready for him. The rich musk called to his beast. He would taste her there before he impaled her upon his cock. Hades released her. Taylor immediately grabbed her breasts and pressed them together, offering herself to him. Hades fought the urge to return for another taste. He had richer valleys to explore.

He slid down her body, kissing and laving her navel before nipping at her hipbones. She jumped and her hips rocked up to greet him. Hades closed his eyes and inhaled. *Definitely in heat.* In the past, he'd always avoided bedding women, when they were in heat. Their scent was far too tempting, but with Taylor it was almost too much to ignore.

Hades growled in frustration. He parted her nether lips quickly and latched onto her clit. The tender bud swelled with blood as he gently bit down. Taylor shuddered.

"Not yet!" he snapped. Hades wanted to lap up her juices, wanted them running down his chin before he allowed her to come. His rough tongue went to work licking and swirling, flicking and flitting.

Taylor's back arched and she moaned.

Hades kissed her inner thighs, then sucked her clit even harder. Taylor's body quaked and she gripped the furs in tight fists.

"Please, Hades," she pleaded.

Her juices pooled. Hades licked them up and went back to feasting. He wasn't nearly finished with her. He'd never be finished with her. For the first time in his life, that thought wasn't frightening. Hades refused to examine why.

He licked her, swirling his tongue around her entrance, until Taylor cried out. Hades felt the ripples from her release, but he refused to stop. He wanted her to beg, to never forget who'd brought her so much pleasure. He wanted Taylor to remember...*him.*

Hades plunged his tongue inside her spasming channel and purred, long and loud. Taylor screamed his name and her body bucked. He held onto her until her heart-rate calmed, then Hades slowly slid his body over hers, settling his hips between her boneless thighs.

He positioned his cock at her dripping entrance. "Taylor, look at me."

Her lashes fluttered, but didn't open.

"Taylor!" She would be with him. She would know who possessed her.

Her eyes snapped open at his tone, but remained unfocused.

"No one will ever make you feel the way that I do. The way that I have," he ground out, as if his words could will it so.

She didn't say anything. She simply stared at him, but Hades read her thoughts easily. Taylor didn't want what he said to be true, but she believed that it was. And for Hades that was enough for now.

He surged forward, burying his cock deep within her body.

Mark her, an insidious little voice whispered.

Hades shook his head to clear it. He couldn't. Wouldn't. His wants and needs didn't matter beyond the physical. But even as the thought trickled through his mind, he knew it was a lie.

Hades pulled back and thrust forward hard. He needed to be closer. Needed to bury himself inside her until they became one being, their two halves making a whole. His mouth latched onto Taylor's. He poured every bit of his frustration, his anger, his passion into the kiss as he fucked her with the power of his beast.

*****

Taylor whimpered and clung to Hades. She wrapped her long legs around his hips and hung on as he fucked her. Each stroke, each thrust bound her to him, until she knew there was no escaping the Dark King. Taylor felt his anger. Felt his frustration. And worst of all, she felt his love. The one thing she could never have. The one thing he would never give her.

It wasn't fair.

Hades was inside her body, inside her head, and had a permanent place in her heart. Each thrust solidified his position. She'd never get him out. Never.

Taylor surrendered to the inevitable. If all she'd ever be was a mistress to the Dark King, then so be it. She'd settle for that, if it meant having Hades in her life.

Her body relaxed, cradling him close. His grunts of passion turned to sighs as he did his best to lose himself inside of her. Taylor ran her hands over his back, careful to avoid his injuries. She held him as tight as she dared, encouraging him to let go. Hades shuddered and reached between their bodies. He strummed her clit and Taylor shattered again.

She gulped in air as the orgasm rocked her.

Hades' body lost rhythm as she clamped down on his thick shaft.

"Let go," she whispered.

"Not yet," he grit out.

"Now," Taylor murmured.

Hades trembled and his hips jerked. "No!" he bellowed, but it was too late. He spilled his warm essence inside of her. The Dark King collapsed, gasping for breath.

Taylor bore his weight easily, willingly. She continued to gently stroke him. His eyes were closed and his face was now lax. The tension that had been there earlier was gone for the time being.

He rose just enough to look down at her face. "What am I to do with you?"

"You know, I've been asking myself the very same question," Taylor said.

Hades slid off her body. "Let me clean you."

Taylor expected him to go into the bathroom and get a towel. So when he slid down her body and settled between her thighs, she was confused. "What are you doing?"

He didn't answer. Instead, Hades gently licked her labia. Taylor fell back on the bed. She supposed that was one way to clean down there. He neared her over-sensitive clit, taking his time to thoroughly cleanse the area. She'd never think about bathing in the same way again.

She quivered as a gentle orgasm rippled through her. "I think you've got everything," she gasped.

"Sorry, I hadn't intended to bring you to release. I only wanted to clean you, but your scent is distracting," he said.

Taylor flushed. "Do I smell bad? Let me take a quick shower."

"No." Hades held her down on the bed. "You misunderstand. Your scent is richer now, sweeter, riper because of your heat."

She sat up. "My what?"

"You're in heat," he said, licking her once more. His eyes fluttered shut in ecstasy.

Taylor gaped at him. "What do you mean I'm in heat?" She wasn't due for another week and a half.

"I believe the term that you use on Earth is ovulating. You are fertile." Hades stuck his nose into the thin line of curls covering her sex and inhaled.

Taylor felt the color drain from her face. "Are you telling me that I might be pregnant?" Her heart slammed against her ribs and panic set in. A wave of calm washed over her a second later. She knew it had come from Hades.

"Would that be so bad?" he asked.

She stared at him, preparing to give a flippant answer, but he looked so serious. Taylor sighed. "No." She shook her head. "It wouldn't be bad, but it would be a surprise. To be honest, I haven't given children much thought." She had no choice but to lie. Hades' opinion on the subject was clear. Taylor didn't want him to think that she was trying to trap him somehow.

Like most women, Taylor had considered having children, but she'd never felt emotionally safe enough to bring the subject up with any of her exes. Taylor had been diligent about her use of birth control. She never slept with any of her boyfriends without a condom unless they'd been tested, and even then she made them wear one.

Did Phantoms even have condoms?

She looked at Hades. He would protect his child, even if the child were initially unwanted. Taylor might not be able to trust him with her heart, but she would trust him implicitly with their child's safety.

He took one last lick, then slid onto the bed beside her, pulling her into his arms. "Do not worry. You cannot have a child with me or any other warrior without being bound."

His words should've been a relief, but all Taylor felt was disappointment.

Hades gathered her close and nuzzled her. His tongue unerringly found the spot where her shoulder met her neck and he lapped at her skin.

"You're going to wear a hole in that spot if you're not careful." Taylor kept her voice light, but thanks to Perseus, she knew that particular spot had significance to the Phantom people and to Hades.

He stopped immediately and kissed the spot. "Get some rest," he said, but she noticed that his tension had returned.

Taylor shouldn't have said anything. She should've just kept her mouth shut. "I'm glad that you're okay," she whispered.

Hades kissed the side of her head. "Sleep, little one. I will protect you through the night," he said. And she believed every word.

The heat from his skin made covering herself in furs unnecessary. Despite wanting to stay awake and talk about what had just happened, it wasn't long before Taylor drifted off. She dreamed of tawny-haired boys and blue-eyed girls, snuggling on Hades' lap while he sat on his hard metal throne.

*****

<h1 style="text-align:center">CHAPTER ELEVEN</h1>

Taylor awoke at dawn. She wasn't sure what had disturbed her sleep, until she saw Hades by the door.

He grinned. "I was trying not to wake you."

She yawned. "I've always been a light sleeper. What time is it?"

Hades gave her an odd look.

"Sorry, I forgot you guys don't have watches."

His brow furrowed.

"Never mind. I need to get up anyway," she said.

"Why?" he asked.

Taylor hesitated. "Um, Opal and I are meeting up this morning. I don't want to be late."

Hades' frown deepened. "Make sure if you go anywhere to take an escort. I still haven't captured the Slavers."

She brightened. "I will."

He continued to stare, regarding her quizzically.

"I promise."

Hades nodded hesitantly. "I will see you later?" He made it a question, even though it wasn't one.

"Sure, we'll catch up, when I return...from seeing Opal."

Hades looked like he wanted to say something more, but

seemed to change his mind. "Until then." He slipped out of the room.

Taylor stretched and couldn't keep the grin from spreading across her face. Her body felt deliciously spent. Hades had woken her during the night and they'd made love again. *Had sex,* she told herself quickly, but it was a lie. A lie she'd concocted to protect her heart.

Love was the only way to describe the slow joining she'd experienced with Hades. He'd been so thorough, so caring, and tender that her heart had nearly swelled with the giddy emotion. He had murmured things in another tongue that had sounded like endearments.

Taylor hadn't asked what he'd said because part of her didn't want to know in case she was wrong. She had not wanted to destroy the precious moment. She wasn't naive enough to believe that making love would make a difference outside of the bedroom. Taylor was the definition of a realist. She'd stopped believing in happily-ever-after long ago, but that didn't mean she wouldn't hold the memory in her heart forever.

A knock sounded on her door.

Taylor jumped out of bed, grabbing a fur as she did so to wrap around her. Had Hades returned? What would that mean if he had? She opened the door to find Opal standing in the doorway. The King's Righthand was frowning.

"I thought you'd be ready by now," Opal said.

"Uh." Her gaze shot to Kon. She blushed, when he smiled. "I just woke up," Taylor said. She wasn't about to mention that the only reason she had was because of Hades. If she hadn't heard him leave, she'd still be out cold.

"I can see that." Opal crossed her arms and tapped her foot. "How long will it take you to get ready?"

"Can you give me forty-five minutes?" Taylor asked.

Opal's frown deepened.

"Make it thirty. I'll be ready as quick as I can," she said.

Opal nodded. "Fine! But hurry. We don't have all day."

Taylor shut the door and raced to her bathroom, determined not to keep Opal waiting for long. Her mood was already questionable. But nothing would ruin Taylor's day. Not after spending last night in Hades' arms.

Opal was standing in the hall, when Taylor walked out of her room twenty minutes later. She seemed surprised, but she didn't say anything.

"Ready?" Opal asked.

"More than ready," Taylor responded.

"Good, let's get out of here."

Kon stepped in front of them. "Where are you going?"

Opal's temper flared. "That is none of your concern, warrior."

"It's my job to watch over her," Kon said.

"Correction," Opal said. "Hades gave me that duty. Your job is to watch over her when she's in her chamber. If you have a problem with that, then I suggest you take the issue to the King."

Kon's face flushed.

Taylor mouthed the word 'sorry' to him.

Opal didn't wait for a response. She led Taylor out one of the side entrances of the Keep, bypassing the main guards at the front.

"This way," Opal said. She opened a door that Taylor hadn't noticed before.

They traveled down a side path that wound its way into the city. The sun was rising quickly in the light green sky, but the air remained comfortable and wonderfully scented.

"I still can't get over the color of your sky or the fact that you have two moons," Taylor said.

"Doesn't Earth?" Opal asked without looking at her. Instead, she continued to scan the area around them.

"No." She shook her head. "We only have one moon. Our blue sky is just as pretty though."

Opal wrinkled her nose in distaste. "I hate that color."

Taylor didn't ask her why, since it was obvious. "This

trail is handy," she said instead. "I'm surprised it's not heavily guarded like the rest of the Keep."

Opal glanced at her. "I use this route often, when I want privacy. Even if someone wanted to storm the Keep from this direction, they wouldn't make it through the Walled City without being spotted. Someone would sound the alarm."

Something didn't feel right. The trail was isolated and devoid of life. Taylor looked around nervously. It seemed like they were sneaking. And there was only one reason to do that. "I thought you said we wouldn't get in trouble?"

"We won't," Opal said.

"Then why are we using this route?" Taylor picked her way over the uneven stones. "Wouldn't going out the front take less time?" She stumbled. *And be less dangerous.* After the night she'd spent with Hades, Taylor really didn't want to jeopardize the intimate gains that she'd made by breaking the rules.

"Going this way lets me avoid unnecessary questions." Opal gave her a pointed look. "Besides, I thought you of all people would appreciate skirting regulations."

"I would have in the past, but the Pit challenge put things into perspective. Hades almost died last night. He needs time to recover. I don't want to do anything that's going to upset him and delay his healing," she said. Not something silly like sneak into town to go shopping. Taylor glanced around again. "Are you sure it's safe for us to journey without a guard into the Walled City? Hades said it was dangerous."

Opal scowled. "I am a guard. Less you forget."

Taylor held up her hands. "I didn't mean anything by it. I just think we should've told Kon where we were going."

Opal glared at her. "You can go back if you want, but I'm going to the sale booths." She pointed to the top of the mountain. The trail zigzagged up the rock face, growing steeper and steeper the higher it got.

Taylor did not look forward to that climb. She'd barely made it going down. "Maybe I'll stay for a few minutes," she said.

Opal rolled her eyes. "Come on, we're almost there."

They reached the Walled City, which was blissfully flat, and weaved their way through the various stalls. The place reminded Taylor of a Renaissance Faire she'd attended a long time ago—if she overlooked the advanced technology humming in the booths.

Rows and rows of stalls lined the main road that led to the Keep. They were four deep and didn't stop until they met the three story dwellings that ringed the massive wall enclosing the city. Handmade goods were advertised on holoscreens. 'Not Replicated Materials' bulletins were posted everywhere.

Taylor stopped and examined the clothing closely, doing her best to ignore all the curious glances coming her way. "What does the 'Not Replicated Materials' signs mean?"

Opal left the stand she'd been browsing and walked over to her. "The Phantom people have special clothing requirements. They need to be able to absorb the fabric into their bodies at will, allowing them to shift any time they like without having to constantly replace their clothing. Handmade natural fiber clothes are better for absorption. Hence the signs and the different prices. Buy whatever you like. Hades won't mind." She picked up a shirt and held it to the sunlight. The iridescent green turned to blue. Opal dropped it onto the table like it had singed her fingers. "It doesn't really matter what you choose because in all likelihood you're going to end up mating with an Atlantean anyway."

"Excuse me?" Taylor arched a brow. Did Opal know something that she didn't? "Why would you say that? I haven't even *met* any Atlanteans." Her exclamation brought even more stares from the crowd around them.

Opal glanced at the people, her gaze narrowing. Most hurried away.

"Atlantean warriors are quite handsome, if you can get

past the blue eyes and other physical limitations." She shrugged, then gave Taylor a calculating smile. "As to your question, Hades and I were discussing your tenuous situation this morning in bed. We decided that you mating with an Atlantean was best for everyone involved. That way you'd get to live in New Atlantis near your sister and there would be no need to *ever* return to the Walled City. His words, not mine."

Taylor turned away from the stall. "What do you mean you were discussing *my* situation? I don't have a *situation*." She did, but that wasn't the point. How dare Opal bring the subject up in public! No one was supposed to know that she was here.

She mentally replayed the rest of what Opal had said. The woman had claimed they'd been in bed while having this conversation, but that was impossible. Unless he had a twin, Hades had been in her room all night. "Where exactly were you, when you were discussing this?"

Opal's smile broadened. "I didn't mean to tell you in quite this manner, but I spent the night in the King's chambers after the challenge," she said. "I told you before, Hades needs a warrior in his bed to fulfill all his animalistic urges."

Didn't mean to tell her... Was she for real? The bitch had enjoyed every second of jabbing that knife into her gut.

As for Hades' needs, Taylor had more than held her own in bed with the Dark King, thank you very much. Just how gullible did Opal think she was? "We are talking about last night, right?" Taylor asked.

"Yes," Opal said without blinking an eye. "I'm surprised I made it to your door on time. As you know the King is quite vigorous."

Yes, he was, Taylor concurred.

Hades had spent the night in her bed. The whole night. Opal was *lying*. If she hadn't known the truth, Taylor would be crushed. No doubt that had been Opal's intent. The question was why had she gone to so much trouble? Opal could've just as easily passed the lie off at the Keep. She didn't have to waste her entire morning shopping with Taylor, waiting for the perfect moment to pounce.

Maybe it was a cat thing?

Taylor rolled her eyes. Whatever game she was playing, it didn't make sense, but it did confirm what she already suspected. They would *never* be friends. No matter how hard she tried to forge a relationship with the woman, no matter what Taylor did, it would never be enough.

She decided not to call Opal on the lie. There was no point. The woman was delusional. Highlighting the fact would only make their time together in the city unbearable, and Taylor was determined to enjoy herself. She kept her expression neutral, when she said, "I'm glad the King won't care if I spend some of his credits. I need to pick up a few things."

Opal stared at her in confusion. "I told you that I spent the night in the King's bed," she said. "Why aren't you upset?"

"Why should I be?" Taylor asked, steeling herself. "He's not 'mated'. I have no legal claim on Hades." *But she wanted one.* The thought escaped before she could stop it. Oh man, she had it bad, so bad. And nothing good would ever come of it.

Opal's expression cooled. "That is correct. Hades is not and will never be—*yours*. It's best that you remember that, though it hardly matters now."

Okay...crazy, table for one. "Are we going to shop or what?" Taylor asked calmly, though her heart was pounding. "If you've changed your mind, we can head back now." *Please say yes. Please say yes.*

"No!" Opal's panicked tone startled Taylor.

"What's going on?" she asked, grateful that there were still people around. She might need a witness if Opal went off the deep end of the galaxy.

"Nothing! Everything's on schedule," Opal said, her

outward countenance calm once more. "I'd planned to stay out all morning. Besides, you haven't found anything yet. You don't want to go back empty handed." She indicated to the row behind the booth they were in front of. "Come." She motioned with her hand. "I know where the best clothes and ornamentations are located. I'm sure you'll find something there that you like."

Opal was right. Taylor found a beautiful emerald green shawl and a matching necklace at the booths near the city wall. The crowds were thinner along the outer circle, giving her room to breathe. It allowed some of the tension she'd been feeling to seep away.

Most of the Phantom people had stopped gawking at her and moved on with their daily routines. Even Opal seemed in a better mood and that was saying something given the start to their morning together.

"I have one more place that we should check before we return to the Keep. It's just outside the wall," Opal said.

Taylor hesitated. Hades said not to go outside. That it wasn't safe. Opal knew this. "I don't think that's a good idea. The Slavers are still out there."

Opal's lips thinned and her brows drew down over her eyes. Her hand moved to her sword. "Do you think that I can't protect you? That I'm not a powerful Phantom Warrior? Just because I am a woman does not mean that I am incapable of doing my job."

"Of course not! I've seen you fight. Remember? You're a badass," Taylor said. "My hesitation has nothing to do with you being a woman." It did, since women were being targeted, but best not to point that out right now.

"We won't be long. It's just on the other side of the wall. If we go now, no one will notice. We'll be back before they even realize that we were gone." Opal was persuasive when she wanted to be. "I saw an ornamentation last week that I really wanted to buy, but I didn't get it. I'd like to do so now."

"You're sure it's safe?" Taylor asked, eyeing the wall nervously. She really didn't want to leave the security of the city. "Why don't you go and I'll wait here?"

"No!" Opal snapped.

Taylor flinched.

Opal took a deep breath. "What I meant to say is that I can't. You're not allowed in the city without an escort. Hades' orders. If I leave you here, then there will be no one to watch over you, no one to guard you if trouble arises."

She was right, Taylor thought, then glanced at the imposing wall once more. If Opal left her, then she'd be disobeying the Dark King. Taylor didn't want to think what the punishment for that would be given Hades' volatile moods.

"Please," Opal pleaded. "I really want to get the ear clamp and matching necklace. It won't take long. I promise."

Taylor felt her resolve crumble. "Five minutes," she said.

"Done." Opal nodded. "Now let's go. And whatever you do, be quiet."

"You don't expect me to climb that wall, do you?" she asked. "I'm not much of a climber."

"Of course not," Opal said. "Follow me."

They crawled out a small drainage ditch to get to the other side of the wall. Taylor had barely managed to squeeze her way through the opening at the far end. No way would a man's broad shoulders fit in the cramped space. She scrambled to her feet and brushed off her clothes, then looked around.

In the distance, lush forests hugged mammoth mountains, but the land surrounding the Walled City was barren like a desert. "Where are the stalls?"

"They're cloaked for their safety," Opal said. "They will appear as we approach them."

Given everything she'd seen, Taylor figured it was possible.

Sweat dripped from Opal's brow and she glanced around

manically.

The skin at the base of Taylor's neck prickled. "What's wrong?" She looked around warily.

"Nothing!" Opal growled. "They should be here."

"Calm down, I'll help you find them." Taylor walked from one empty space to another, waiting to see if a stall appeared. But no matter where she stood, nothing happened. "Maybe they moved? Maybe we missed them back in the city?"

Opal shook her head vehemently. "No! They have to be here."

"There were a lot of pretty necklaces at the last stall we went to. I'm sure you can find something there," Taylor said.

Opal looked at her as if she were mad.

"Or not." It was time to leave. Something wasn't right. Taylor took a step back and collided with a solid object. "I think I found the booth." She turned, but instead of finding the stall she came face to chest with a man. He had long, dark braided hair and golden eyes that seemed to look straight through her. His head rose and his molten gaze locked onto Opal.

Taylor jerked her head around and told Opal to run, then she opened her mouth to scream. The man's hand crushed her lips before she could utter a sound. She shoved at his chest and kicked him in the shin. He grunted, but didn't release her.

"Next time, my Little Cat. You will not be so lucky," he murmured, but he wasn't looking at Taylor when he said it. He was staring at the spot Opal had been in.

Relief flooded Taylor. Opal had gotten away. Help would be coming soon. Her ears strained. Why weren't the alarms going off in the city? Where were the Phantom guards?

The golden-eyed man bound her, then tossed Taylor into a ship that she could not see. She landed hard on a cold metal floor and immediately struggled to sit up. The second she did, she saw that she was surrounded. He wasn't alone.

There were several other men with him and they were all staring at her.

The ship rose, then sped across the desert, whisking her away from the city. Taylor screamed until her throat hurt. She'd heard the stories. She had no doubt that these were the Slavers that Hades was hunting. How long before they sliced her up and sold her parts?

Her stomach convulsed and she nearly threw up.

"We're almost there," he said.

Taylor looked at him and realized that the Slaver was speaking to her, not his men. "You are in so much trouble," she said. "Hades is going to rain hell down upon your heads, once Opal informs him about what you've done."

The man actually had the nerve to laugh. "Is that her name? Opal?"

Taylor hesitated, but she saw no reason to keep the information from him. He'd be dead soon. "Yes, she's the Dark King's Righthand."

"Now that *is* interesting," he said. "Too bad that you are mistaken."

"No, I'm not." She shook her head. "Hades put me under his protection, when I arrived at the Keep. He gave his word to the Phantom people. The Dark King never breaks a vow. He will come."

The man stared at her. "I've never met an Earth woman before. I had no idea that they were so easily led astray. Had I known, I would've sought them out sooner."

"What are you talking about?" Despite her faith in Hades, dread engulfed her. Why wasn't he worried? The Slaver should be panicking by now.

He scooted closer to her and lifted a strand of her long hair. "Such a unique color. She was right, you will fetch a handsome price."

She? What was he talking about?

"How do you think we found you?" he asked.

"You were hunting for women." She shrugged. "I was in

the wrong place at the wrong time." It happened to some victims, though it was rare.

The golden-eyed man shook his head. "If it weren't for the Phantom woman's assistance, we wouldn't have even known that you existed."

Bile rose in her throat as the full extent of the betrayal hit her. How could Opal do such a thing, knowing that these people might kill her? No wonder the man was confident that he'd get away. No one knew that she was missing. So there'd be no rescue attempt. By the time Hades was aware that something was wrong, she'd be halfway across the galaxy.

"Opal said that you'd fetch more credits on the slave blocks if you were whole. Looking at you, I'm sure that she's right. But I haven't ruled out dissecting you," he said matter-of-factly. "Especially if you turn out to be more trouble than you're worth."

A tremor shook her body. Thanks to Opal, she was on her own. But unlike her sister, Taylor had always been a survivor and she'd somehow figure out how to save herself. When the doors to the utilitarian ship opened again, they were in the woods.

"Come," the man said. "We have much to do before departure." He pulled her inside another ship that was just as sterile and invisible as the last one. As they approached, a man near the door came to attention.

"Captain Hawk," he said.

So her captor had a name, Taylor thought, filing the information away for later.

"Take her to holding bay four and secure her for departure," Hawk said.

He grabbed the restraints on Taylor's wrists. The man yanked her, nearly pulling her off her feet. "Hurry," he said. "I do not have time for your games."

She wasn't playing any games. Not yet anyway. Taylor made herself appear weak, vulnerable. It was easy to do.

She'd done it in her act many times. She whimpered as he led her over to a strange sort of elevator. He shoved her inside, then followed her in. The thing dropped rapidly, leaving her stomach on the ceiling. Within seconds they were in the holding bay.

Several metal doors lined the bay. More than Taylor could count. Each had a small high window, but the interiors were dim. Whimpers and cries rang out as they passed the chambers. Taylor thought she glimpsed movement inside. Fear slowed her steps. How many women had they captured?

The Slaver strode to a metal door that looked just like the rest and pressed his hand against the center just below the window. The door rose with a hiss like a crypt being unsealed. Stale air blew her hair back and a coppery odor smacked her in the face, gagging her.

There were a few unmarked crates in the room and a series of rods lining what looked like bloodstained walls. A large discolored drain sat in the center of the floor, surrounded by rust-colored tentacles. The stained *paths* branched out, leading to various rods around the room.

What in the hell had they done in here? Her mind screamed in silent horror.

Taylor's body locked in place, refusing to enter. If she went inside, she'd have to acknowledge the truth of her situation. She'd been betrayed and in all likelihood here was where she would die. Taylor couldn't do it. Wouldn't do it. She'd fight this man to the death if need be.

Before she could act out her half-baked plan, the man put his hands between her shoulder blades and pushed her into the room. The stench of desperation and pain was worse inside. It made breathing difficult.

Her panic increased. She had to get out of here. She had to escape before they did to her what they'd so obviously done to the others. The Slaver prodded her over to the far wall and slotted Taylor between two of the metal rods.

"Hold out your hands," he said. "And don't move."

Taylor shook as she extended her arms.

The Slaver scissored his fingers between her restraints. They separated instantly, but remained attached to her wrists. He secured one hand to a metal rod on the right, then the other to a rod on the left. Her feet remained unbound. Satisfied, the man grunted and walked off without a backwards glance.

The lighting dimmed when he reached the doorway, threatening to go out. Taylor's heart stuttered in her chest. The flickering stopped and something like emergency lighting kicked in. Shadows crouched in the corners, but she could still make out the crates in the room.

Taylor waited until the door closed behind him, then examined her restraints and pulled. The rods didn't budge. She tried again. Nothing. Her shoulders slumped and she felt her left wrist slip down a notch. In her desperation, Taylor thought that she'd imagined the movement, so she didn't immediately respond. It was only when her right hand moved that awareness dawned.

She could move up and down, but would that matter if she couldn't break the bonds? Taylor glanced up, expecting to see the rods attached to the ceiling.

They weren't.

She glanced at the distance between the rods, then looked toward the sky and thanked God once more for her long legs. Taylor kicked off her shoes, then got to work on her escape.

*****

Opal returned to the Keep after spending another hour shopping in the Walled City. It had been hard to appear like everything was normal, but she was pretty sure that she'd pulled it off. When she'd seen Captain Hawk, Opal had almost changed her mind about the plan. The way he'd looked at her had left her shaken. Men didn't look at her like that. Ever!

Fear and excitement thrummed inside Opal as she entered the front gates, but she kept her expression pained.

The guards stiffened. "What is wrong?"

"Where is Hades?" she demanded, purposely not answering their question. Opal didn't want them sounding the alarm. Not yet.

"He is in his chambers," one said.

Opal pushed past them and rushed on. "I must speak to him. The Earth woman has been captured."

The guards immediately moved to the hidden com devices beneath their hair and called for reinforcements. They also sent out a message to the King, before Opal could stop them.

*****

Hades sat in his chambers rifling through requests. He wondered when Taylor would return. He longed to see her again, even though they'd only been apart for a few hours. He'd just picked up another request, when a surge of panicked energy struck his temples, causing blinding pain.

He clutched his head and tried to filter some of the words so he could figure out what was happening. Were they under attack? Had someone died?

She's gone. The dark message floated in his mind. Hades froze, unable to move.

"No!" His denial was swift.

He couldn't have lost her. Not Taylor. They hadn't had enough time together. The Goddess would never be that cruel. But in his hearts, Hades knew that wasn't true. Life did not operate that way. Loss could be instantaneous and irrevocable like when his father had been killed. His mother had never recovered from her grief. She'd died a few years later of a broken heart.

The hollowness Hades felt from Taylor being gone was

quickly filled with ice-cold fury. No one took what was his and lived to see another moonrise. Hades shot to his feet, toppling his chair. He compressed the pain threatening to hobble him into a seething ball and rushed toward the door. It opened before he reached it and his guards poured inside the room.

"What happened? Where is she?" he shouted to mask his fear. He couldn't lose her. Hades could still smell her sweet scent upon his skin, taste her essence on his tongue. He had to find her, even if it meant journeying into the land of the dead.

"They have her, Sire," the guard said. "Your Righthand just reported the news at the front gates. She's on her way here now."

Hades didn't need to ask the guard who he was referring to. He knew. His gut clenched at the thought of what the Slavers were doing to Taylor. She was so soft. So weak. So very human. He'd vowed to protect her and he'd failed.

"How did this happen?" Hades bellowed. It would be easy to blame another, but he could only blame himself. He should've never left her side this morning. He should've made her come with him. He'd known she was up to something, but he'd given Taylor her privacy and not pried into her mind. Now he wished that he had. Maybe he could've prevented this whole situation.

The guard lowered his head and spoke. "She was snatched from within the Walled City."

"What in Zaronian fire was she doing in the city?" Hades asked. "I told her it wasn't safe."

"Shopping, Sire," Opal said as she stepped around the guard. "I took her shopping. It's my fault that she was taken."

"She was grabbed within the city?" he asked.

"Yes, Sire."

"That's impossible. No one can get past our energy field to enter the city without tripping an alarm," Hades said. "It would've been detected immediately." He turned to the other guard. "Have there been any perimeter breeches?"

He shook his head. "No, Sire. Nothing."

Hades gaze landed on Opal.

She stared at him beseechingly. "I don't know how they did it, Sire, but somehow they managed. I was a couple of booths away, when I heard Taylor scream. I rushed to her aid, but by the time I reached her location, she was gone. I am sorry."

"No!" Hades shouted. "She cannot be gone. They couldn't have left the planet so quickly without being detected. Even with their advanced cloaking device, we knew that they were here." He turned to the first guard who'd entered his room. "Expand the energy field. I don't want a single ship taking off from this planet until Taylor is found. Better she die…" He choked. "Than her fate be left in the hands of a Slaver."

"Yes, Sire. Right away." The guard sprinted out of the room. Hades could hear him barking orders as he did so.

He turned to Opal. "I want you to tell me exactly what happened. Leave no detail out. Then I will decide if any disciplinary action shall be taken."

*****

Opal nodded solemnly and tried not to quake under his regard.

Hades' face was a mask of fury as he stared at her. She had never seen him look so angry. Not even when he was challenged for his throne. His aqua eyes shifted from blue to red so quickly that she could barely keep track of the rapid color change.

Phantoms rarely lost control of their Other halves, but the King's body trembled as if he'd burst at any minute. The unanticipated level of violence hovering just beneath his skin truly frightened her. This was a side of the Dark King that Opal had never seen before. And hoped to never see again.

She'd thought she was doing the right thing. Knew she

had done what was needed to protect the Kingdom, protect her position, but would Hades ever see it that way? From the furious look on his face, she doubted it.

"We were in the city shopping. I thought she could do with some fresh air," Opal said. "She's been cooped up for days and her clothes aren't exactly acceptable attire."

"Why didn't you take a guard like I ordered?" he asked through clenched teeth. Teeth that appeared to grow sharper and longer as she watched.

Opal's chin rose. "I didn't need one."

"The facts say differently," he said.

She blanched, but met his hard stare.

His gaze started at her feet and worked its way to the top of her head and back down again. "Why aren't you injured? It was your duty to protect her." He shook with emotion. "At the very least, I'd expect to see battle wounds."

"I barely got away, my King." Opal bowed her head to appear distraught. "If Taylor hadn't warned me, the Slavers would now have us both."

Hades' eyes narrowed. "So she saved *your* life and forfeited her own?"

Opal nodded and managed to muster a tear. "I am sorry, Sire. I know that you vowed to protect her."

Hades' jaw tightened. "As did you, but it looks like we both failed." Claws sprang from his fingertips and stripes appeared beneath his skin. He threw his head back and roared, the sound deafening.

Opal jumped. She'd expected the Dark King to be upset, but she'd underestimated the violence of his reaction to losing the Earthling.

"Shall I notify her sister of the loss?" Opal asked.

Hades' expression arrested her. "No, because I intend to find her and retrieve her. She is mine," he said with so much vehemence that Opal took a step back.

She tried not to let the shock from his declaration show on her face, or the pain that followed. "I fear she's long gone by now, Sire," she murmured. Soon her troubles would be over and everything would return to normal.

"If the energy field doesn't prevent them from taking off, then I shall follow the Slavers across the galaxy until they land on another planet," he growled. "They are not self-sustaining. They'll have to stop eventually. When they do, I'll be ready."

Opal's eyes widened. "You would declare war over the loss of one human female?"

Hades' blue eyes frosted. "I will tear this galaxy apart and every being who stands in my way, until I find her. And if in the end I discover that Taylor is truly gone from this mortal realm, then Goddess help those who took her from me."

Opal shivered as cold fingers of fear trickled down her spine. For the first time since she'd concocted this plan, she was truly terrified. Hades would *never* forgive her. There was nothing that she could do that would atone for this act. If he found out that she was the one behind Taylor's abduction, he would rip her apart with his claws and feast upon her entrails. Her mind raced. What could she do? Where could she go?

She only had one chance at saving herself.

Opal forced herself to look at the Dark King. His fury beat at her, battering her senses, until she was ready to turn tail and run. "I-I believe I have located the Slavers' last position. I cannot guarantee that they will still be there, but it's a place to start the search."

"We have no time for your guesses," Hades said.

"This isn't a guess. I am positive I have found their location." Opal gave the King the coordinates.

His eyes narrowed in suspicion. "Then let us go and stop wasting time."

Opal had never been more grateful that she could block the Dark King's probing mind than at this moment. She could 'feel' him reaching for her thoughts, searching for the truth. If he even had an inkling that she was lying, Opal would be dead. She had only one chance to make it out of this situation alive. She had to reach Taylor before Hades did. If she killed her before the Dark King got to her, then he'd never learn the truth.

*****

Taylor straddled the two rods that kept her arms spread and hands bound. Sweat dripped from her forehead, running along her face. She'd been trying to shimmy up the poles since the Slavers had left her. Her efforts thus far had been fruitless. It was hard to hold the splits between poles, when you could barely move your hands.

The ship's engines purred beneath her feet. She could hear men rushing back and forth outside the door. If even one of them looked in, she'd be caught. But if she didn't get out of here soon, Taylor would be trapped. There'd be no escaping. And thanks to Opal, no help would be coming.

More shouts sounded from inside the bay. Taylor held her breath and prayed they didn't enter the holding room as she gripped the rods and jumped once more, spreading her legs wide until her feet touched the poles. Her muscles shook as she forced her body to climb.

"You can do this," she grunted.

Inch by inch, Taylor worked her way up. Twenty feet had never looked so high. What if when she got to the top she couldn't slip her wrists free? Her arms trembled. She thought of her twin, Tabby. She thought about the bad decisions that she'd made in her life. But most of all she thought about Hades.

Taylor couldn't fathom never seeing him again. She loved him. Funny how being in danger had put everything into perspective. She'd never had such clarity in her life. Too bad the epiphany came so late.

Her body quaked and she dropped an inch. Sweat covered her palms, but somehow Taylor kept from falling even further. She squirmed her way up the last seven inches, arms and legs quivering, lungs gasping for air.

When she reached the top, Taylor paused. Doubt crept in. What if it didn't work? What if she'd done all this for nothing? It had to work! She strained, pulling herself up the last inch. The rods tugged at her wrists, almost as if they were magnetized. Maybe they were. She pulled harder and her left wrist slipped free.

Taylor swung her body over to the right rod and wrapped her straining thighs around the pole. She climbed until her torso was above the right rod and yanked both hands up with all her strength. Her hands slipped free of the rods. Taylor cried out in relief and quickly covered her mouth with her palms, so the Slavers didn't hear her.

She slid down the rod. The second her feet touched the ground, her legs gave out. Tears streamed down Taylor's face. She'd done it. She still had to figure out a way to get out of the room and make it past the guards, but at least she'd freed herself.

Taylor couldn't afford to rest for long. She rubbed her legs, then staggered to her feet. Her thighs protested, but she remained standing. She ducked as a dark shadow passed in front of her door. Taylor dropped to her hands and knees, and crawled across the floor. There had to be something inside of the crates that would work as a weapon. Was it too much to hope for a baseball bat?

She rifled through the crates and found mostly clothing. Clothing of various sizes, shapes and colors. Taylor's gaze strayed to the dark stain, circling the drain in the middle of the floor. How many women had died? How many had been tortured? She shoved the clothes away and moved onto the next crate. She would not give up without a fight. Taylor had learned that much from the Phantom people.

*****

CHAPTER TWELVE

Hades suspected there was more to Opal's story, but he couldn't for the life of him figure out what she could be lying about. She disliked Taylor. Felt threatened by her. That much was obvious, but that didn't explain the events that had occurred in the Walled City.

He tried to probe her mind once more to uncover the truth, but failed again. Her mental blocks were some of the strongest he'd ever encountered. That strength had been a bonus when he'd made her his Righthand, but now it served only as frustration.

Opal led them directly to the Slavers' location, which only added to his growing suspicions. How had she known? She couldn't have just found out, which meant she'd been keeping the information from him. Why hadn't she given him the coordinates right away? The only logical reason for her to keep this from him was if she was the spy they'd been searching for.

The thought pained him. Hades had taken Opal into his bed. He'd trusted her with his life. Depended on her to protect the Phantom people. He'd considered her a *friend*. And this was how she'd repaid him. He had been so worried about challenges from the outside that it never occurred to him to take a closer look at his inner circle. It was a mistake that had cost him dearly. Hades would have to wait to find out the extent of her betrayal until after the raid. It was not something he looked forward to.

The ships' engines roared to life.

Fear beat at Hades' chest as he watched the Slavers prepare for takeoff. He couldn't let them get away. If they gained altitude, they'd blow up when they hit the energy field. There was also a chance that they'd kill Taylor, when the Phantoms attacked. Either way, she would be dead. His beast roared in anguish inside of him. Hades might be uncertain about his feelings, but his beast was not.

With a mental push, Hades told his army to spread out. He planned to take as many of the Slavers as he could alive, if only to torture them later in the Pit. He wanted them to know that the Dark King would not tolerate them in his Kingdom. Would not tolerate them taking what was his.

Once his men were in place, Hades gave the signal and roared. The sound echoed through the woods, signaling the attack. The Slavers' heads shot up and they scrambled to pull their weapons, but it was too late. Phantom Warriors poured out of the trees, shifting as they went. Bears, cats, misshapen wolves, and two-legged vipers rained down upon the Slavers, tearing a swath through their numbers as they fought to reach the ships' open doors.

Hades' claws ripped the head off one man, then he backhanded another. Bone crunched as the Slaver crumpled and fell to the ground. Rage turned his world into a red haze. If he couldn't save Taylor, he would avenge her. His two hearts nearly stopped in his chest at the thought of her being gone forever. She had to be alive. He would accept no other outcome.

More Slavers appeared in the doorways. They rushed out to assist their fallen brethren. Hades tore a bloody swath through the re-enforcements, leaving shattered bodies and twisted limbs in his wake. He no longer cared about survivors. He just needed to reach Taylor before it was too late.

He continued to fight, pushing his way closer and closer toward the ships. Blood dripped from the Dark King's torso and ran down his claws. The Slavers tried to retreat inside the lowest craft, but his men cut off their escape. Hades' beast leapt through the open door and quickly scanned the surroundings. He inhaled, searching for that sweet aroma that he knew so well. Hades caught Taylor's faint scent, but could not tell where it was coming from due to the stench of death and excrement filling his nostrils.

"Fan out!" he bellowed. "She is here. Find her."

*****

Opal rushed through the doors behind Hades in a panic. She had to locate Taylor. She'd told the Slavers that she was worth more alive, than dead. Now she prayed to the Goddess that they hadn't listened to her. If they'd killed her, then all her troubles would be over. Hades would slaughter the Slavers, and then they would return to the Keep. The Dark King would go through a short period of mourning out of respect for Linx and his mate, then things would return to normal.

She kept to the back of the group as they worked their way deeper into the ship. It would be easier to slip away unnoticed, when the time was right. Smooth metal walls wound their way in concentric circles, growing tighter as they neared the heart of the first ship.

Opal had never been inside a Slaver craft, except to examine its wreckage. Intact, the ship looked completely different. She could hear a battle taking place on the deck below her and on the one above, but she didn't have time to worry about who was winning. Opal waited until the halls split, then made her escape.

She used her knowledge of wrecked Slaver' ships to work her way toward the cargo area. The sound of heavy boots hitting metal reached her. The pounding grew louder as the men approached. Opal ducked into the shadows and watched the Slavers and Phantoms rush by.

She waited for the hall to clear, then took a step to her left. A *whoosh* sound came from behind her. Before Opal could turn to see what the noise was a large hand came down upon her shoulder. She was jerked into a hatch that she hadn't even noticed was there.

Opal spun, her clawed hand ready to eviscerate her assailant. Captain Hawk struck like a viper, easily catching her wrist and stopping her attack. He tsked. With a squeeze, he warned her how easy it would be for him to crush her wrist, then slowly released her. Opal's hearts stuttered in her chest as she stared into his uncompromising face and her hand fell to her side.

"I should've known that you were behind the betrayal," he said. His golden eyes simmered in the artificial lighting, but he made no move for his weapon.

Opal blanched. He wasn't referring to the Dark King. He was talking about himself. "You don't understand." She shook her head. "I gave you over an hour to escape with the Earthling. I'd expected you to be long gone by now."

He used his big body to cage her against the smooth wall. "And I seem to recall telling you that I'd see you again. I just hadn't expected it to be so soon." His voice lowered. "I should gut you where you stand."

Heat poured off his body, raising the temperature around them. Awareness flared between them, before being quickly banked. "You could, but I'm not the reason the Dark King is here. At least not entirely," she stammered. "He's here for her. But I need to get to her first. You could help me."

Hawk's raven brow arched. "You attack my ship, then have the nerve to ask for a favor?"

She ran a shaky hand through her short hair. "I know I

ask much of you."

He snorted. "You ask everything, yet offer nothing in exchange." Hawk's gaze scrolled down her body. He reached out and touched her hair. It slid through his fingertips. "So soft," he said. "I knew it would be the first time I saw you in the tree."

Opal's stomach lurched. She'd thought he'd seen her, but had convinced herself otherwise. "Why didn't you raise the alarm?" It was the question Opal had been asking herself since she'd first spotted him.

"It would've driven you off," he said. "I wanted you to think that you were safe, so that you'd come back. I pride myself on being a patient *hunter*."

Opal swallowed hard. "We don't have much time," she said, her voice breathless despite the urgency of the situation.

Hawk shook his head. "No, *you* don't have much time."

"Please," Opal pleaded. He appeared unmoved by her begging. Given the amount of Beings who'd probably begged him for their freedom, for their very life, she wasn't surprised. "I'm sure we could come up with some sort of arrangement."

"Now you're speaking my language," he said. "What exactly do you have in mind?"

"If you tell me where the Earthling is being held, I will make sure that the Dark King leaves your ship and whatever's left of your people," she said.

His gaze became calculating. "You can guarantee such a thing."

Opal gave him a shaky nod. "Y-yes! The King will go the second he finds her."

It was a lie and they both knew it. Once Hades found Taylor's lifeless body, he would leave no one standing.

Hawk's sensual lips peeled back in a feral smile. "You smell of deceit...and fear. Deceit, I can appreciate, but your fear does nothing for me." There was more than a little disgust in his voice. He closed the distance between them until only a breath separated them.

Opal thought all Slavers lived for the fear that they created in their captives, but she didn't think that Hawk was lying to her—at least not about that. Why would he? He had her right where he wanted her.

Right where she wanted to be. The insidious thought crept through her mind before she could stop it. "Don't." It was a plea and a command.

Hawk leaned forward, creating a faux intimacy that Opal didn't want to feel. He paid no heed to the fighting going on outside the door or her demands. "If I hadn't scented your fear before you knew I was here, then I would've believed it was caused by me." Hawk exhaled. His warm breath fanned over her face, leaving her light-headed.

Opal tried to flatten herself against the wall, but the move was ineffective. She couldn't escape him.

"Now I know otherwise." He cocked his head and took another deep breath. The movement caused his massive chest to brush against hers. Awareness returned with a vengeance and so did his smile. "No." He shook his head. "Your fear does not come from me. You feel something altogether different, when I am near. Don't you, Little Cat?"

"I don't know what you're talking about," she snarled and glanced away.

His knowing smile told her that he'd easily caught the lie. "If you're not afraid of me, then there is only one other powerful Being on this ship that could be causing your distress." He brushed his knuckles over her jaw. "Looks like I'm not the only one caught in a trap."

Opal jerked her head away. He was too close to the truth. Hawk was too close period. "I have to go. I have to reach the Earthling before the Dark King does."

"And what will you do, when you get to her?" he asked with genuine curiosity.

"Kill her, of course," she said matter-of-factly.

"That's quite a profit you're talking about disposing of. What are you going to offer me to make up for the loss?" he asked.

"What do you want?" Opal asked, glancing at the sealed hatch door.

Hawk's brow rose even further as he studied her. "You really are in trouble, if you're so eager to bargain with the enemy," he said.

"I won't be, if I get to her first," Opal said.

"Betrayal costs, Little Cat. No one gets away without paying the price," Hawk said.

"Please, I'll do anything you ask," she said.

Hawk cocked his head to the side to study her. "Anything?"

"Yes," she hissed.

He grabbed her chin and tilted her head up until their eyes met. "I plan to hold you to your word," Hawk said. "Best you remember that. The woman is being held in cargo bay four. I suggest you hurry. I've just received word that *your* people have reached level three."

Opal scooted away, but he stopped her before she made it to the door.

"This is not over between us," he said.

She gave him a curt nod.

Hawk pressed a button on the wall and the door opened. He stuck his head out the hatch and looked around. "All is clear." He grabbed Opal's arm and pulled her into the hall.

"Let go of me," she demanded.

Hawk took one step and was struck from the side by a massive liger. The cat ripped Opal from his grasp and knocked him off his feet. The powerful blow sent him sailing through the air, end over end. Instead of slamming into the wall, Hawk twisted at the last second and landed lightly on his toes.

One moment he was standing there, shaking his head to clear it. The next he was gone. A monstrous black beast with yellow eyes, deadly claws, and sharp teeth stood in his place.

Opal flinched as the creature took a step forward, its claws clacking on the metal floor. What was he?

He wasn't a Phantom, but there was no denying that he was some kind of shifter. The hair on Hades' back stood on end as he prepared to attack. Opal stepped forward, then stopped short as she realized what she'd been about to do. Why had her first instinct been to step between them and stop the fight? One look at Hawk told her that he didn't need her assistance.

Hades launched himself at the black cat, raking his claws over the Slavers' flank.

The black beast snarled, then whipped around so fast that Opal barely tracked his movements. He latched onto the Dark King's ear and bit down. Hades cried out, then they rolled. Claws, teeth, and fur went flying as the two evenly matched beasts engaged in battle. Blood splattered the walls and made the floor slick. Opal's hearts were in her throat as she watched them tear at each other, but she couldn't stay. She had a job to do. With Hades distracted, this was her last chance.

Sheer force of will turned her from the fight. Opal rushed down the hall until she found a transport cylinder. She stepped inside and shouted, "Level Four!"

The door closed and the transport dropped. Within seconds, she was standing outside of cargo bay four. Opal poked her head out the door. The bay was empty. She drew her sword and stepped into the cavernous chamber. Her boots sounded vulgar in the silence. Opal scanned the room. Metal chambers lined the walls. So many that it would take her forever to search them all. But what choice did she have? She had to try.

*****

Hades barely reached Opal in time. When he'd seen the

Slaver's hands on her and heard her cry out, a protective instinct overrode his need for stealth and he'd pounced. He'd torn the Slaver away from his Righthand, sending him flying.

He hadn't expected the Slaver to shift. Nor had he expected the beast to be so damn strong, but he should've known. Nothing was ever that straightforward in the world.

They fought for supremacy, each cat trying to get the upper hand. Every move Hades made was countered by the black beast. Scratch for scratch, bite for bite, they exchanged strikes, neither gaining ground. If he weren't a Slaver, the King might've had respect for the man. He was quite a fighter. Too bad he'd chosen the wrong path.

Hades circled him once more, looking for an opening. His side hurt from where Perseus had injured him last night, but he didn't let it show. "Where is she?" he growled.

The black beast snarled, but didn't answer.

"I will make your death swift if she is unharmed. Otherwise you'll experience torture like you've never known existed," Hades said.

The Slaver snorted out what sounded like a laugh.

Movement caught Hades' attention. His men were approaching from the opposite hall. Hades kept the Slaver's eyes on him, until they were near enough to strike.

"Have it your way," he said, then shouted. "Take him!"

The black beast went down as five Phantoms leapt onto his back.

"Bind him and bring him with us," Hades said, then raced down the hall. It was only as he was leaving that the King noticed that Opal was missing.

*****

Opal moved to the nearest door and pressed her hand against the metal to open it. The hatch rose revealing four women tethered to the walls. They cried out in relief when they saw her. But their cries of joy quickly turned to shouts of disbelief as Opal stepped back out and shut the door. She didn't have time to free the women now, not until she found what she was looking for.

She opened room after room, searching for Taylor, only to find more and more women. Some were Atlanteans. Most were of unknown origin. How long had the Slavers been here? How many other planets had they culled? It took time to gather this many females.

It wasn't until Opal reached the doors on the far part of the bay that she found her. She peeked through the glass and saw Taylor against the wall. The second the door slid open, Taylor lunged for her. Opal was so surprised by the move that she nearly dropped her sword. She dodged to the side at the last second and twisted out of the way.

"How did you get free?" she asked, stunned that one so inferior had managed such a feat.

Taylor pointed to the rods. "I'll give you one guess?"

Opal glanced at the poles and cursed under her breath, then looked at Taylor's hand. She wasn't holding a proper weapon. Instead, she had what looked to be a bolt tool. "What do you think you're going to do with that?"

"Smash you over the head, then get the hell out of here," Taylor said. "I can't believe you did this to me. What could I have possibly done to deserve this? And don't you dare say sleep with Hades because that answer isn't going to fly, bitch."

Opal lifted her sword, studying the blade as she spoke. "I admit that I initially concocted my plan because of what was happening between you and the Dark King. I hated you for taking him from me. Hades was mine. Is mine," she corrected. "But the reason I despise you, truly despise you has to do with the Kingdom. I would do anything to protect the Phantom realm. If that means getting rid of distractions like you by nefarious means, then so be it. Your mere presence reflects poorly on the Phantom people and weakens the Dark King. As long as humans like you are around, we are vulnerable."

Taylor raised her tool in defense. "You are insane."

Opal swung her weapon in a wide arc, barely missing Taylor. "I am not crazy," she said.

"Yes, you are, if you believe that you've done this," she indicated to the bloody walls around them, "for any other reason than spite and jealousy," Taylor said.

Opal rushed her.

*****

Taylor dodged left, then pivoted on her right foot, striking Opal in the back. The King's Righthand lost her balance and went flying forward, but didn't fall.

"Nice shot." Opal rolled her shoulders. "I taught you well, but it won't save you."

"Don't flatter yourself. I learned that move from Perseus," she said.

Fear focused her. Taylor concentrated on what else Perseus had taught her. She could hear the battle taking place around them, but just because Hades was on the ship didn't mean that she'd survive the next few minutes.

She held up her makeshift weapon. It wasn't nearly as effective as a wooden sword, but it was better than nothing. Taylor jumped over the crates and grabbed a handful of clothes as she went. She threw them into Opal's face, but it barely slowed the Phantom woman down.

Opal lunged, her sword jabbing forward. She sliced through the material, cutting her way to Taylor's arm.

Taylor cried out and staggered back.

Blood welled from the wound, but Taylor's grip on her weapon remained firm. She saw movement outside the door. Had the Slavers returned? Her heart slammed against her ribs, but she didn't dare take her eyes off Opal. She needed a sword or a longer weapon. Anything to give her a fighting chance.

"Why did you do it?" Taylor asked again to buy herself some time. She kept the crates between them as Opal tried to reposition herself for a kill shot.

"I told you," Opal said. "I did it for the King, for the Phantom people. Now stop stalling. You are only delaying the inevitable. The sooner you die, the sooner things can return to what they were before you arrived." She lunged for her.

Taylor had her weapon raised and ready, but there wasn't much she could do against a sword.

A loud menacing growl filled the small compartment. The growl quickly turned into an outraged roar.

Opal stopped mid-charge. They both turned to find Hades standing in the doorway, covered in blood, his large body trembling with barely contained rage.

"Sire." Opal sheathed her sword. "As you can see, I've found her. She's alive, but appears to be suffering from delusions. She thinks I'm trying to kill her. Perhaps now that you're here, you can talk some sense into her."

His red eyes followed her movements, then slowly shifted to Taylor. "What I see is that I've arrived just in time." His words were guttural and in no way human.

Opal's composure cracked and she dropped to one knee. "My King, I did what was best for the people. Having a human in our court will weaken us, weaken you. Can't you see that? This foolish raid proves it. How many warriors have we lost for one Earthling? Five? Ten?"

"We wouldn't have lost any had it not been for you." Hades' fury entered the room before him. The heat from it boiled over, making it hard to breathe. He stepped forward and held out his hand. "Taylor, come to me." Bloody claws had replaced his fingertips, but she didn't hesitate.

Taylor rushed into Hades' arms. He inhaled, taking in her scent, then slowly examined every inch of her. When he reached the injury on her arm, he leaned down and licked the blood off. He cleaned the wound thoroughly, then examined it again. His eyes were glowing, when his gaze returned to Opal.

"You have betrayed me," he growled. "Betrayed my trust. Betrayed the Phantom people by working with the Slavers. What have you to say for yourself?"

Opal shook her head in denial. "Sire, I did it for you. And for the people—"

"Cease speaking this instant! I shall listen to no more of your lies. You did this..." He held up Taylor's injured arm. "All of this, for yourself."

"But, Sire..." Opal beseeched. "I love you."

Hades' gaze flicked to the dried blood on the walls. "This is not love. This is madness."

Taylor squeezed Hades' hand to reassure him that all was well. His touch remained gentle, but firm.

Opal rose to her feet. "Will you challenge me in the Pit?" She swallowed convulsively as she awaited his answer.

"I will," Taylor said.

Satisfaction flashed in Opal's eyes, but quickly diminished when Hades looked at her.

"No." He slowly shook his head. "I have a better idea." Hades turned to his nearest guard. "Bring him to me."

A Phantom Warrior pushed Captain Hawk forward. Opal's eyes widened and her color drained.

"Remove the shackles from her," Hades said.

Hawk did as he asked.

Taylor rubbed her wrists. They were sore from the climb, but they didn't appear to be bruised. Not that it mattered. She'd heal.

"Because I am a fair King, I will allow you to take what is left of your people and leave this planet." Hades pointed to Opal. "You will take her with you."

"No!" Opal shouted.

Hawk gave her a feral grin. "It would be my pleasure. I'm in need of a new pet."

Hades' free hand curled into fist. "The only reason you are alive is because she is unharmed." He ran his knuckles over Taylor's uninjured arm. "If you ever return to Zaron, I will find your home planet and declare war upon it." His glacial voice cut through any remaining doubt of his sincerity. "I will not stop, until all that remains is a memory of your planet and its people. Do you understand?"

Hawk's battered gaze moved to Opal and his smile widened, making his split lip bleed even more. "Agreed," he said. "What about the others?" He indicated to the containers around them.

Hades' eyes narrowed. "The others shall be freed. They can either remain here on Zaron or they will eventually be returned to their homes. Accept my decree or die where you stand."

Hawk hesitated, then nodded. "I don't have much of a choice."

"No, you do not."

Hades' cold blue eyes pinned Opal in place as they left the compartment. Hawk raised his hand and pressed a panel on the right. Opal rushed forward as the door slammed shut.

"You can't do this. It means death. Please, Sire." Her fists pounded on the metal. The clang, clang, clang echoed in the silence.

"It is done," Hawk said.

Hades glanced one more time at the sealed compartment, then slowly turned away. He pulled Taylor close, then issued the order to leave. The Phantoms freed the enslaved women, then escorted them off the ships.

The Slavers took off an hour later.

Taylor and Hades watched them go. Even after everything she'd done to her, Taylor felt bad for Opal. She'd feel bad for anyone stuck in that horrendous chamber of horrors. As the ships left the atmosphere, she turned to Hades.

"I'm sorry," she whispered.

He tensed, but didn't look at her. "So am I."

"Do you think he'll kill her?" she asked.

Pain flashed across his face. "He had the opportunity to do so before and didn't."

Taylor glanced at him. "What does that mean?"

He met her gaze fleetingly. "It means her fate is now in his hands."

*****

Hades watched the ship leave. He'd done the right thing, but couldn't stop the feelings of sorrow and guilt from carving chunks out of him. It was his fault that things had come to this point. Had he not lain with Opal, she would've never believed that there was more to their joining than just pleasure. He'd been a fool and hadn't even known it until Taylor's arrival in his Kingdom.

He did his best to hide how relieved he felt having her back in his arms. He'd come so close to losing her. Too close in his mind. When he'd seen Opal rush her, sword drawn, his hearts had stopped.

For a second, he'd thought he was too late. Even now Hades resisted the urge to crush Taylor to him. To reassure himself that she was real and not just a yearning desire that he'd somehow conjured in his mind.

It was in that moment when he realized that he might not get to her in time, that Hades had faced a hard truth about his feelings for the Earth woman.

He *loved* her. He loved her with both his hearts. It was a feeling he never thought he'd ever experience. Had never planned to experience. Even now he could barely believe what the Goddess was telling him, but Hades knew it was true.

The volatile emotion made it all the more difficult to do what must come next. Hades had failed in his duty to protect Taylor. And because of that failure, he'd nearly lost her. He could no longer guarantee her safety in the Walled City, which meant that he had to contact Linx. Taylor would be safe in New Atlantis. Safe and alive. In the end, that's all that mattered.

*****

Taylor nearly collapsed when they reached the Keep. Word had already spread about Opal's deceit. The guards' reactions to the news and to her in general ran from blame to sympathy. Taylor bore it all as she made her way to her room. Her muscles ached and her arm stung, but those were minor concerns given the weight of what had just occurred.

Hades didn't come to her room that night. Initially, Taylor had been disappointed, but later she'd been relieved. She needed time alone to process everything that had happened. She also needed time to sort through her complicated emotions. And boy were they complicated.

She loved the Dark King. Of that there was no doubt, but Taylor had no idea what to do about it or if she should even tell him.

Hades had been through a lot. He had not only gone to battle, but he'd lost his most trusted guard to treachery. Opal had been in his life and in his bed for *years*. She'd been his ears, his eyes, and his confidant. The loss was a lot to digest for anyone, much less a King with so many responsibilities.

Taylor had been here for what, five days? And in that short period of time she'd managed to sleep with the King, get kidnapped, and start a war. Hades didn't need, nor would he appreciate, having her unrequited feelings dumped on him right now. It would not help the King's mood or the situation. He had enough on his plate.

Hades might not blame her for this mess, but Taylor blamed herself. Had Linx not brought her here, Opal would still be on Zaron, Hades would have quickly found the Slavers, and all of his men would be alive. The Dark King wouldn't have had to rescue her and he wouldn't have lost anyone. Hades wouldn't have had to go through any of this, if she hadn't always been such a screw up.

Opal was right about one thing. Taylor was a distraction. A dangerous one.

Taylor sighed. Her life here was out of control. She wasn't a Phantom, but she no longer felt like an Earthling. Her old life seemed so far away, a hazy dream that was fading fast. Taylor couldn't imagine returning to Earth now.

In a couple of days, Linx would return to take her away, Eventually Taylor would forget all about her short time on the Slavers' ship, the bloody container, and being shackled. But she'd never forget about the Dark King.

Hades would haunt her forever.

*****

<h1 style="text-align:center">Chapter Thirteen</h1>

Taylor awoke the next morning to the sounds of heavy boots thudding up and down the halls. Fear enveloped her and her heart pummeled her ribcage. She glanced around wide-eyed as she searched for blood on the walls. It took her panicked brain a second to process that she was no longer on the Slavers' ship. That she was back in her room at the Keep. Safe.

She slipped out of bed and made her way to the door. Taylor poked her head out to find Kon at his post. "What's going on? What's with all the noise?"

He watched more men race by. "The King has increased the guards on duty. Your abduction has pointed out holes in our security. They are being plugged now," he said. "You should pack. Phantom Warrior Linx is waiting for you."

"What do you mean 'waiting for me'?" Taylor asked. She had at least a day before she had to leave.

"The King summoned him early. He believes you'll be safer in New Atlantis," Kon said.

"So Hades just plans to pack me up and ship me off without saying goodbye?" The thought hurt.

Kon opened his mouth, then closed it again. "I thought

after all that had occurred, you'd want to leave this place," he said cautiously.

"I did. I mean I do...just..." *Not yet. Not like this.* Taylor's voice trailed off.

What did she want? That was the million-dollar question. She thought she'd have time to speak with Hades. Linx's early arrival changed everything.

"Where is Linx now?" She had to get to him before he spoke with the King. She didn't want him hearing about Opal and the Slavers secondhand. No telling what he'd relay to her sister, Tabby.

Kon glanced at a couple of guards who rushed past. "Phantom Warrior Linx has been temporarily confined to one of the spare chambers. He's none to happy about it, hence the extra guards and sense of urgency."

"Confined? What did he do?" Taylor asked. She wouldn't put anything past the silly cat. Linx liked to cause trouble and walked a thin line between right and wrong, but he'd only crossed it once to her knowledge, and that had been to save her life.

Kon cocked his head and gave her a curious look. "Nothing, other than be his annoying self." He hesitated. "The Dark King summoned him, but has refused to meet with him now that he is here."

"Why?" Taylor's brows arched.

Kon mirrored her expression. "Why indeed?"

"Can he do that?" Taylor asked.

Kon snorted. "He is the Dark King. He can do whatever he likes."

"That may fly with Linx, but Hades can't just ship me off," she said.

"Yes, he can." Kon gave her a pointed look.

"No, he can't," she said, then added, "Take me to him right now."

"I do not think that is such a good idea," Kon said. "The King's mood has been most unpleasant ever since he received word of Linx's arrival."

"Why should Monster Kitty be upset? He's the one who called him," she said.

"Why indeed?" There was a wealth of meaning in Kon's words.

Was it too much to hope that Hades actually cared whether she stayed or left? There had to be a way to find out quickly. Taylor slipped back into her room.

Linx was here to take her to New Atlantis because Hades didn't think she was safe. Taylor pressed her hand to her racing heart and tried to slow her breathing. She should be thrilled. Excited even, that she'd get to see Tabby soon. But all she felt was panic. She couldn't leave here until things were settled between her and Hades, until they'd talked everything out, until they'd made love one final time.

"Hades, Hades, Hades, what am I going to do with you?" she muttered under her breath.

Don't panic. Don't panic.

Taylor ran across the room and grabbed some clean clothes out of her closet. She had to get to the Dark King before he did anything else insane. She wasn't exactly sure what she'd say to him when she saw him, but she'd think of something.

In her mind, it no longer mattered whether Linx found out about the kidnapping. More important things were at stake. She showered quickly and threw her clothes on, then pulled her long, red hair back into a tight braid. Taylor rushed out of the room, only to be stopped short by Kon.

"Where's the King?" she asked.

"I told you that his mood is less than optimal at present," Kon said.

"Well I don't think waiting is going to make it any better, especially if he's pissed off about Linx being here. Now where is he?"

Kon hesitated.

"Please, Kon." She choked back a sob. "I need to talk to

him, before I go. It's important." It was more than important to her. Taylor couldn't leave, until she knew the truth.

"He is in the Great Hall meeting with his tactical advisors and does not want to be disturbed," he said.

So it wasn't only Linx that the King was trying to avoid. He didn't want to speak with her either. Well too bad. Taylor dodged left, then cut right and ran. Kon cursed and started after her. She could hear his heavy boots hitting the stone behind her. With his long legs, he should've been able to catch her easily.

Taylor glanced back. He was letting her get away. What was the warrior up to? There was no time now to find out. She ran straight for the Great Hall and rushed inside.

Like the first time she'd saw him, Hades was seated at the foot of his throne, dressed in black fabric that molded his hard body, making him appear menacing. Several guards surrounded him. Their heads were bent over a holographic map, which had been spread out in front of them. They all looked up as she rushed inside with Kon hot on her high heels.

Kon skidded to a halt when he caught sight of Hades, and bowed. "I'm sorry, Sire. I told her that you were not to be disturbed, but she would not listen. She insisted on coming here immediately to speak to you." He didn't sound sorry, but he did look contrite.

Hades' cool gaze moved from the guard over to Taylor. There he began a slow appraisal of her body. By the time the Dark King finished his examination, Taylor's face was flushed and her temperature had skyrocketed.

She took a step forward. "We need to talk."

Hades stared at her. "I do not have time right now. As you can see." He indicated to the men around him. "I am in a meeting."

He had time to call Linx, he had time to get her packed up, he had time to turn her on, but he didn't have time to talk. Yeah, so not happening. The King was not going to get rid of her that easy. "Make time," she growled.

Taylor steadfastly ignored the shocked expressions of the guards and continued her approach. In all likelihood, this was her last and only chance to speak to Hades before she had to leave. The strategy meeting could wait. Linx could wait. Hell, they all could, until she had her answer.

Something flared in Hades' blue eyes, before being carefully shuttered. "Then by all means, speak!"

Here? In front of everyone? She thought she'd get to talk to him in private. *You're the one who interrupted his meeting. What did you expect?*

Taylor made her way to the throne and stopped below the dais. If he wanted to talk in front of his friends, then so be it. Though he might be sorry he did, by the time she was finished.

"Why didn't you let me challenge Opal in the Pit?" The question was out of her mouth before she realized she was going to ask it. Sure, she'd thought about it. She'd wondered why he'd denied her the right, but that hadn't been the first thing Taylor had wanted to know.

Hades blinked in surprise, then said slowly, "Because you would've died."

"It was my choice," Taylor said.

"No!" He shook his head. "It was *my* choice. You are not from here. You do not know our ways."

She crossed her arms over her chest and called it like she saw it. "Bullshit!"

Hades' jaw clenched.

Taylor leaned forward. "I may not be from here, but in the short period of time that I've been here I have gotten a pretty good grasp of your ways. It was my right to challenge Opal after she betrayed me. You denied me that right."

The Dark King stood so abruptly that everyone took a step back. Angry white lines bracketed his cruelly sensual mouth. "I decide who has rights in *my* Kingdom. And I will not allow your rash behavior to get you killed. I vowed to keep you safe. I failed once. I will not fail again."

"You did not fail," she said.

"Yes, I did," he said. "But it was for the last time." He slammed his fist against his chest. The thud echoed in the silence. "I will not watch you die. For that, you ask too much of me."

Taylor's heart skipped a beat. What was he saying? Was the King admitting that he cared? She didn't know. Couldn't tell. She had created so many imaginary relationships over the years by projecting her emotions onto every man she cared about in hopes that they would one day love her in return that it made recognizing the truth difficult. Taylor didn't want to make the same mistake with the Dark King. He was different from the rest. She wanted what they had to be real, not just wishful thinking on her part.

"So let me get this straight, your solution for this whole situation is to pack me up and ship me off to New Atlantis," she said.

"Yes." He nodded. "You'll be safe there. I won't have to—"

"You won't have to what? Worry? Care? Think about me ever again?" she asked, glaring at him. Taylor had come here for an answer, had come here for the truth, even if it wasn't what she wanted to hear. Hades hadn't exactly made a clear declaration. She wasn't sure that he ever would.

The Dark King's expression hardened. "It is done."

Taylor brushed her hands together. "Just like that, eh? Didn't even think to ask if it was okay with me? If it was what I wanted? Just poof and I'm gone."

Hades' nostrils flared. "I did not need your input."

"I see," she ground out. "First you tell me that I'm not one of your people, then in the next breath you tell me I have to follow your orders. Make up your mind, Monster Kitty. You cannot have it both ways."

"I already have," he said, his voice tight.

"Fine!" She shrugged. "Have it your way." Taylor made

like she was going to leave, then swung around at the last second to face the King and his warriors. "I, Taylor Shelley, formally challenge you, Hades, the Dark King in the Pit tonight." Desperation made her open her mouth to utter the outrageous proposition, but it was love that fueled her conviction. Taylor's body trembled as she declared her intentions.

She'd obviously lost her mind. Taylor clearly and vividly recalled what Hades had done to the last person who had challenged him in the Pit, but what choice did she have? She couldn't let him kick her out. Not yet.

The guards stared at her in disbelief. But they weren't nearly as shocked as Hades.

"Take that back," he demanded.

Taylor set her jaw and stared at him. "No!"

Hades stepped down from the dais and approached her, his gaze searching her face. "You've seen what I become and what I can do. You have no hope of winning. You must know that."

Oh she did know. There wasn't a snowball's chance of her beating Hades in the Pit, not in a *fair* fight anyway. She couldn't even beat him if she cheated, but that wasn't the point. She needed to break his iron-fisted control. Only then would the truth come out.

"You never know," she said, knowingly baiting him. "I might get lucky."

"Or you could die." He'd said it to scare her.

It worked. She was well and truly terrified, but Taylor wasn't about to back down. "There's always a chance."

His brow furrowed and his expression grew mutinous. "You cannot possibly win the throne." He growled and gnashed teeth. "Even if you did manage the unthinkable, there's no way you could hold the seat for long."

Poor, poor Dark King. He was so used to people trying to get his seat of power that it didn't occur to him that she might be after something else entirely. Taylor met his hard gaze with one of her own. The tension in the Great Hall became stifling. The guards shifted, their unease growing.

Taylor eventually took pity on their unwanted audience. "Who said anything about wanting your throne?" she asked.

Hades' eyes widened and he reared back in surprise. "What else could you..." His words cut off abruptly and his expression closed down, but not before she saw the admiration in his eyes. Or was that *anticipation*? Knowing Hades it was probably a bit of both.

"Fine!" he said. "I accept your challenge."

"Good." Taylor grinned and pivoted to leave.

Hades caught her arm, stopping her short. She glanced at his hand, then at his handsome face. He gave her a wicked grin that sent a shaft of heat straight to her core. "Be prepared to bow before the Dark King," he said.

Taylor sniffed. "I bow before no man," she replied, even though the thought had her pulse racing and parts of her body moistening in anticipation.

"You'll bow before me." The King inhaled and his feral grin widened. "I'll have you on your knees before the night is through."

She pressed her lips together and bit the inside of her cheek to keep focused. "I'm not the one who'll be on my knees tonight. See you in the Pit, Monster Kitty." Taylor strolled off, making sure to rock her hips seductively as she went. She had never been more scared, more excited, or more turned on in her life. She might not be able to win the challenge. Okay, no way would she win the fight. But maybe, just maybe she'd be able to win the man.

*****

Hades couldn't tear his eyes away from Taylor's lush ass. If there weren't so many guards around, he'd take her to the ground and fuck her where she stood. His cock ached to have her, especially after he'd come so close to losing her.

The challenge only fueled his need. Her sweet scent lingered on the air, teasing him long after her departure.

For a moment he had feared, that like all the others who had come before her, Taylor was after his throne. It was a ridiculous thought. He was ashamed that it had even crossed his mind. One look in her eyes had revealed her true motives. And the truth he'd seen there had left him shaken.

So shaken, that even now Hades refused to accept it for fear it wasn't real.

The little fool had lost her mind. That could be the only logical explanation for her erratic behavior. No sane person would challenge him in front of his men. They would petition him in private. That way if Hades turned them down, they would save face.

He should've ignored her clumsy attempt to prick his temper, but Hades had never been able to ignore Taylor. Something about her held his attention, refusing to release him. It was why he'd refused to see Linx, even though he'd summoned him. He wasn't ready to let the little Earthling go yet. He knew he should, but Hades wasn't sure that he'd ever be.

He stared at the closed door, until he heard murmurs of concern coming from his guards. Their low voices a painful reminder that he wasn't alone. *And whose fault was that?* Hades cursed under his breath. He should've known that Taylor was up to something, when she stormed into the Great Hall. He should've stopped her before she opened her exquisite mouth. But he hadn't. Something had stayed his tongue.

With his men present to witness Taylor issuing the challenge, Hades had no choice but to accept it or lose face. *At least that's what he told himself...though he'd never worried about such things before.*

He turned to find all his guards wide-eyed and gaping at him. "What are you looking at?" he snapped.

They all ducked their heads. "Nothing, Sire."

"Good, then let's get back to work."

*****

Taylor thought she'd have a heart-attack before she made it out of the Great Hall. If Kon hadn't met her halfway, she would've collapsed. What in the world was she thinking? She'd just challenged Hades, the Dark King to meet her in the Pit. Really bad things happened in that place. Really bad and really...*decadent* things.

She needed to be ready for both. Taylor turned to Kon, who'd kept pace beside her.

"You must have a plan," he said, giving her sanity the benefit of the doubt. "Why else would you do something so foolish?"

Did she have a plan? Not really. It was more of a spur of the moment, not fully formed, idea that had seemed good at the time. Hades had rushed her by calling Linx. In response, she'd done something rash. Now Taylor had to live with her decision. "I'm going to need a few things for tonight."

Kon nodded. "What is it you need?"

"Do you guys have spray bottles?" she asked.

He frowned and shook his head in confusion.

Taylor described what she meant.

"Ah, not exactly," he said. "But I believe I might have an adequate substitute."

"Good enough," she said. "I also need the training poles distributed throughout the Pit. Four should do, if they're spaced evenly enough." If she could reach any of the poles, then there was a good chance Hades wouldn't be able to catch her. At least not right away.

"What do you need the poles for?" he asked, then added. "They are not weapons." This time his tone did question her sanity.

"I realize that," Taylor said. "Can you just do this for me?"

"I will," Kon said hesitantly. "If you tell me what you're really up to."

Taylor stopped walking. "I can't leave here with Linx. Not yet. Not when there's a chance..."

Kon continued to stare, then his red eyes softened. "You love the Dark King," he said. "I mean really love the Dark King. Not for his title, but for who he is." He sounded amazed...and *relieved*. "I thought as much. Your scent changes when you're around him."

"I didn't say—"

He smiled. "You didn't have to. Only love could explain the madness of your plan," he said.

Taylor's face heated and she lowered her voice. "You're not going to say anything, are you?"

Kon shook his head. "There is nothing to say."

"I haven't told Hades." She sighed. "I don't know if he feels the same. I won't know for sure until tonight."

His expression was sympathetic. "Hades is a complicated man. Being King makes him more so. It takes complicated men time to sort through their emotions. Do not give up on him. You have me and the Phantom people behind you, pulling for your success."

"Thank you." Taylor grinned.

"No, thank you." Kon gave her a short bow.

*****

Hades called an abrupt end to his meeting. There was no use even pretending to pay attention. He ordered his men out, then returned to his chambers and summoned Linx. Hades did his best to hide his impatience, but something must have shown in his demeanor because the wily cat stopped in the middle of the room and looked at him.

"What's happened? What has you so tense, Sire?" Linx's lips twitched in amusement. "I could guess, but that wouldn't be nearly as much fun as you coming right out and telling

216

me."

"Nothing," Hades said. "Now state your business."

Linx's brow furrowed in confusion. "You called me, remember? You told me to get here right away. I've come to pick up Taylor like you asked," he said. "After I received your message, I went directly to King Eros. He is eager to meet her. So eager that he's scheduled an appointment to do so tomorrow. He intends to make his decision about her future before the gathering."

Hades didn't know what gathering he was referring to and didn't care. He had much to think about before he entered the Pit tonight. He didn't have the time, nor the inclination to explain himself to Linx.

"You'll have to wait or better yet, come back tomorrow. Taylor is currently unavailable." Hades picked up a random document off his desk and pretended to read it.

Curiosity overrode self-preservation, causing Linx to step deeper into the room. "What do you mean she's unavailable? She's still here, isn't she? Nothing has happened to her."

"Of course she's here. Where else would she be?" Hades' mind flashed to her in the bloody chamber and his stomach recoiled. Thankfully the blood hadn't been hers. But it could've been.

"Just checking." Linx's expression was deceptively lazy. "I thought for a minute that you were going to tell me that she was gone."

She nearly had been. Even now the fear threatened to claim him. Hades resisted the urge to go to Taylor's room to check on her. As it was, he'd stopped by twice while she slept just to poke his head in the door to be sure she was safe.

Linx watched him closely. "When might she be able to see me?"

"As I said, she won't be available until tomorrow," Hades said, doing his best to keep the aggravation out of his voice. "I'm afraid you and the Atlantean King will have to wait."

Linx's gaze turned calculating. "Why tomorrow? What's so important about tonight? I know you're not telling me something."

Hades took a deep breath and tried to rein in his temper. Wasn't shouldering the blame for what had occurred enough? Must he explain himself to the warrior? He needed to think, to plan, to ultimately decide what course of action he would take. Hades couldn't do that with Linx filling his ears with nonsense.

"Tonight Taylor is otherwise engaged," he said.

Linx blinked. "Doing what? What could possibly occupy her so thoroughly that she doesn't have time tonight to speak with me?"

Hades stood, nearly knocking over his chair. "This may come as a surprise, but not everything revolves around you and your needs," he said. "Taylor has other commitments tonight. Commitments that cannot be rescheduled."

"Sire, I think you need to explain what's going on," Linx said. "You called me here to come get her. I came right away. I deserve an explanation. What has changed?"

A red haze covered Hades' vision. "Perhaps you should rephrase that 'statement'."

Their gazes held for a few seconds, then Linx slowly looked away. "What am I suppose to do until tomorrow?" he asked.

Hades' eyes narrowed. "Attend the challenge in the Pit like everyone else in the Kingdom."

Linx's chin shot up. "Sorry, Sire. I didn't realize. Who's challenged you now?" His bored tone wouldn't remain so for long.

Hades let the silence stretch.

"Obviously a fool who's never seen you fight," Linx added to fill the quiet and perhaps soothe his temper.

Hades thought about not telling him. It would be worth it just to see the look of surprise on the cat's arrogant face. If he thought the challenge would remain a secret, then he would've, but Hades knew word of Taylor's folly was already spreading throughout the Kingdom. No way would Linx remain oblivious for long.

When it looked as if Linx's curiosity might burst, Hades spoke. "Actually, the fool *has* seen me fight. To the death no less," he said.

Linx balked. "And they still wanted to challenge you?"

The King nodded. "Evidently, yes."

"They must have a death wish," he said.

"I am not entirely certain of their motives, but I do have my suspicions."

"I suppose going to the Pit is one way to kill an hour," Linx mused.

Hades tilted his head. "I doubt that this particular challenge will take an hour. In fact, I'd be surprised if it lasted for more than five minutes."

"Five minutes!" Linx snorted. "Then why bother?"

Hades met his affronted gaze. "Taylor didn't give me much of a choice."

For a full minute, Linx just stood there too stunned to say anything, then he shot forward and leapt upon Hades' desk. The King caught him around the throat, stopping his charge. He shook the feline in warning, his claws raking his vulnerable neck.

"You cannot allow a human female to fight in the Pit," Linx gasped as Hades squeezed.

The beast rose inside of the Dark King. "Do not tell me what I can and cannot do in my Kingdom, Warrior, or you might find yourself facing me in the Pit next."

Linx paled, but remained undeterred. "She's a woman!" he spat.

"I am well aware of that fact, Phantom. It's quite hard to miss. Now stand down." Hades shoved Linx back, but like most cats when he fell, he landed on his feet.

Linx shook his head. "I will not let you do this. I cannot."

Hades' brows rose to his hairline. "Excuse me?"

The warrior rubbed his throat as if to remove the claws that had been there only moments ago. "What I meant to say is that King Eros will not be pleased when he hears about this."

It was a thinly veiled warning. One that did nothing to deter Hades from his course.

His eyes narrowed. "That sounded suspiciously like a threat against the Dark King. But I must be mistaken, because I know you would never do anything like that without expecting a swift response."

"No, Sire. It was no threat." Linx swallowed hard to choke down the lie. "But I am saying that it's wrong for you to accept a challenge from a female. Especially a human female, who is under your protection."

The King glared at him. "You've met Taylor Shelley. You knew her on Earth, while you were courting your mate. Did she strike you as tame in any way?"

"No." Linx shook his head. "Not in the least."

"Then what in Zaronian fires makes you think that I have *any* control over what that wildcat does?" He grit out, then ran a hand through his hair in frustration. If he'd had control, she would never have been kidnapped by Slavers. No, if he had any say over her whatsoever, she would've never left his bed. That was his biggest mistake. One Hades planned to rectify tonight.

Linx conceded his point, then quietly said, "I cannot let my mate's sister die in the Pit. Tabby would *never* forgive me."

Hades re-stacked the documents on his desk. "Who said anything about dying?"

How could Linx even think such a thing? He might be the Dark King, but he wasn't a monster. Hades had never killed a woman in a fight in his life and he didn't intend to start tonight.

The tension between them grew. "Death is only one of the ways to lose in the Pit. Or have you forgotten?" His voice was pitched low, but it held an edge, an edge they both heard.

Linx's eyes widened, then widened some more. "You can't mean...Surely you wouldn't...Not in front of everyone." He blew out a heavy breath. "She's human," he said as if that should explain everything.

"Yes, she is." Hades gave him a feral grin. "But you forget that I am the Dark King."

*****

Chapter Fourteen

The pounding of the drums beat at her nerves. Taylor had only brought a couple of her old costumes with her when she'd left Earth. She'd made sure that she'd grabbed her favorites. And now she was glad that she had. She stared at her reflection and slowly ran her hand over the red and white sequins.

Beneath her short skirt and cropped top were a matching red thong and tassels. She didn't bother with a bra. Her tactic for tonight was to distract for as long as she was able. Since the audience in the Pit consisted mainly of men, nudity was a safe bet to do the trick. Taylor had no idea if Hades would immediately shift into Monster Kitty form or if he'd fight as a man.

She hoped his cat came out to play. She'd prepared for that possibility, not for the other. As scary as he was in his Other form, his human form scared her more. Taylor wouldn't be able to hold him off for long, but she didn't need long to get her answer. His actions tonight would tell her how he truly felt.

She rechecked her skimpy costume and her makeup, then slipped on her high heels. "Shatter his control. Shatter his control," she repeated the words, until they became her mantra.

Taylor knew what would likely occur if she succeeded. She'd seen Pitticus in action after he won his challenge. And though it had embarrassed him to no end, she had confirmed her suspicions with Kon. He'd given her an abridged version of Phantom mating rituals just in case the tone in the Pit moved from sex to something else. It wasn't a lot of information, but it was enough.

Was she really going to go through with this? Could she do this? It was one thing to strip before an audience, quite another to have sex.

A soft knock sounded on the door.

"Come in," she said.

Kon poked his head in. "Are you ready?"

"No," she said honestly. "But let's go anyway."

He nodded and held out his arm for her to take. Taylor slipped her hand on top of his and allowed him to escort her to the Pit. The drumming grew louder upon their approach, making her even more jumpy.

"Everything is as you requested," Kon said, giving her arm a reassuring squeeze.

"Good," she said. "Were you able to get the spray bottles?"

He pulled a container out from a side pocket. "There are others in the Pit, when this one runs out. I've placed them near the poles. Are you sure you just want water in them?"

"As opposed to what? Acid?" Taylor glanced at him.

He grinned. "There are certain plants that can disrupt a Phantoms' senses."

She laughed. "I appreciate the thought, but water will do nicely, thanks."

"It won't stop him," Kon said. "It won't even slow him down."

"I know." The bottles weren't meant to stop him. They were just one more way to distract the King and draw out the challenge so she could get her answer.

They reached the entrance to the Pit. The drums suddenly stopped, but her heart continued its cadence.

"Wow, there are a lot of people here," she said, staring at the packed arena.

"Are you sure you want to go through with this?" Kon asked. "No one will think unkindly of you, if you've changed your mind."

Taylor was sure his tone was meant to be soothing, but it was hard to miss the concern in his voice or the worry that she might back out. Kon obviously didn't know her well. None of them did.

They looked upon her as a human. And to them, human was synonymous with weak. But Taylor was determined to show them that despite her human 'handicap' that she was strong. Strong enough to challenge the Dark King and walk away unscathed...she hoped.

A roar of excitement filled the arena as Hades stepped into the Pit. This time he wasn't wearing the leggings he'd had on when Perseus challenged him. His chest was bare and so were his long legs. Taylor's gaze rose and she squinted.

What was he wearing?

It looked like a *loincloth*.

The King took a step forward and the material split all the way to his hips, revealing his nakedness.

Taylor gulped. Heaven help her. She'd never seen anything so smoking hot in her life or anything so tempting. How could she be expected to fight with all that lusciousness on display? Her fingers itched to touch his hipbones and feel the flex of his muscled thighs.

She obviously wasn't the only one who'd dressed in hopes of distracting their opponent. The King looked like he'd stepped out of her darkest fantasies. Taylor had to fight the overwhelming urge to run across the arena and jump on him.

Kon released her. "Good luck! That is what the Earthlings say, right?"

"Yep! Thanks! I'll need all I can get." She stepped into the Pit. The crowds' volume rose to deafening. "Winner take all," Taylor murmured under her breath.

*****

Hades couldn't pull his gaze away from Taylor. For a moment, he'd feared that she had changed her mind and that he'd have to give chase. But after a breath, she'd released Kon and stepped into the Pit.

When the light hit her, her clothing sparkled like a shooting star. Every step made Taylor glisten. Her endless legs were encased in those silly high shoes that she insisted on wearing. Her short skirt barely reached the top of her firm thighs, while her shirt played peekaboo with her mid-drift, giving him tantalizing glimpses of her flawless bare skin. Hades had no idea what she was wearing, but he knew that he liked it. A lot. And he'd like it even more, when he peeled it off.

His gaze moved to the stands. Howls and roars filled his ears. It appeared that most of the warriors appreciated Taylor's scraps of clothing, too. Hades growled at the audience and caught Linx's wry grin. The warrior was seated front and center, giving him quick access to the Pit. The cat obviously didn't trust him to keep his word.

Hades shrugged off the unwanted distraction and glanced at the poles situated around the Pit. What would she need with those? It wasn't like Taylor could lift one and hit him with it. And this wasn't a *dancing* challenge. At least he didn't think so.

He continued to look around. There were small containers scattered throughout the ring. Hades walked over to the nearest one, picked it up, and sniffed. Water? What was she going to do with water? He frowned in confusion. Had he completely misunderstood her reasons for this challenge?

Maybe he'd read her wrong. Maybe Taylor didn't have a plan. He looked at her once more. She proudly lifted her head and met his unwavering gaze.

Strike that—she definitely had a plan.

He hoped her strategy became clear shortly, and that for once his plans corresponded with hers.

Hades stepped forward and nodded to Kon. The Phantom raised his hands into the air to quiet everyone. "An unusual challenge has been put forth by Taylor Shelley. Since humans aren't normally allowed to compete in the Pit, the Dark King has made an exception this one time, but Phantom rules still apply."

This brought a fresh round of grunts and growls from the crowd. Hades ignored them. He had no intention of losing this particular fight.

*****

Would they say ready, set, go? Taylor sure hoped that Kon did. She needed time to reach the pole before Hades got to her.

"Begin," Kon shouted.

Crap! Taylor didn't hesitate. She ran straight for the pole. When she reached it, she put the spray bottle in her mouth and climbed as fast as she could.

Tawny fur sprouted from Hades' skin, spreading quickly over his body. Claws and sharp teeth grew at an alarming rate. His body shifted and morphed, tripling in size until all resemblance to the man was gone. Hades roared, then Monster Kitty ran across the arena toward her.

Taylor screamed and climbed higher. She'd barely made it to the top, when Hades leapt. She spread her legs just in time. He barely missed her. The pole screeched as his sharp claws tried to grip the hardened, sealed wood.

She wrapped her legs around the pole and grabbed the bottle that Kon had given her. Hades jumped again. Taylor dropped back until she was hanging upside down, exposing her bare stomach and long legs. The crowd went wild as she undulated.

Hades' head snapped to the left to look at the warriors as he slid down the pole. He hissed in warning, but the crowd ignored him. Taylor continued to gyrate, playfully running the bottle over her body. She held her arms down, just out of reach. The moved worked. Hades snarled and tried to scramble up the pole once more, his red-blue eyes narrowed and intent.

When he neared, Taylor pressed the button and sprayed. Water hit Hades straight in the face, surprising him and sending him falling back. The Dark King shook his massive head and snorted. The liquid dripped down his whiskers and onto his sharp teeth. His long tongue darted out and he quickly cleaned himself.

An agitated swish of his tail told Taylor that she would pay for that one, but it had been worth it just to see the look on the Dark King's face. She dropped the bottle and moved to the fastenings on her top.

Hades' gaze remained locked on her as she stripped off her shirt, revealing the red tassels beneath. She dropped the material onto his head. The sounds coming from the stands turned guttural as Taylor put on the performance of her life in hopes of provoking the King into revealing his feelings.

*****

Hades roared in anger and rumbled at his men, but they refused to take their eyes off the human dangling precariously from the pole. Not that he could blame them with her perfect breasts on full display and those odd things twirling from her nipples. She was luscious and flawless and...*his*.

Didn't they understand that?

He didn't want his men looking at her, staring at every

last delectable inch of her body. That was for his eyes only. And it was time Taylor learned that.

Hades stretched, allowing his muscles to reshape and his claws to retract. Within seconds his beast was gone and he was once again standing on two legs.

"Come down this instant and fight me," he demanded.

Taylor had the nerve to smile at him and twirl the things on her nipples even faster.

Hades' hands rested on his loincloth-covered hips in feigned patience.

Taylor shrugged, then slowly swirled down the pole, but stopped short of touching the ground. By the time she neared the bottom, Hades' shaft was as hard as the rod she was straddling.

Instead of dropping down the last few feet, Taylor leapt to the side and grabbed a wooden sword. She spun around quickly and prepared to attack.

Hades didn't give her the chance. He leapt across the distance separating them and tackled her, taking her to the ground and covering her nakedness with his body. The second she caught her breath, he pinned her in place and demanded that she yield.

"Never!" Taylor shouted.

"I warned you what would happen if you challenged me." Hades flipped Taylor onto her stomach and ripped her skirt away, revealing a strip of red cloth and her bare bottom.

The roars around the Pit became a mixture of encouragement and surprise. Hades fingered the fragile red material that was cradled between her ass cheeks, then impatiently snapped it in half.

"It's never smart to bait the Dark King," he murmured in her ear, then licked the tender flesh. "I told you that you'd end up on your knees this night."

He yanked Taylor up until she was on all fours and lifted his loincloth. Without any warning whatsoever, Hades thrust forward and entered her.

The crowd went insane as the Dark King claimed victory.

Hades had expected to meet resistance, but there was none. Warm moist woman surrounded him, taking the breath from his lungs. He thrust again to be sure and glided deeper into her body. Goddess bless, she felt good. So good. So right. So utterly perfect.

He closed his eyes, reveling in the truth. Taylor wanted him. Wanted this. And Goddess forgive him, but he wanted her, too.

"Yield!" he roared, but the harshness had all but diminished, its remaining edges lost amongst the voices of the masses.

Taylor shook her head and bit her lip, but her hips rocked back to meet his thrusts.

Hades' teeth sharpened as his urge to dominate her grew. He waited until his incisors resembled fangs, then latched onto the skin of her fragile neck where it met her delicate shoulder. "I said yield." The words were garbled, but still intelligible.

Taylor shuddered beneath him and her feminine musk filled the air.

His sudden aggression caused the crowd to grab the sides of the cage surrounding the Pit. They shook the metal with all their might and chanted, "Claim her!" at the top of their lungs.

Hades' gaze moved to Linx. The arrogant cat smirked, then gave him an 'I knew it' look and laughed. As much as he'd like to strangle the feline, he wasn't about to let his 'prey' go in order to do so.

The Dark King was so intent on holding Taylor in place that it took him a moment to notice that she'd gone limp beneath him. She'd finally *submitted*. Tension he didn't know he was holding left his body in a rush.

"You are mine now." Hades kissed her neck tenderly, then bit down hard, breaking the skin. He thrust forward at the same time, burying his cock deep inside her willing body. The second he tasted Taylor's sweet blood in his mouth, something inside of him snapped.

Hades' beast took over and went into a frenzy. He pounded into Taylor, his thick shaft stretching her, working her soft folds, making sure she knew exactly who she belonged to. The ramifications of what he'd done entered his mind, but were quickly dispersed. This felt right. She felt right.

He purred and lapped up her blood, while his body continued to claim hers.

Taylor tightened beneath him, her wet channel fluttering sporadically as she neared completion. Hades slipped his hand between her legs and slowly circled her clit, then flicked it with his thumb. Taylor jerked, then cried out as her release broke. But Hades refused to stop. He was just getting started.

*****

Taylor felt overwhelmed as Hades fucked her in front of the Phantom people. Blood dripped from her neck, but she barely noticed the sting. All she could feel was the Dark King surrounding her, cradling her, shielding her as he laid claim to her body, her heart, and her soul.

An orgasm struck, but Hades didn't give her time to catch her breath. He immediately rebuilt the tension. Taylor's nipples were so hard and sensitive that they actually ached. Hades pinched them mercilessly. The pain only added to her pleasure.

Taylor clawed at the dirt, trying to get away from their intense connection before she shattered into a million pieces. Hades released her neck and licked the blood off, but his grip didn't ease. He seemed harder than ever.

"You shouldn't have challenged me. This is what happens when you challenge the Dark King." He grabbed her hips and shoved his thick, hot length as deep as it could go.

Taylor cried out and her body quivered. One second Hades was behind her, the next he was beneath her, kissing her breasts and biting her nipples. Everything inside of her tingled. Taylor closed her eyes and shook her head. How had he done that?

In a blink he was behind her again.

"What's happening?" The tingles increased until her whole body felt electrified.

Hades didn't answer. He simply faded into nothingness.

Taylor's skin felt as if it were wired to her funny bone. She had no idea what was happening, but whatever it was sent the crowd into hysteria. The Dark King reappeared beneath her long enough to kiss her soundly, then disappeared.

When he reappeared, he was behind her once more. Hades rocked his hips against her bottom, his massive cock branding her flesh.

Taylor felt...weird. Off. Not sick, but different. "What did you do to me?" she asked.

"I claimed you as a Phantom Warrior does. Now we will join in the Atlantean way," he said, brushing a hand over her temple.

Heat flashed through her head before she could utter a sound and a loud pop detonated in her ears. Taylor would've collapsed had it not been for Hades holding her up.

It is done, he said.

The words whispered in her head.

Holy crap! What have you done now? Taylor wasn't even aware that she hadn't asked the question out loud, until Hades answered.

I have bound us in the ways of my mother and my father. It is done. He pulled Taylor to her feet, then lifted her from the ground, while somehow managing to keep their connection. Hades walked them over to the fence. Each step sent his shaft deeper into her weeping channel.

Taylor's eyes closed and her head fell back onto his

shoulder as another orgasm swept through her. Hades carefully set her feet down on the ground, then gently bent her over.

"Grab the fence." His harsh words were at odds with his tender touch.

Taylor reached out blindly, until her fingers grasped the metal.

"Now don't move!"

*****

Hades thrust deep, his body trembling with the need for release. Not yet. Not until he'd followed the rules of challenge. He grasped Taylor's neck and carefully adjusted it, until his mark was clearly visible to the bulk of the crowd.

Their voices quieted instantly.

"I claim this human female as my mate," Hades bellowed.

"What does that mean? I'm not going to sprout a tail and fur, am I?" she asked, only half kidding.

"Eventually, but not right this minute."

Taylor's expression told him that she didn't believe him. But she would soon. Soon there would be no hiding the changes taking place in her body.

Roars and howls filled the air once more. He waited for them to cease, then continued.

"Are there any objections to my claim? Speak now! But know that if you do, that you'd better be prepared to enter the Pit. For I shall kill any male who tries to take her away from me or attempts to stand between us." Hades scanned the arena, then locked gazes with Linx.

The feline's brow rose, but he remained silent.

"Then as the Dark King, I declare this union accepted!" He grasped Taylor's lush hips and released his beast once more. His shaft grew and guttural noises came from his throat, but somehow Hades managed to keep his humanoid form as he claimed his new mate.

His hearts swelled as the word 'mate' wafted through his mind. Taylor was his. Would always be his. Now no one would ever be able to take her away.

Blood roared in Hades' ears. His sac tightened and he increased his speed. He nuzzled Taylor's neck, nibbling the spot he'd marked. He released one of her hips and slid his hand between her parted thighs. She wiggled when he neared the bundle of nerves at her core, drenching his fingers. Hades pressed down hard.

Taylor screamed. Her channel tightened, then convulsed in endless ripples, taking Hades with her. His big body jerked once, arching his spine, then his essence shot out. His legs trembled as he filled her with his life-force. Already Hades could sense the changes taking place in Taylor's body. Soon she would be more Phantom than Earthling.

Hades brushed the soft curls that covered her sex and rested his large hand over her flat abdomen. It wouldn't be flat for long, he mused as a new life blossomed within her. He reluctantly withdrew from her body. His shaft was still half erect. He'd need to take her again. Soon.

He glanced around at the smiling faces of his people. Hades acknowledged their happiness and encouragement, but he wouldn't be claiming Taylor in front of an audience again.

No, the next time he had Taylor it would be in a bed. His bed. *Their bed.*

He kissed her shoulder and carefully unwound her fingers from the fence. Taylor's knees gave out, but Hades caught her, lifting her into his arms. He pressed another kiss upon her moist brow.

"I love you," she murmured, but he heard her all the same.

"I know." Hades grasped her hand and brought it to his hearts. *You reside here. Now and always.*

She cracked one eye open. "You were kidding about the tail and ears, right?"

Hades didn't answer. Some things she'd have to learn firsthand. He carried Taylor out of the Pit with every intention of going straight to his room. Linx stepped in front of him, blocking his retreat.

"King Eros would still like to meet with her," he said. "It is an official summons."

Hades set Taylor down, making sure that she was steady before he released her. He then stepped in front of her and growled menacingly at Linx.

"I see," Linx said. "In that case..." He reached into his pocket, pulled out a document, and handed it to Hades.

"What's this?" Hades clutched the missive, crumpling it in his fist.

"It's an invitation to the Christmas party tomorrow night."

"Leave!" he snapped.

Linx chuckled.

Hades roared, but the sound was cut short when he received a squirt of water to the face.

"Tone it down, Monster Kitty," Taylor said.

He turned to find her holding one of the bottles she'd positioned around the Pit.

Hades brushed his hand over his wet face and flicked the water off. "What was that for?" he asked.

Taylor didn't answer. Instead, she looked to Linx. "Tell the King and Tabby that we'll be there."

Linx grinned. "I'll do that," he said, then left. "You're welcome," he added as a parting shot to Hades, before he slipped through the door.

"I hate that cat," Hades said.

Taylor laughed. "No, you don't. If you did, he'd be dead already. Admit it, you like him."

Hades scowled at her. "No, I don't."

"Come on." Taylor grabbed his hand.

"Where are we going?" Hades allowed her to drag him along.

She glanced over her shoulder at him. "To your room."

He pulled her to a stop. "Don't you mean *our* room?"

Taylor grinned, then bit her lower lip, drawing his gaze to her mouth. "I guess I do."

Heat burst inside of him and his cock lifted his loincloth. "I should warn you that the Dark King can be *very* demanding."

She released his hand long enough to run her fingertips over his shaft. "So can I," Taylor said. "It's why we're perfect for each other."

"Prove it." Hades hurried them down the hall toward their chambers.

"I already have." Taylor touched the mark on her neck and winked.

*****

EPILOGUE

New Atlantis's roads were lined with blue crystals that sparkled in the sunlight and glowed beneath the moonlight. If the Emerald City were based upon fact, then this would be its inspiration. Taylor had never seen anything so beautiful or so intimidating in her life.

The transport slowed and eventually came to a stop in front of a crystal palace. Like a jewel in a crown, the massive building took center stage. She had only seen the city in the distance when she'd first arrived. Up close it didn't look real.

This was where Tabby lived.

Taylor ran a hand over the new dress that Hades had purchased for her. The dark red should've clashed with her hair, but somehow it didn't. The dress dipped in the front, exposing the swell of her ample bosom. Taylor tugged, feeling underdressed and outclassed. It was a feeling that she was used to on Earth, but somehow seemed wrong here on Zaron.

The Dark King stood beside her in a matching tunic, but his legs remained encased in his usual black 'leather'. His aqua blue eyes glowed as they climbed the steps and entered the Atlantean Palace. If Hades was nervous, Taylor couldn't tell. He exuded strength and quiet confidence.

Hopefully he had enough confidence for them both.

Taylor tried to straighten her clothes again, but Hades stilled her hand. "You look beautiful. In fact you are the most beautiful woman in this place."

"I don't think you've looked around," Taylor said.

His brow arched, but he didn't respond.

Whispers of the Dark King's arrival spread through the crowd. The people's expressions ranged from shock to thinly veiled disgust. Several men jockeyed for position to get a better look. But it was the women that caught Taylor's attention. A few of them sauntered forward, not bothering to disguise their interest in Hades. They ignored her as if she didn't exist.

Taylor glared at the brazen women and an unexpected growl came out. The women's eyes widened and they looked away immediately. She cleared her throat.

"Sorry, I don't know why I did that," she said to Hades. "I've obviously been hanging around you too long. I'm starting to sound like you."

His approving gaze slid her way. "Like a lioness, you were protecting what is yours." He gave her a mysterious smile that caused her stomach to flutter.

"Yeah, well, don't let it go to your head," she murmured under her breath.

Hades laughed. "You would never allow such a thing, my Queen." He kissed her hand.

A muffled scream rang out.

Taylor and Hades turned as one to see a flash of movement. Taylor would recognize that red hair anywhere. She left Hades' side to meet her sister halfway. She pulled Tabitha into her arms and hugged her until she gasped. "I've missed you so much."

"I've missed you, too," Tabby said.

"I thought I wasn't going to get to see you again." Tears pricked Taylor's eyes.

"Me, too," Tabby said. "Linx carried you off so fast that I didn't even get to say goodbye. I gave him an ear-load for that one."

Taylor laughed. "I bet you did. Goodness knows he deserved it." A large shadow fell upon them.

Tabby's gaze moved past her. "Is it true?"

Taylor looked at Hades, then motioned for him to come closer. "Yes," she said.

"It's awful fast. Don't you think?" Tabby asked, not bothering to disguise the worry in her voice.

"This from the woman who picked up an alien on Earth?" Taylor asked. "Pot meet kettle."

Her sister pulled a face, but Taylor ignored her.

"Tabby, I'd like for you to meet the Dark King," she said.

Hades inclined his head in greeting.

Tabby didn't immediately acknowledge him, nor did she extend her hand. Instead, she studied Hades closely, searching for signs of trouble. Taylor couldn't blame her twin. She didn't exactly have the best track record when it came to men. The scrutiny continued.

"Knock it off, Tab." Taylor nudged her with her elbow.

"Sorry," she said, but she didn't look sorry. "It's just that I've heard a lot about him and most of it wasn't good."

"From Linx no doubt," Hades said.

Tabby nodded.

As if uttering his name would make him appear, Linx materialized next to Tabby.

Hades paid no attention to him. "You shouldn't believe everything you hear," he said, then his expression hardened and he became the Dark King before their eyes. "On second thought, maybe you should."

Taylor looked at her sister, then at her 'mate'. The tension rose between them as they continued their stare down. "Knock it off, you guys!" she snapped. "We're family now, so you might as well suck it up and get along."

Hades grinned and his aqua eyes sparkled mischievously.

"I thought we were."

"Yeah, me too," Tabby said. "Stop causing trouble, Tay."

*****

Taylor's sister did resemble her. In fact, they were nearly identical, but she lacked a certain something to his mind. She didn't have the same vitality or the same fire, but she was loyal. And that was all that was important to him. Hades scanned the crowd and caught sight of the Atlantean King.

Some instinct must have warned him, because Eros' head rose and their gazes locked. They stood like that for a full minute, then he slowly nodded, acknowledging the Dark King's presence and rank. Hades did the same, then gently touched Taylor on the elbow.

"It is time," he said.

"Now?" she asked, clearly torn between duty and her twin.

"Yes, but we'll be back later." Hades' gaze brushed his mate in reassurance.

"Okay, we'll catch up in a little while." Taylor gave her sister another hug.

"We'd better," Tabby warned, then released her. The withering look she sent Hades told him that she was watching him, watching out for her sister.

They made their way across the room. The place was full of Atlantean and Phantom warriors that Hades recognized. He stopped and said hello to Ares, who wrestled with a blonde woman and a little boy.

"Hades!" Ares shouted. "I cannot believe that Eros got you to come."

"He didn't," Hades deadpanned. "She did." He pulled Taylor forward.

"Ah," Ares said, his grin growing wider. "I should've known. Glad you made it anyway. Have you met my wife, Jac?"

The blonde's mouth snapped shut in mid-tirade and she turned to greet the new arrivals. "It's nice to meet you," she said. "Glad you could make it to the party."

Ares' brother, Orion strolled up with his very pregnant wife, Brigit. The lower half of her body was covered in what appeared to be a giant lizard. Despite the unusual choice of clothing, Hades didn't miss the longing in Taylor's eyes as her gaze rested on the woman's protruding stomach.

"I can't believe it," Orion said. "I would've never in a million galaxies believed that I'd see you at one of these gatherings."

"Hi, I'm Brigit." The small red-headed woman stepped forward with her hand out.

Taylor shook it. "I'm Taylor."

"It's so nice to meet you. We've heard so many conflicting stories that we thought you'd been made up. Glad to see that you're real." Brigit giggled, then grasped her stomach. "Honey, I need to sit down. The baby is kicking my bladder again."

Orion rushed to her side. "Excuse us," he said. "Hades, it was nice seeing you." He ushered his wife away.

"If you'll excuse us, we need to speak with Eros," Hades said.

Ares nodded in understanding. "Don't let another five years pass before you come back."

Taylor looked at him after they left the Atlantean couple. "Has it really been that long?"

Hades shrugged. "Time passes quickly, when you're trying to rebuild a kingdom."

They continued on, but didn't make it far before they were stopped once more by a group of Phantoms huddling together. One man stood a head higher than the others. His tiny mate clung to his side.

"Riot," Hades said in acknowledgement.

The Phantom Warrior dropped to one knee. "Sire." His action caused the others to turn and do the same.

The fair-haired Phantom rose first and stepped forward. "It's nice to see you here, Sire."

"And you, Arctos." Hades' gaze moved to the woman watching their exchange.

Arctos held out his hand. "This is my mate, Caitlin."

"I remember," Hades said. "This is my *Queen*, Taylor."

The four men bowed to Taylor in unison, causing her to blush.

"So it is true." A fifth Phantom stepped through the crowd, his snake-like eyes missing nothing.

"Yes, Bacchus, it is so. I have finally taken a mate. *Mast Moon* has officially frozen over."

Bacchus laughed and shook his head. "It happens to the best of us, Sire." He walked over to his mate, Carrie and kissed her. Like Brigit, her stomach carried the next generation of Phantom.

"Daddy, daddy!" All the Phantoms turned to see which child had called out.

Phantom Warrior Kegar caught the little boy and pulled him close. "Mason, where is your mother?"

"She's coming." He pointed through the crowd. "She said that you would tuck me into bed and read me a story."

"She did, did she?"

His dark hair fell into his face when he nodded. "Yep."

Kegar grinned and pressed his lips to his son's temple. "Sire, if you'll excuse me. Duty calls."

Hades watched the Saber-tooth wander off with a wiggling child in his arms.

"Sire?"

Hades turned as Talon approached.

"Congratulations!" he said.

The Dark King's eyes moved to the ample woman behind him.

"This is my mate, Lynn," Talon said.

"Nice to meet you," Taylor said.

They exchanged pleasantries, then continued on. King

Eros was waiting for them toward the back of the room. The crowd sensed the tension in the air and everyone's voice dropped as the two men faced each other for the first time in years.

"Hades," Eros said.

"Eros," Hades replied.

"Is this the female who missed our appointment today?" Eros asked.

Hades grasped Taylor possessively. "No, this is my Queen."

"Oh for goodness sake." A dark-haired woman broke away from a nearby group and approached. "Kiss and make up already," she said.

*****

Hades looked horrified by the suggestion. Taylor would've laughed, but she didn't think that he'd appreciate it.

"I'm Rachel," the woman said and hugged her.

"Taylor," she said, hugging her back.

"This is my husband, Eros," Rachel said. "He doesn't normally have such a stick up his butt."

Taylor cracked up. "I wish I could say the same."

Hades gave her a warning glare.

"Men." Rachel rolled her eyes. "Did you get cake?"

"No, I haven't seen any food," Taylor said. "But I am starving."

Rachel squeezed her one last time, then released her. "Well, we need to fix that." She led Taylor over to a table that she was surprised hadn't collapsed under the weight of the feast.

"The orange colored ones taste like chocolate. Trust me, you'll love them. How are you enjoying the Christmas party?"

Taylor ran her hand over her arms. "It's lovely."

Rachel smiled knowingly. "I'm not great with crowds

either, but you do get used to it. So tell me all about yourself."

Taylor hesitated.

"Don't worry, I've heard it all. And seen it all since I arrived here." Rachel pressed her hand.

Taylor felt herself relax. Soon she was spilling her life story. She'd looked at Rachel a time or two expecting to see revulsion or at the very least judgment, but there'd been none. Rachel simply stood there and listened to her. Really listened. In that moment, they became fast friends.

By the time they returned to Hades and Eros, the men were laughing and exchanging war stories. Taylor had eaten until she was ready to burst and now she was tired. She looked at the Dark King.

Without a word, he reached for her. "We will hammer out the details of the treaty in the coming weeks."

King Eros nodded. "It shouldn't take long. After all, our fathers were able to work together peacefully for centuries. Why should we be any different?"

Taylor promised to visit Rachel soon. It felt good to have a friend on the planet.

They found Tabby and Linx long enough to let them know that they were heading back. Her sister had begged them to stay, but Taylor knew where she belonged. Hades escorted her out of the Atlantean Palace.

"I'm sorry, but between the crowd and the food I am beat," Taylor said.

"Do not apologize," Hades said. "I was looking for an excuse to go." His smile faded when they reached the top of the stairs. "Are you sure you want to leave?"

"The party?"

Hades shook his head. "The Keep is not nearly as grand as this place. It never will be." He looked around. "And your sister is here."

Taylor pulled away from him. "Are you trying to get rid of me again?"

He snorted. "Why would I do that, when I've only just found you?"

Taylor melted inside. "This place is incredible. Magnificent." She reached for his hand. She needed his warm touch. "I love my sister and I plan to visit her a lot, especially now that I've met Rachel. But like you," she looked around, "I don't belong here. This isn't me. Besides, you wouldn't be here."

The tension in his big body eased. "Then let us go home, my Queen."

She grinned and playfully shoved him forward. "Right behind you, Dark King. Race you to the transport." Taylor lifted her skirts and took off.

Hades roared, then jumped down the stairs. He landed at the base of them before her foot hit the last rung.

"You cheated," she huffed, then laughed.

"You know what happens, when you tease the Dark King," he purred, pulling her close so he could nuzzle her ear.

Taylor's eyes widened and she grinned. "Yes, and I can't wait."

# # #

After the Happily Ever After
Bonus Material

Taylor rolled out of bed and promptly threw up on her stilettos. Not another pair. She scowled. This made four mornings in a row that she hadn't been feeling well. *How long did food poisoning last anyway?*

She glanced over her shoulder. Hades side of the bed was empty—thank goodness. Nothing brought an end to the romance quicker than barfing in bed.

Taylor wiped her mouth with the back of her hand and stumbled to the bathroom. She turned on the tap and splashed some cold water over her face.

Between shoring up their defenses against the Slavers and pounding out a treaty with Eros, the Atlantean King, Hades had been working long hours. When he finally made it home, often late at night, he'd made sure that they never left the bed.

Her big cat was insatiable and seemed to be even more so lately. It was like he couldn't get enough of her, but Taylor wouldn't have him any other way.

Her stomach gurgled ominously and she gagged. She shouldn't have eaten that fish-like creature. She thought it had smelled funny. Taylor ran for the waste basin and barely got her head over it in time before she barfed again. This was getting old—fast.

After several more minutes of tossing her cookies and a lot of dry-heaving, Taylor was able to climb into the shower. She needed to pull herself together.

The Dark King wasn't the only one who had meetings to attend today. Thanks to her new position as Queen of the Phantom Warriors, Taylor had her own set of required duties.

With the nausea behind her, she got dressed in a pencil skirt and semi-conservative blouse. Taylor pulled her long red hair back and tied it at her nape. She smoothed her clothes and glanced at her appearance. Other than her complexion being a lovely shade of light green, she looked okay.

Before she left for her office, Taylor cleaned up the mess she'd made on the floor. It pained her to do it, but she had no choice but to dump her stilettos in the trash. She sighed and tried not to think about the cost.

Her first appointment started in ten minutes. If she hurried, Taylor had just enough time to make it.

A group of Phantom women were already seated around the conference table at the far end of the office by the time Taylor arrived. Hades had set the office up for her after he'd made her his queen. It was the first time she'd worked in an office, but it didn't take long to get the hang of it.

The women seated around the table handled the bulk of the trading that occurred within the Walled City. Today's agenda would cover expanding the trade market to include the Atlantean's Crystal City. If successful, the move would bring in a lot of revenue to the Walled City and its people.

The women rose to their feet and bowed their heads when she walked into the room. Taylor blushed. She still wasn't used to her new position, even though it had been a couple of months since Hades had claimed her as his mate.

"Please be seated," Taylor said, then grabbed the back of a chair to steady herself.

The woman seated next her glanced up. "My Queen, are you well?"

Taylor waved away her concerns. She wasn't the first woman to fall ill and she certainly wouldn't be the last. "Just a little food poisoning."

There was a collective gasp from the women around the table. "Someone is trying to harm you?"

Their eyes glowed red and claws sprang from their fingertips. Suddenly they looked less like business heads and more like predators.

"No! No, no." Taylor held out her hands to quell their need to shift. "That's not what I mean."

"But you said you were poisoned," the dark-haired woman said.

Taylor sighed. There were still some things from Earth that didn't translate well on Planet Zaron. She mentally added food poisoning to her growing list of terms.

"Please, ladies, take a seat," Taylor said. She turned to the woman next to her. "What's your name?"

The woman straightened. "I am called Mari."

"Mari," Taylor said. "On Earth, when food gets old or has not been properly handled and prepared, it can cause what's known as food poisoning. If you eat food like that, it'll make you sick." She paused. "It's not done deliberately. It just happens."

Mari watched her closely. "So you are saying that the food caused your illness."

Taylor smiled weakly. "Yes." She nodded, grateful that the woman understood. "That's exactly what I'm saying."

Mari's dark brow furrowed, then she glanced at the other women around the table. They seemed to reach some kind of silent consensus.

"My Queen," she said. "That's simply not possible."

Not possible? The endless fountain of vomit said

otherwise. "I beg to differ," Taylor said. "It happens all the time on Earth."

Mari slowly shook her head. "No, I beg your forgiveness, but tis' not."

Taylor rubbed her forehead. Maybe she hadn't been clear. She'd thought for sure that Mari had understood.

"Why not?" Taylor asked, while she tried to come up with a different way to describe what she meant.

"All food eaten on Zaron has been treated to destroy the *kutza*. Nothing harmful can survive the process," Mari said.

What was a *kutza*? Taylor's stomach gurgled and churned. Was that the fish she ate the other night?

"Maybe something slipped through the cracks," she said. There was nothing else it could be. She'd hardly eaten a thing since that particular dinner.

The women's gazes dropped to her abdomen as the gurgling and rumbling noises increased in volume.

"Excuse me," Taylor said, covering her stomach.

"Even if it wasn't the law," Mari said. "No Zaronian would allow untreated food to be consumed. The *kutza* makes its home in your intestines. It devours all the waste your body produces and...it *grows*. It grows so large that eventually your body cannot produce enough waste and it has to eat its way out."

Taylor's stomach flipped and she swallowed hard to keep from throwing up on the table. "Are you telling me that I have an alien growing inside me?"

Her mind leapt to the old movie where the alien burst out of unsuspecting chests. Taylor glanced down at her well-endowed physique. She didn't want any alien breaking her ribs to escape.

Uh-huh! No way! She wasn't about to lose her best asset because of bad fish. Her mouth watered. Taylor gulped, then gulped again. It took great effort to keep everything down.

"Someone should notify the Dark King that the Queen has been poisoned," Mari said.

"No!" Taylor let go of her stomach and straightened. Hades was stressed enough without adding her tummy troubles to his problems. They were overreacting. "I'm sure it's just a bug. Not a *kutza*," she added quickly. "Just a regular old virus. I'll be right as rain in a day or two. Now please everyone calm down and let's get back to the meeting."

*****

Two days later, Taylor felt even worse. She'd had no choice but to cancel her appointments. The women might think that food poisoning didn't exist, but Taylor wasn't convinced. It was either that or she had the flu.

She pressed her hand to her forehead, but her skin was cool to the touch. Okay, so no fever. Other than the occasional nausea, she felt all right. So maybe it wasn't the flu after all.

Whatever was plaguing her certainly hadn't dampened her appetite. She'd eaten the Zaronian equivalent of a chicken and a box of earth chocolates, and Taylor was still hungry. If she kept this up, she'd be as big as the Keep.

On Earth, not having a fever or body aches would mean something, but this was Zaron. The bugs here were different. Taylor had no way of knowing if illness behaved the same way here as it did at home.

She sat down in a comfy chair and closed her eyes. She just needed to rest for a minute, then she'd be okay. An hour later, a roar rattled the walls.

Taylor's eyes opened in time to see the picture of her and her sister, Tabby fall to the floor. A door slammed, then a giant Liger-looking cat prowled into the room.

"I take it the meeting with Eros isn't going well," she said, climbing to her feet.

A warm glow surrounded the beast's pale fur. It grew brighter and brighter until Taylor had to look away. When the light faded, she glanced back and saw the Dark King standing in the doorway.

Hades was naked.

Gloriously so.

His muscles flexed as he ran a hand through his tawny hair, leaving it disheveled. "The Atlantean is as stubborn as a Zaronian boarram," he snarled. "He refuses to listen to reason. Maybe I should try ripping his head off and shouting in his ear."

Taylor laughed and closed the distance between them. "You have to remember that he's not as adept at war as you are. You must be patient with him. Eros doesn't fully appreciate the threat the Slavers bring. He needs more time. He'll come around." She brushed her hand over his cheek.

Hades caught her fingers and brought them to his lips. "I didn't think you'd be here."

Taylor hesitated, then said, "I finished early."

Hades' nose twitched. "You smell good. Did you put something different on your skin?"

"No." She shook her head. "I just showered."

He growled. "You smell really good." Hades pulled her into his arms until their bodies were flush. He rubbed his head against hers and pushed his nose into her neck.

A hard ridge pressed against Taylor's abdomen.

"I can't seem to keep my hands off you," Hades purred. He nibbled on her ear.

Taylor felt her bones melt. It was like this every time they got together, fireworks and puddles. "You've never been able to keep your hands off me," she reminded him. And Taylor was grateful for it.

"I know." Hades kissed her nape. "But now all I want to do is tie you to the bed and have my way with you."

Taylor giggled. "Didn't we do that last week?"

Hades' purr turned into a growl. He ripped his mouth away from her neck and captured her full lips. His hands seemed to be everywhere at once as bits of her clothing fell to the floor. He never cut her with his claws, not a single scratch. It always amazed her how accurate he could be with those deadly weapons.

Taylor's body softened to counter his growing hardness. By the time he backed her into the bedroom, she was naked.

Hades' hands slid past her waist to knead her bottom, then they continued on their journey south. His rough palms settled against her thighs, his fingers stroking her sensitive skin. He suddenly grabbed her and lifted.

Taylor tumbled onto the bed.

He clasped her foot and kissed the inside of her ankle, then slowly made his way up her inner thigh. "Your scent is driving me insane. It's so sweet that it makes me want to devour every inch of you." He licked her to prove his point, then parted her legs and made good on his promise.

His rough cat tongue had Taylor clawing at the covers as he sent her soaring into the air. Hades didn't stop feasting until she was limp and panting for breath.

"You are a very bad kitty," Taylor said.

His aqua eyes flashed, then slowly smoldered. "You love it when I am." He licked her juices off his lips and grinned.

"Yes," she said. "I do."

"I'm not finished," he said.

Taylor laughed. "I'd be disappointed if you were."

Hades crawled between her legs and positioned his large shaft at her moist entrance, then slowly impaled her.

Taylor would never tire of the feel of him. He filled her like no other could. It was sheer ecstasy. He was sin incarnate.

Hades rolled his hips. The move took him even deeper.

Taylor groaned and clasped his back, wrapping her thighs around his waist. Blindly, she sought his lips, then rose up to meet him thrust for thrust.

The slow beginning quickly devolved into a frenzied mating. Hades grunted in her ear as he rode her body into oblivion and beyond. Taylor shattered in his arms once more.

"Mine!" Hades bellowed as she went boneless beneath him. One final plunge and he followed her over the edge.

A short time later, Taylor awoke to soft kisses being placed upon her stomach. She smiled as one particular kiss tickled and ran her fingers through Hades' soft hair. He purred and arched his neck so she could do it again. She closed her eyes, enjoying the simple pleasure of touching him.

"I'd love to lay here all day, but Eros is going to be mad that you've kept him waiting," she said.

"He'll get over it." Hades kissed her again. "Why didn't you tell me?"

Taylor opened her eyes.

Hades looked up and their gazes met. The emotion swimming in his aqua depths made her breath catch. His thumb lazily circled her navel as he stared at her.

Taylor's fingers stilled. "It's no big deal—"

"No big deal!" Hades leapt to his feet naked, angry, and aroused. "How can you casually dismiss such a thing?"

"Did Mari tell you?" Taylor's temper rose to match his. She'd told the women not to bother him. Obviously one of them had gone behind her back and blabbed.

"You told others, but you didn't think to share the news with me?" Some of his anger faded. It was quickly replaced by hurt.

Now Taylor was confused. "Surely people here on Zaron don't have to report to the Dark King every time they get sick."

"Of course not," he said.

She scrambled to her feet. "Then why should I?"

They stood in the center of their massive bed, facing each other.

Hades' tawny brow furrowed. "You're ill?"

"That's what I've been trying to tell you," Taylor said. "I've had a little stomach bug. It's not a big deal. You've been so busy. I didn't want you to worry. It's nothing. I am sure it'll pass soon."

Hades blinked, then his blue eyes widened. A second later, he threw his head back and roared with laughter.

Taylor went from confusion to anger. He was laughing at her. She didn't think there was anything funny about throwing up and ruining perfectly good shoes.

"Sometimes you can be a real jerk! You know?" Taylor tried to climb off the bed, but Hades caught her before she could escape.

He gently clasped her face and drew her to him, then his lips tenderly touched hers. "You continue to surprise and delight me, mate," he said, then kissed her again.

Taylor frowned at the change in his demeanor. "I do?" *What was he up to now?* She didn't trust this sudden turnabout. This was Hades after all.

He brushed his nose across hers, then nuzzled her ear. "Yes, you do," he said. "My love for you grows stronger every day."

Tears welled Taylor's eyes. *Why was she crying? She wasn't a crier.* "I love you, too." She sniffed.

His hand slid from her cheek and settled on her belly protectively. "Thank you for giving me the gift I did not know I needed or even wanted until now." Hades brushed his thumb over her bare skin.

"What?" Gooseflesh rose as warning bells went off in Taylor's head. She swayed and her legs threatened to give out. "You mean I'm...I'm...I'm pregnant!" She couldn't be. It wasn't possible. Okay, it was possible, but she wasn't ready.

Hades' feral grin widened. "Mine," he snarled and spread his fingertips.

The room spun on its axis. If it kept that up, Taylor was going to be sick. "I can't be pregnant," she sputtered as panic set in.

Hades dropped to his knees and buried his nose in her

abdomen. He inhaled deeply. "There's no mistaking the scent—my scent," he growled. "Our child grows inside of you." His tone was fierce, but when he looked up at her it was love that shone in his crystal blue eyes.

In an instant, Taylor's fears vanished. She wasn't in this alone. Hades wouldn't abandon her like the men had in her old life on Earth. He was different. This was not a man kneeling at her feet. This was a warrior.

Looking at the fierce determination on his handsome face, her heart knew that she'd always have the Dark King by her side.

Hawk's Slave: Excerpt

Some days, being the captain of a slaver ship wasn't all it was cracked up to be. Sure, flying through space and kidnapping unsuspecting women was thrilling, but most days were spent trying to find ways to kill time between planet jumps.

That's what Hawk was doing today, as he found himself strolling across the cavernous cargo bay to the row of doors along the ship's hull.

He went straight to the containment unit on the end and peered into the holding tank where his favorite slave resided. She was seated on the floor with one long leg bent and her arms resting on her knee. Her head hung forward like she was asleep, causing her dark, shoulder-length hair to obscure her face. But Hawk knew she wasn't. She always knew the precise moment he arrived.

Unlike the other slaves he had, this one hadn't been captured. The Dark King had given her to him. Which was probably why she hadn't bargained for her life or offered her body in exchange for her freedom.

Not that Hawk had expected the woman who'd betrayed her king to roll over so easily, but he was *surprised*. And perhaps, a *tiny* bit disappointed.

Opal...her name hinted at her rarity and conjured all kinds of fantasies.

Fantasies he intended to live out—once he tamed her.

Thus far, getting Opal to bend to his will hadn't been as easy as he'd anticipated, but Hawk had a new plan. One that would push her control to the very limits. He glanced at the room on the other side of the cargo bay.

It was a special room. A room he'd personally designed for this exact situation. The space held unique equipment. Equipment geared to handle the most stubborn of slaves...and the wildest females.

No one had ever left that room without begging him to ease their *suffering*. No one. Eventually, everyone surrendered.

Hawk had no plans to injure this woman or any of the others occupying the nearby cells. No, he intended to use the tools in the room to explore Opal's limits. He planned to take her through galactic levels of pleasure, and if need be, staggering realms of frustration. Hawk was prepared to do whatever it took to tame her because he had no intention of releasing her.

"Why don't you just go in there and command her to obey?" his First said as he came up beside him in the cargo hold. "You're the captain. She has to listen."

For all his experience, Fallon knew *nothing* about women. He was from a planet where all the females were subservient. The males took their behavior for granted and believed women of every species should follow suit.

If the men on his planet wanted a female, they simply went to her family and demanded that she be given to them. With the men's war-like natures, that wasn't always the best course of action to take, but they accepted that it was the way things were done.

Hawk glanced at the green-skinned man beside him. "Your horns are sticking up."

Fallon's yellow gaze shot up to see, even though it was physically impossible to do so. "I just sharpened them. Thought I might pick out a female to test them on later."

Hawk's dark brow rose, along with the beast lurking inside of him. Fallon's horns could be used for pleasure or savagery, depending on where he stuck them in a woman.

"And you thought this one would do?" Hawk asked. It was a simple question that was loaded with Zaronian explosives.

Fallon's yellow eyes narrowed and his green skin darkened. "I'm not that foolish," he said. "Everyone knows this slave is yours, Captain."

She was...and his First had better not forget it. If he stuck Opal with those horns, Hawk would rip them off his head and shove them where they were bound to hurt.

Hawk's lips twitched. "You know I don't play favorites with my chattel," he said, which had been true until Hades, The Dark King had given him Opal. Ever since she'd landed on his ship, she'd occupied much of his free time, but she'd yet to grace his rest pad.

"True." Fallon stroked his horns, testing the tips' sharpness. "But she isn't exactly our usual cargo."

He was right. As a shifter, Opal was unique and extremely valuable. Sure, she had done her best to set up the woman who'd captured the Dark King's heart. She would have succeeded too, if she hadn't underestimated the King's feelings for the golden-haired Earthling.

Hawk had taken one look at the Dark King's face when they were fighting and had known he'd go to war for that woman without batting a whisker.

As a Slaver, Hawk had no interest in war, but he did care about the credits his cargo would bring, which was why they'd had to raid two more planets after leaving Zaron.

The Phantoms hadn't allowed them to leave with any female but this one. Hawk had seen what giving her to him had cost the Dark King, but the Phantom ruler had no choice.

It was either act decisively or be seen as weak in front of his people.

Hawk knew something about that and had the scars to prove it. He tapped his finger on the front of Opal's container. Her dark head never moved, but she did shift her lithe body giving him another tantalizing glimpse of her long legs. She never acknowledged his presence. It was a game they played. A game he was determined to win.

He closed the window to her door. "Have you set a course for the next solar system?"

"Yes, Captain," Fallon said. "We're just awaiting you on the flight deck."

"Well, let us wait no longer." Hawk glanced once more at the closed door before striding toward the transport cylinder.

"She'd fetch a fair price on Farn. They're always looking for pets," Fallon said. "Her cat form would make a good one."

"That it would," Hawk replied. "If she were for sale."

Fallon smartly kept his silence.

"Have her transferred to the pleasure room," Hawk said.

Fallon blinked in surprise, then his face carefully blanked. "Yes, Captain."

*****

Opal knew he was there. Felt him lurking outside her cell like a big cat stalking its cornered prey. Hawk came to her every day. Had been ever since he'd taken her captive. He never said anything to her directly. He simply stared at her like the predator he was and waited.

For what? She had no idea.

She could still recall the moment she'd laid eyes on the Slaver. Opal had been crouched in a tree, when Hawk stepped out the door of his ship. His long black hair had been braided at the sides of his head and tight leather pants hung low on his trim hips, exposing a sliver of his light blue skin.

He'd looked right at her cat form with those golden eyes of his and seen straight through her. Opal could still feel the heat of that stare on her skin. The distance didn't diminish Hawk's presence then, and it sure as heck wasn't now, even though he was on the other side of the metal door.

One glance had told her that Hawk was going to be trouble. Her first instinct was to run for her life, but Opal rarely listened to her gut when it came to men. She'd always been drawn to dark ones. The more dangerous they were, the more alluring she found them.

It was why she'd worked so hard to become part of the Phantom Warrior royal guard. She'd found Hades, the Dark King attractive and was determined to get close to him. Opal had succeeded in more ways than one. She'd become Hades' right hand, a position normally reserved for men, and over time, ended up sharing his rest pad. Too bad the latter position turned out to be temporary.

Her obsession with the Dark King had cost Opal her position, her home, and her freedom, which was why she found herself here on this ship, under the watchful eye of a handsome Slaver.

The constant observation was beginning to get to her. Opal wasn't sure what she was going to do about it, since she wasn't exactly in a position to stop him, but it couldn't go on.

What did he want?

Stupid question, she thought.

Opal knew exactly what Captain Hawk wanted from her. He wanted the coordinates to Earth. If that were all he wanted, they might be able to strike a mutually beneficial agreement, but he wanted so much more.

The only true mystery was why he hadn't taken her yet. He was a Slaver after all. They weren't known for their restraint or for their compassion. If he'd wanted her bound and on her knees, then that's where she'd be—willing or not. Yet it had been a month and he had not made a move. All he did was *watch*.

Why?

Opal's body tightened and her skin stretched as her cat side threatened to surface. The sensation was occurring more and more frequently—thanks to the sexy, dark-haired bastard continually prowling outside her door.

To get Hawk off her mind, Opal thought about Zaron and Hades. When she did, a fresh wave of anger struck. The Dark King had betrayed her.

Hades had left her to the Slavers with no thought of whether she'd live or die. It mattered not that she'd betrayed him *first*.

That was different. His motives were selfish. Hers were not.

Opal had done what she'd done for the Phantom people, even if the Dark King didn't see it that way. Given the chance, she'd do so again. Which Opal supposed was why he'd abandoned her in the first place. And to think, she used to *love* him.

She snorted at her own foolishness. Time and distance had allowed her to re-evaluate her feelings and they'd come up severely lacking. If her experience with the Dark King had taught Opal anything it was that she couldn't trust any man with her two hearts, whether she loved him or not. Captain Hawk may be darkly appealing, but trusting a Slaver was out of the question.

Opal glared at the door as the voices rose. Who was he talking to this time? She strained to listen, but their footsteps were already fading.

"She'd fetch a fair price on Farn," the man said.

Fear swept through Opal. Farn was known for its skin trade, exotic pet market, and sex slavery. Was Hawk planning to kill her and sell off her parts? Or did he have something else in mind for her, something far, far worse than death?

Blood roared in her ears. Opal tried to catch Hawk's

response to the question, but the thick metal door and the distance muted his words.

How long would it take to reach Farn?

She didn't know, which meant she'd have to come up with a plan fast. Unlike Hades' new mate, Opal would do whatever it took to survive...even if that meant seducing the enemy.

Opal pictured Hawk lying naked on a rest pad and quivered. The shape-shifting Slaver had featured in far too many of her dreams.

Nightmares, never dreams. Nightmares.

On the surface, seducing him wouldn't be a hardship, but the captain was no fool. He wouldn't trust her no matter what she claimed, which was good since Opal didn't trust him either.

Her cat might be ready to lift its tail up to his beast, but Opal would never allow her instincts to override her good sense. Not anymore.

The only thing working in her favor was that the Slaver desired her. Oh sure, he needed her to give him directions to Earth, but his lust was a strong motivating factor behind his daily visits.

Heat practically rolled off Hawk's hard body when he was around her. Opal smiled coldly. She would play on his attraction. Convince Hawk that she wanted him, then the first opportunity she got, Opal would betray him and escape.

She glanced around her cell. There were only a few boxes of clothes and the basic necessities, but they were enough to work with, enough to catch a Slaver's attention. If need be, she'd wear nothing.

After all, men were men. And if Opal knew anything, it was how to manipulate male shifters. She'd been doing it her whole life. She'd had no choice but to in order to get ahead in the Phantom patriarchal society.

She heard footsteps coming toward her containment pod. Was Hawk returning so soon? She dropped her head so she wouldn't be caught looking his way if he peered through the viewer hatch.

The door to her cell opened suddenly, sending glaring light into the room, temporarily blinding her. When her vision cleared, Opal saw two men standing outside the door. Neither of which were Hawk.

The tall and lanky of the two had fair hair and violet-colored eyes. He smiled at her, flashing two-inch fangs. Despite the color of his eyes, Opal inhaled, expecting to catch the scent of a Phantom Blood Clan member. It wasn't there. Whatever he was, he wasn't from Zaron.

Her gaze shifted to the man beside him. Ice green eyes with snake-like pupils stared back at her. The man's head was shaven and had been imprinted with a multitude of symbols. None of which she recognized.

"Come with us," the fanged one said.

"Where's Hawk?" she asked.

The symbols on the man's bald head shifted and his green eyes narrowed. "That's Captain Hawk to you, slave," he snarled and his body pulsed with power.

The small wave hit her and Opal spasmed. Her eyes widened and her hearts began to pound. There was only one being that she knew of with that kind of power—a *Sorce*.

She'd never met one in person. Most people who did ended up dead. Opal tried to hide her fear, but wasn't sure she succeeded. Magic wielders were some of the most lethal beings in the galaxy. Their skills as assassins were legendary.

"Where are we going?" her voice cracked.

Had Hawk ordered his men to kill her?

"Just get on your feet or we'll bind you and carry you," the fair-haired man said.

Opal reluctantly climbed to her feet. She wasn't a coward and she wasn't stupid. Fighting these two men would most certainly lead to her death, but warriors didn't just roll over and die without a fight. If they planned to kill her, she wouldn't make it easy for them.

Her fists clenched at her sides. "I'm standing. Now what?"

"This way." The man's violet-colored eyes began to glow.

As she watched, Opal's head grew fuzzy and she found herself wanting to comply with his order. Her muscles strained to resist the compulsion, but it was no use. It was too strong. She walked into the cargo hold. A quick glance told her no one was around.

"Where are you taking me?" Opal clutched her temple and tried to focus. There was a reason she didn't want to go with them. What was it?

"You'll see." The Sorce put a hand between her shoulder blades and shoved.

Opal stumbled forward but kept her feet under her. They didn't go far. The men walked her to the other side of the hold and opened the lone door along the hull.

"Get in," the Sorce said, watching her closely.

Opal poked her head in the door and saw a table with straps anchored to it and chains secured to the wall. Below the chains were...she squinted...various instruments.

It took her a moment to recognize what they were. Oh no. Not that. Opal took a step back. She didn't get far before a strong hand came down upon her shoulder.

"I'm not going in there," she snarled. Death was preferable to what Hawk and his men had planned for her.

# # #

Other Books by Jordan Summers

Phantom Warriors 1: Bacchus
Phantom Warriors 2: Saber-tooth
Phantom Warriors 3: Talon
Phantom Warriors 4: Arctos
Phantom Warriors 5: Linx
Phantom Warriors 6: Riot
Hawk's Slave
Phantom Warriors Anthology Volume 1
Phantom Warriors Anthology Volume 2

Atlantean's Quest 1: The Arrival
Atlantean's Quest 2: Exodus
Atlantean's Quest 3: Redemption
Atlantean Heat 3.5
Atlantean's Quest 4: The Return
Atlantean's Quest 5: The Dark King
Atlantean's Quest Bundle Volume 1
Atlantean's Quest Bundle Volume 2

Dead World Prequel: Raphael
Dead World Prequel: Kane
Dead World 1: Red
Dead World 2: Scarlet
Dead World 3: Crimson

Moonlight Kin 1: A Wolf's Tale
Moonlight Kin 2: Aidan's Mate
Moonlight Kin 3: Nic
Moonlight Kin 4: Tristan - Coming Soon

Tears of Amun
Heat of the Night
Gothic Passions
Rose's Rapture
Paris After Dark

Ghost Hunter: Solomon's Seals

Private Investigations
Mesmerized
Hot Shot
Ride Em' Cowboy
Off Limits

About the Author

Jordan Summers has thirty-one published books to her credit and has sold over 145,000 ebooks. She's a member of The Horror Writer's Association, International Thriller Writers, the Author's Guild, and Novelist Inc.

Connect with her online:
Twitter.com/jordanwriter
www.facebook.com/authorjordansummers
www.JordanSummers.com
Join the Endless Summers Newsletter to find out about upcoming releases and author signings.
http://www.jordansummers.com/contact/